midnight
dolls

Also by Kiki Sullivan
The Dolls

midnight dolls

KIKI SULLIVAN

BALZER + BRAY

An Imprint of HarperCollins*Publishers*

Library of Congress Cataloging-in-Publication Data
Sullivan, Kiki.
  Midnight dolls / Kiki Sullivan. — First edition.
    pages cm
  Sequel to: Dolls.
  Summary: When Eveny Cheval, seventeen, is attacked by Main de
  Lumière, her father whisks her, her sister zandara queens, and their
  protectors to his home on Caouanne Island, where Eveny learns more
  about her andaba heritage and feels torn between the two magical
  traditions—and between two boys.
  ISBN 978-0-06-228150-0 (paperback)
  [1. Voodoo—Fiction. 2. Identity—Fiction. 3. Friendship—Fiction.
  4. Love—Fiction. 5. Fathers and daughters—Fiction. 6. Louisiana—Fiction.
  7. Georgia—Fiction.] I. Title.
PZ7.S9524Mid 2015   2015005744
[Fic]—dc23   CIP
                                                                 AC

Typography by Torborg Davern
15 16 17 18 19   PC/RRDH   10 9 8 7 6 5 4 3 2 1
❖
First Edition

TO MY OWN SOSYETE, HOLLY ROOT, NICK HARRIS, SARA SARGENT, AND VIANA SINISCALCHI: WE MAY NOT HAVE ACTUAL POWERS, BUT WE CREATED A WORLD ON THE PAGE, AND THAT'S PRETTY MAGICAL TOO.

AND TO NICK'S WIFE, MELISSA, AND HIS DEAR CHILDREN, NOA AND DASH: I WAS FORTUNATE TO HAVE EXPERIENCED NICK'S DEEP KINDNESS AND BIG IMAGINATION FOR A LITTLE WHILE, AND THIS BOOK IS JUST A VERY SMALL PIECE OF THE LEGACY HE LEAVES BEHIND. THE THREE OF YOU WERE HIS EVERYTHING. HE LOVED YOU DEEPLY, AND I KNOW HE'LL ALWAYS BE WITH YOU. WHEN HE TALKED ABOUT DREAMING BIG, I KNOW HE WAS DREAMING OF YOU MOST OF ALL.

*T*wilight falls crisp and clean on the first day of spring in Carrefour.

As the light seeps from the sky, I stand in the garden behind our mansion, my eyes closed, trying to picture my mother standing here fourteen years ago today, just before she died.

It would have been an important day for her, the way it is for me. In this town, the arrival of the vernal equinox means a lot, because zandara, the type of voodoo-like magic we practice here in secret, is most powerful in spring. Then again, thanks to the magic cloaking the town, there's no real winter, so the roses, lavender, fennel, and thousands of other plants and herbs we use to cast zandara charms flourish year-round.

I take a deep breath and try to reach out to the nether, the world between life and death where some souls get stranded for a while. Later tonight, just past midnight, I'll meet Peregrine and Chloe, my two sister queens, in the middle of the cemetery for a ceremony to strengthen our bond with the spirits who help us. But for now, I'm trying to reach them alone. I've felt unsettled for the last couple of weeks, since the night in New Orleans when I played a role in the death of Drew Grady, someone I'd thought was a friend. Instead, it turned out that he'd been recruited to kill me. Now I can't help but feel like the incident was merely the prelude to something darker and more sinister that's about to unfold. I need to ask the spirits to protect me and those I love.

"Come to us now, Eloi Oke, and open the gate," I chant. "Come to us now, Eloi Oke, and open the gate. Come to us now, Eloi Oke, and open the gate." Eloi Oke is zandara's gatekeeper, a spirit who opens the lines of communication each time my sister queens and I ask for help. The air around me suddenly feels eerily still, and I know that the words, which we use to begin all but the smallest of charms, have worked.

I put my left ring finger on my Stone of Carrefour, the powerful rock that hangs from my neck. It was imbued with magic more than a hundred years ago, when the town was founded, and now it allows me to cast charms without actually holding the things I'm invoking. As long as I'm touching it, I can draw power from any plant in the world.

I do my best to clear my mind and summon some of the

herbs I've been learning about. "Sage and yarrow, I draw your power. Spirits, please help me to see the threats against me and the people I love, and to bravely face any coming danger." I concentrate hard on my requests, and then I murmur the standard words of gratitude for the spirits' help.

"*Mesi, zanset,*" I say. "*Mesi, zanset. Mesi, zanset.*" Ceremonial words are meant to be repeated three times whenever possible, because three is the most powerful number in zandara. It demonstrates respect for the spirits by symbolizing heaven, hell, and the space between.

The air pressure returns to normal, the way it always does when communication with the spirits has ended, but something still doesn't feel right. There's a gnawing in the pit of my stomach, and I have the sense that something is lurking in the garden.

"Hello?" I say tentatively. "Is anybody out there?"

It's not until the words are out of my mouth that I realize I'm hoping the answer is yes, that it's Caleb Shaw in the shadows. I've barely seen him since Drew's funeral a couple of weeks ago, when he kissed me passionately and then pulled away to tell me it was over between us. I'd known it was coming; the rules of zandara forbid us from being together, even if we're drawn to each other like magnets. His family is sworn to protect mine, and any romantic feelings between us get in the way. He attempted to explain it to me a couple of months ago by comparing the link between us to a Wi-Fi connection that grows fuzzier as it gets overloaded. In other words, the more feelings he has for me, the less able he is to sense when I need his help. "Caleb?" I call now.

Something rustles behind the wall that separates the garden from the cemetery, and then the night goes still again. I hold my breath and try my best to listen, but I'm forced to admit I'm imagining things. Caleb isn't out there. I'm on my own.

"Eveny?"

I look up to see my father standing in the doorway of the house, backlit by the dim lamplight of the living room.

"Out here!" I call. He closes the back door and makes his way down the deck stairs and out through the twisting path of the garden toward me. I still can't get used to him being here, and I haven't quite decided whether I can trust him yet. Despite his claims that he has always kept an eye on me from afar, it feels strange that after seventeen years, he's suddenly back in my life. Still, I know my mother loved him until the day she died. I owe him the benefit of the doubt.

"What are you doing out here?" he asks, sitting down on the stone bench in front of my mother's roses and gesturing for me to join him. "You disappeared after dinner."

"I was just thinking," I say, settling beside him.

"About your mom?"

I nod.

"You miss her a lot, don't you?" my father asks.

"She was my whole world when I was a kid. Losing her was like losing everything."

"I felt the same way. When she was still alive, knowing

that I had to leave her and go back to Caouanne Island . . . It was torture for me."

I nod and look away. My parents had decided before I was born that my dad would return to the island where he'd been raised, just off the coast of Georgia. My father is a king of andaba, the magical sect based there, and he and my mother feared that if an anti-magic organization like the murderous Main de Lumière realized they were together, their child would become an instant target. Never before had a king from one voodoo-derived magical sect and a queen from another produced an heir. My father's absence seemed to work for a while, although it broke my mother's heart. But now she's dead, and our enemies know about my heritage anyhow.

I only learned a couple of weeks ago that Main de Lumière considers me the most powerful queen in the world because I have a rare combination of magical blood—andaba from my dad's side and zandara from my mom's.

"Dad?" I say after a moment. It still feels strange to call him something so familiar.

"Yes, honey?"

"Do you think I'm still in danger?"

I watch a shadow pass over his face. "I think that we have to assume you are." He speaks slowly without meeting my eye. "I can't imagine that a group as strategic as Main de Lumière wouldn't have a backup plan. But that's why I'm here, Eveny: to protect you. To make sure you're not harmed."

"I thought that was Caleb's job." I sound more bitter than

I mean to. I shake my head and look off into the distance. I'm frustrated that I know so little about the traditions that make me who I am, and I'm overwhelmed by everything I'll need to learn in order to be any good at either form of magic. I have the sense that my father is waiting patiently until I ask about the details of andaba before he explains everything. The thing is, learning I'm a zandara queen was jarring enough, and I'm not sure I'm ready to know any more just yet.

"Want me to bring you out some of that chocolate chip lavender cake your aunt Bea made for dessert?" my father asks me after the silence has stretched on too long. "I think there's some vanilla ice cream in the freezer too. . . ."

"I'm not hungry," I tell him. "I'm just going to sit here for a while, I think."

He nods. "Being with your mom's roses has always brought me peace too," he says. "It's a little bit like she's still here with us." He stands, kisses me on the top of my head, and smiles at me sadly before striding back toward the house.

Exhausted from a long day of studying zandara charms and sapped of energy after asking the spirits for help, I doze off on the garden bench and dream of Caleb emerging from the shadows in New Orleans a couple of weeks ago to save me. I'd gone there to take part in my sosyete's annual possession ceremony, but as we danced in the streets among Mardi Gras revelers, Drew had emerged from the crowd, brandishing a knife, and forced me into an alley. He would have killed me if Caleb hadn't shown up just in time.

Suddenly, in the midst of the dream, I hear a woman's voice in my head, clear and sharp: "Save yourself." I awaken with a start, my heart pounding, but before I can figure out if I'm hearing things or if the warning was just part of the unsettling dream, a hulking shape comes at me from the left at lightning speed, slamming my head down onto the stone bench. I hear a loud grunt, then a mumbled phrase in what sounds like French.

I start to scream, but a man's hand, rough and hairy, clamps down over my nose and mouth, cutting off my air supply. I struggle and choke, clawing at him, but he's much bigger than I am, and he swats my hands away. I strain to see his face, but he's wearing a ski mask, and he's shrouded in darkness. The only thing I can make out are his pale blue, bloodshot eyes, rimmed with blond lashes.

Keeping one hand over my mouth, he uses his other hand to lift me up by my hair until I'm dangling several inches above the ground. "Good girl," he hisses. "Be nice, now."

I try to scream again, but he shakes me so hard that I can almost feel my brain banging against the inside of my skull. I'm temporarily silenced as the world goes fuzzy. I blink a few times, forcing myself to focus, and I begin to kick wildly, aiming for my assailant's midsection. But he's larger than I thought, and he's easily holding me far enough from his body that my kicks aren't even close to connecting.

"Stop struggling!" the man says, giving me another violent shake.

A moment later, my vision clears, and I can see that we're

moving rapidly toward the back wall. The man still has me by the hair, one hand over my mouth, and he's dragging me across the dirt almost effortlessly. My head throbs, and I feel dazed, but I'm coherent enough to realize that the farther we get from my house, the less likely it is that anyone will find me. Just as we reach the brick wall separating the garden from the cemetery, I gather all my strength, force my jaw open as if I'm about to scream, and clamp down as hard as I can, biting the man's hand.

"Merde!" He jerks his hand away from my face and loosens his grip on my hair a little. It's enough for me to twist away from him and begin screaming.

"Help! Caleb! Dad!" I yell, but it's all I have time for before the man pounces on me again, shoving me to the ground and pinning me with the weight of his enormous body. In the distance, from the direction of the house, I can hear footsteps and shouting, and I know that someone's coming for me. But I might not have that much time.

"You little bitch!" My attacker tries to pull me up by my hair again, but I jab backward with my right elbow, connecting with his face, and hear a sickening crunch. "Damn you!" he cries as blood spurts from his broken nose.

He doesn't let go, though, and a moment later, his hands are around my neck. "I'm not supposed to kill you, but I think I can ignore orders just this once," he growls. "And believe me, I'm going to make it hurt." In one deft motion, he presses down on my right arm until I hear it snap. Pain sears through me like I'm on fire.

I scream as the agony takes over my body. Suddenly, I hear the voice from my dream again. *Save yourself,* it whispers, and I realize suddenly that I don't have to fight like a normal person. I'm *not* a normal person. I'm a zandara queen.

I stop struggling, which seems to startle the man. He pulls away slightly, and in the instant before he reaches for me again, I touch my Stone of Carrefour with my left ring finger and murmur, "Asafoetida, I draw your power." It's a repellent herb I read about yesterday, and I think it could be just the thing to push him back. "Please, spirits," I add quickly, "keep this man away long enough for me to escape from him."

Right away, he stops fighting and rolls to the side, limp. I don't know how long the charm will work, so I scramble out from beneath him, kick him once more in the face for good measure, and take off toward my house. I'm breathless and bruised, and my right arm sends pain ricocheting through my entire body with every step I take, but I run as fast as I can until I almost collide with my father and Caleb. Relief sweeps over me.

"He's that way!" I point with my left hand. "I think he's Main de Lumière. Be careful."

"You're okay?" Caleb hesitates, his sky-blue eyes ablaze with concern.

"I'll live," I say. He hesitates for another millisecond before running in the direction I pointed.

My father reaches for me, but I cry out when he touches my right arm. "The man broke it," I say, and his eyes widen.

"Let's get you inside. I'll call Peregrine and Chloe."

I nod, but already I'm feeling woozy, and I'm not sure if it's from the pain of my snapped arm or if the man shook me hard enough to give me a concussion. Either way, I sink gratefully into my father and let him lead me gently back toward the house. In the distance, I can hear Caleb shouting and then the screams of the man who tried to kill me.

After that, silence.

2

"You know, you're always getting yourself into things like this," Peregrine says twenty minutes later, after she and Chloe screech up to my house in her vintage Aston Martin. Her snake, Audowido, is draped over her shoulders like a shawl, and the way he's staring at me unsettles me, as usual. "I was right in the middle of getting a manicure, you know. Now I've chipped the polish on three nails, Eveny. Three nails!" But despite her words, I know she's worried. She's chewing her bottom lip almost hard enough to draw blood.

"So sorry to inconvenience you." I turn slightly, wincing as I jostle my broken arm.

"Well," she says, looking me up and down. "You'll owe me for the manicure anyhow. Twenty dollars." Audowido hisses his agreement.

I just glare at her until she sighs and crosses her arms.

"You know, we can't be here to keep you from getting hurt all the time, okay?" she says. "And you can't be so irresponsible. This town is counting on all three of us."

I roll my eyes. "Gee, really? I hadn't realized."

Peregrine opens her mouth, but Chloe cuts her off with an elbow to her ribs. "What Peregrine's trying to say," Chloe says, "is that we're both very glad you're okay. You must have been really scared."

I nod, which sends pain shooting through my arm again. "Caleb got the guy," I say. In the corner, Caleb, who is scratched and bloody, looks up and meets my gaze. In his eyes, I see both fury and anguish; protecting me is his job, but taking a life still carves a piece out of your soul.

"The bigger problem," my father says, striding into the room with a handful of herbs, "is how the hell this monster got into Carrefour. Isn't the wall supposed to be protecting us from people like that?" He bends beside me and hands me the herbs. "Are you okay, honey?"

"She will be," Peregrine says before I can answer. "If you go away and let us do our thing." Peregrine's bought into the viewpoint her mom has held for a long time: that my dad is indirectly responsible for causing the trouble that has plagued Carrefour, beginning with my mother's death. The mothers' sosyete seems to believe that things were fine in town until my father arrived for the first time two decades ago, and that he somehow opened us up to attack from the outside. In other words, if he hadn't come here, danger wouldn't have found us.

"I can speak for myself, Peregrine," I say.

She shrugs and flicks her hundreds of snakelike curls over her shoulder while giving my father a dirty look.

"Peregrine—" my father begins, but then he seems to realize this isn't the time to argue. He closes his eyes briefly and says, "I know that if the three of you work together, you'll be much more effective at healing Eveny than I could be by myself. So please, just help her."

Peregrine turns away without replying and grabs the herbs from my hand. She takes a quick inventory of what my father has brought—white oak bark, althea, bay leaf, and walnut leaf. "Good choices," she says grudgingly. My father nods and walks away.

"You're going to have to do this one without holding my hand," I say, turning to Peregrine. Typically, when the three of us cast together, our power is strengthened when we join hands. But with my broken arm—the very thing we're here to heal—I don't think I'll be able to hold on without excruciating pain.

"Don't worry," Peregrine says, and for an instant, her defenses are down, and I see concern in her eyes. "I think if Chloe and I both grab on to your waist, we can still complete the circle. Okay?"

I nod, and she reaches for me more gently than I would have expected, inching one side of my shirt up to my rib cage and gesturing for Chloe to do the same. Once they're both touching me, Peregrine grasps the handful of herbs and takes Chloe's hand, so that the plants are between them. "Come to us now, Eloi Oke, and open the gate," she murmurs. Chloe and I join in on the second and third repetition, and as always, the air pressure in the room shifts as soon as we've said the phrase a third time.

Audowido hisses softly as Chloe begins to hum. Music isn't always necessary in a ceremony, but the spirits like it, so when you're asking for something big, it doesn't hurt. She keeps humming a single note as Peregrine chants, "White oak bark, althea, bay leaf, and walnut leaf, we draw your power. Spirits, please heal Eveny's broken arm and the other wounds she received at the hands of her attacker."

We all hum for a moment, our three voices combining to send a sweet sound into the universe. I'd like to imagine our singing heading up toward heaven, but the truth is, we only deal with spirits trapped in the nether, and those spirits live beneath us. Not exactly hell, but close. So I look down and concentrate, and after a moment, I feel a warm buzzing in my shoulder that spreads slowly down my arm like honey. Then there's the sensation of something pulling gently at me, and I can feel the pain being sucked out.

Finally, the room seems to vibrate with energy, and I don't hurt anymore. Audowido looks me up and down and, apparently sensing that the charm has worked, hisses in Peregrine's ear. She nods and stops humming. *"Mesi, zanset,"* she says. Chloe and I repeat the words, which mean *Thank you, ancestors.*

The air pressure regulates after we've said the phrase a third time, and the three of us look up at each other. As usual, I feel exhausted; the spirits draw on our energy to complete charms, so performing zandara always leaves us tired.

"You okay now?" Peregrine asks, looking me up and down.

I touch my arm gingerly, then shake it out. I sigh in relief. "Yeah, I think so."

"Good," she says. "Then let's talk about what the hell just happened. How did Main de Lumière get in?"

"We don't know for sure it was Main de Lumière," I remind her. But in my heart, I know there's no other option. High-ranking Main de Lumière soldiers—such as Aloysius Vauclain, the man who tried to kill me last month—are descended from the same line of magic haters, and they tend to be startlingly pale, with white-blond hair and almost translucent blue eyes. That's exactly what my attacker looked like behind the ski mask.

"There's no doubt," Caleb says from the corner. I turn, startled. I'd almost forgotten he was there. He crosses over to us and stands beside me, so close that I can feel the heat radiating from his skin. "When I took off his mask afterward . . ." His voice trails off and he looks at the ground. "He was definitely Main de Lumière."

"Okay. But how did they get in?" Chloe says.

"I don't know," I say. "But this isn't good." Since Carrefour's founding in 1904, the town has been protected by a magically charmed gate. It's what keeps us safe; only residents can enter, using a special key, and when they bring visitors in, which is rare, those people are powerless to harm anyone. The fact that a Main de Lumière intruder has gotten in—and succeeded in hurting me—means that something's wrong with the charm.

"We'll have to cast again as soon as possible," Peregrine says. "We're in danger all the time until we can fix this."

"Should we leave town until we figure it out?" Chloe asks. "This has never happened before."

Peregrine and I look at her in surprise, and I can see Caleb's head jerk up too. "Leave Carrefour?" I ask. The town has been a safe haven for our families for over a hundred years, and on top of that, leaving would put all of the innocent townspeople at risk, because we wouldn't be here to protect them. Abandoning it is unthinkable.

"Just for a little while," Chloe says. "Until we know we're safe?"

"Let's talk to our mothers about it," Peregrine says. "Ready to go?" she asks Chloe.

Chloe shoots me a concerned look. "You going to be okay?"

I nod. "Yeah. And thank you. For healing me."

"Of course," Chloe says.

"That's what sisters are for," Peregrine says, and I'm not sure whether or not she's being sarcastic until she gives me a quick hug good-bye and whispers, "I'm glad you're feeling better."

They disappear out the front door in a cloud of perfume,

leaving Caleb and me alone in the parlor.

"You're really all right?" he asks. For a second, all I can think about is the last time he kissed me and how amazing it would feel if he did it again. But then he takes a big step backward and says, "Look, I'm sorry."

"For what?" I say.

"I failed you—again."

"No, you didn't. Why would you ever think I'd be in danger in my own backyard? And you were here in an instant, Caleb." It suddenly occurs to me just how quickly he arrived. "Wait, how *did* you get here so fast?"

"I was meeting with your dad," he says, avoiding my gaze.

"Meeting with my dad? Why?"

He looks away. "There were some things he wanted to talk to me about."

"What things?"

Caleb shakes his head. "That's between me and your dad, Eveny. We're just concerned about keeping you safe."

I stare at him. "Yeah, heaven forbid you guys let me in on that plan."

Caleb sighs heavily. "Look. It's better this way, okay? I know I have to . . . separate myself from you. It's what your dad wants, and I agree. So just let it go. Okay?"

My stomach lurches. "I can't. You know I can't."

He sets his jaw. "And you know where I stand. I'm glad you're okay this time, but I should have sensed it before I heard you scream. It's exactly why I can't be with you, Eveny. My feelings are still getting in the way of our protectorate link."

"Which I should never have agreed to restore," I mutter. I'd let Caleb and my father persuade me, a few days after Drew's funeral, to reverse the charm I'd cast to sever the bond between Caleb and me. *If you die*, my father had warned, *this town will be in serious danger, because you won't be here to protect it.*

Caleb shakes his head. "Knowing I let you down . . ." He pauses and draws a ragged breath. "It's horrible. And I won't let it happen again."

"Caleb—" I begin, but he's already walking away. My heart sinks as I watch him go. I understand where he's coming from—he's trying to do the right thing—but I'm getting tired of century-old rules dictating who I'm allowed to love.

"Look, you can't just come back into my life and start trying to change it," I say a few minutes later as I walk into the kitchen and find my father sitting at the table.

He looks up. "Eveny, I'm not trying to change your life."

"Then what do you call talking to Caleb about me behind my back?"

"That isn't about changing your life, Eveny. That's about protecting you."

"Don't you think I should have a say in what happens to me?"

"Of course. But it's my responsibility to make sure you're okay."

I laugh. "Seriously? You're gone for almost my entire life, and then you turn up when I'm seventeen, and suddenly I'm *your responsibility*?"

He stands up and takes a step toward me. "Sweetheart, I know how you must be feeling, and I'm so sorry for any pain I've caused. But like I've told you, I was never really gone."

I cross my arms and try not to feel so torn. The problem is, I can't just jump into a warm father-daughter relationship with a man I hardly know. Since my mom died, the only parent I've had is my aunt Bea, who has avoided my father as much as possible since he's been back. I know that she, like Peregrine's and Chloe's mothers, believes he's at least partially to blame for bringing trouble to Carrefour.

"Look," I finally say. "I know you're trying to do the right thing here and that you want to protect me."

"Of course I do, Eveny," he says.

I hold up a hand. "Let me finish. What I'm trying to say is that this is hard for me, okay? I've spent the last fourteen years taking care of myself, with Aunt Bea's help. And whether you were looking out for me or not, that's not the same as being here."

He looks at me for a minute. "Of course. I understand."

"And you have to trust that I can look out for myself too. I'm not a kid anymore."

"I didn't mean to imply that you're not capable of taking care of yourself, Eveny. But you are a kid—*my* kid. And I'm going to do all I can to protect you."

I stand there in silence for a moment, and I'm surprised to feel tears in my eyes. I blink a few times and change the subject. "So what did you say to Caleb anyway?"

"I wanted to remind him of his responsibilities." He

doesn't meet my eye. I wait for him to go on, and finally, he adds, "It's his job to protect you. Nothing more."

"Don't you think he knows that?"

My father shakes his head. "He's let himself get distracted by his feelings for you. Not only is that a bad idea, but it's forbidden by the rules of zandara. Caleb needed to hear that again. And frankly, so do you."

I bristle at this. "That's not your business."

"I'm sorry, but it's just not something I can ignore," he says. "Not when it comes to your safety. In fact, I'm thinking about bringing someone else in to help keep you safe."

"I don't need anyone else!"

"Yes, well, there's going to come a day when being in the right place at the right time isn't going to work anymore for Caleb Shaw."

I settle into bed just past eleven to study my mother's herb journal, which I've been reading and rereading every night, trying to absorb the things she had learned about practicing zandara. She never had a chance to finish filling the journal out, because she was killed when she was only twenty-eight. Seeing all the empty pages at the back always makes me sad; they're like a symbol of her incomplete life.

The words are just starting to blur in front of my tired eyes when Aunt Bea appears at my open door and knocks lightly.

"Hey." I feel a little hurt that she didn't come to check on me earlier. She must have heard hours ago about my encounter with the Main de Lumière soldier.

When she just stands there, I say, "Did you hear about what happened?"

She nods, her expression oddly flat. "Yes. I heard."

"Caleb went after the guy."

"But I also understand that you got away from him yourself."

I nod and gesture to the journal, open in front of me. "I've been studying Mom's herbs. It's important that I learn everything I can about zandara."

"I suppose." She stares at the ceiling, her gaze somewhere far away. "But is that what you believe? Or is it what you're being told?"

"What?"

She shakes her head. "I mean, why are you suddenly so intent on buying into what the sosyete is telling you? Maybe you should slow down, give yourself some time to think about this before you jump in headfirst."

I stare at her in disbelief. "Are you trying to get me killed? I'm *already* in the middle of this, whether I like it or not. And Caleb's not going to be there every time I'm in trouble. I need to start relying on myself."

"Or you could walk away."

"How can you say that?" I demand, frustrated. "You're the one who brought me back here!"

"Because I thought it was the right thing at the time. I thought I was giving you back a piece of your birthright, something your mom would have wanted for you. But look what I've done! I've put you in danger. There's no way to know who to trust anymore or whose motives are pure. Everyone has their own agenda."

"And you don't?" I ask before I can stop myself.

She blinks a few times. "My only agenda is to protect you."

"And to discourage me from trusting anyone else."

"I'm just warning you," she says, looking away. "You believe in people too easily, and I think it's going to get you hurt."

She gives me a long look and walks away without another word. I watch her go, feeling more confused than ever.

I'm still sitting on my bed, staring after her, when my father appears in my doorway. "I've talked to Peregrine's and Chloe's mothers. After the attack today, they finally agree. It's time we all make a trip to Caouanne Island. We leave first thing in the morning."

3

"Couldn't we have just done a conference call?" I ask with a yawn as we drive past the town gate into the murky, swampy forest that surrounds Carrefour. We're on our way to the Baton Rouge airport, where Peregrine, Chloe, and their mothers are planning to meet us.

"Carrefour's defenses have obviously been breached, so you're not safe here at the moment," my father says, glancing over. "You'll be protected on Caouanne Island. Besides, my sosyete brothers are eager to meet you and show you how andaba works."

In the backseat, Caleb makes a huffing sound, but he doesn't say anything.

"It's part of who you are, Eveny," my father continues, "and the way we practice magic is very different from what you do in zandara. Besides, if the spirits we deal with see us allied with your sosyete sisters from Carrefour, they might be willing to give us all a little more assistance."

"Why?" I ask.

"Because our two sects have never worked together before," my father replies. "And I have to believe that the spirits will consider us more powerful—and therefore more useful to them—as a result."

His logic makes sense, and I can feel my heart thudding with anticipation as we park and hurry toward the airport entrance. The three of us just have carry-on bags, so we make a beeline for security. We're about to get in line when we hear a big commotion behind us. I turn, and my jaw drops when I realize it's my fellow queens arriving. Peregrine, Chloe, and their mothers, all wearing high heels, huge sunglasses, and full makeup, are striding into the airport, trailed by their protectors—Patrick, Oscar, Patrick's father, Benjamin, and Oscar's father, Anton—each of whom is pushing a cart overflowing with Louis Vuitton luggage.

Like Caleb's great-great-great-grandfather, Patrick's and Oscar's ancestors made a pact with the queens' ancestors over a hundred years ago, promising that their descendants would always guard the Queens of Carrefour, in exchange for fortune and good social standing. Apart from that, though, Patrick and Oscar couldn't be more different from Caleb: they chew tobacco, spit, and sometimes talk in Cajun accents so thick it doesn't sound like they're speaking English. But they're reliable guardians and take their jobs seriously.

Peregrine and Chloe are wearing minidresses and leather jackets, while their mothers are in silk pants and low-cut tops. They look like they're jetting off to the French Riviera. Caleb and I exchange looks as the group of queens gets closer, and although I know they're the ones being ridiculous, I feel frumpier than usual in my faded jeans, vintage Ramones T-shirt, and Converse.

"Is that another one of your ironic outfits, Eveny?" Peregrine asks, looking me up and down before air-kissing me on both cheeks.

"It's just comfortable for flying," I say, looking down self-consciously.

My father puts a hand on my back and says, "Come on, let's get to the gate. The others will be right behind us."

By the time the other queens and their protectors check in and make it through security, the flight is about to close. They just barely make it onto the plane, and I try not to laugh as they step aboard one by one and realize that not only are they not sitting together, but they're all in middle seats.

"We requested first class," Peregrine's mother says stiffly to a flight attendant.

"First class is full, ma'am," the woman replies. "You're in 28B."

Peregrine's mother looks horrified, but she manages to squash her Louis Vuitton tote into an overhead and climb over a hefty woman who's sitting on the aisle. "This is not what I'm accustomed to," she says, but everyone ignores her.

The flight takes off, and somehow Peregrine manages to talk the man next to me into letting her switch seats. I'm sure it doesn't hurt that she's batting her eyes like crazy, talking in a high, breathy voice, and leaning forward to give him a view of her cleavage. As soon as the fasten seat belt light goes off, she unbuckles and slides in next to me as the man, still staring at her appreciatively, wedges himself into her just-vacated seat across the aisle.

"I'm sure your father's sosyete brothers are eager to sink their claws into you," Peregrine says once she's strapped in. "So are you planning to cross over to the dark side and abandon us?" She reaches casually into her tote and pulls Audowido out, placing him on her lap. He fixes his beady eyes on me and hisses in greeting.

"Of course I'm not going to abandon you. And how on earth did you get your snake through security?"

Peregrine shrugs. "Flirtation gets me a long way. You should try it sometime."

Chloe turns around and peers at us between the seats. "Actually, she cast a charm on the TSA agents," she whispers, just as the woman sitting on my right sees Audowido and recoils in horror.

"Peregrine . . . ," I say in warning.

She sighs and reaches for her Stone of Carrefour. "Ceylon moss to make him unseen, black mustard seed to confuse onlookers. Spirits, please make Audowido disappear to anyone who's not in on the Secret of Carrefour."

I feel a subtle shift of air pressure—which is unsettling at ten thousand feet—and instantly, the woman beside me relaxes. "How strange!" she says. "I could have sworn you were holding a snake. But it's only your sweater."

"A mistake anyone could make," Peregrine says with a cold smile. "Now," she says, turning back to me, "where were we? Oh yes, I was talking about how your father's sosyete brothers were going to try to poach you. What, are we not good enough for you?"

"Peregrine, you're being ridiculous. I'm not going anywhere."

She gives me a look. "And yet we're all on a flight to Georgia, aren't we?"

"Look, it's complicated. But Carrefour is always going to come first, okay? It's where my mom's from, and that means everything to me."

Peregrine is quiet as Audowido slithers around her shoulders. "Time will tell, I guess."

Four hours and one connection in Atlanta later, most of our entourage is striding through the main doors of the Savannah/Hilton Head International Airport while Oscar, Patrick, and their fathers wait at baggage claim for the queens' luggage.

A white stretch Hummer pulls up to the curb less than a minute after we step outside into the humid afternoon. A tall man in his forties with light brown hair and deeply tanned skin gets out of the back, wearing chinos, boat shoes, and a button-down madras shirt. "Matthias!" he exclaims, pulling my dad into a hug.

My father looks happy to see him, and after they back away from each other, he introduces the man to us. "This is Simon, my sosyete brother," he tells us. "He's one of Caouanne Island's kings, like me."

"Guilty as charged," Simon says with a grin. There's something vaguely familiar about him, but I can't put my finger on what it is. "We're all so grateful that y'all made the trip here so quickly. Didn't you bring your protectors?"

"Eveny's protector, Caleb, is here," my father says as Caleb nods in greeting and shakes Simon's hand. I see Simon looking Caleb up and down as my father adds, "The others are retrieving the luggage."

"You checked luggage?" Simon asks. "But it's just a two-day visit, right?"

"*We* didn't check luggage," my father says, glancing at Peregrine, Chloe, and their mothers, who are standing in a cluster on the sidewalk. Chloe's mom is absentmindedly filing her nails; Peregrine is putting on lipstick in a compact mirror, and her mom is reapplying powder. It's like they're deliberately being disrespectful. Suddenly, I can feel the beginnings of a headache coming on.

Simon exchanges looks with my father, then he opens the door for us and gestures to the inside of the SUV limo. "No time to waste. Get in. I'll go check on your things."

It takes fifteen minutes for the Louis Vuitton bags to come off the conveyor belt and another hour to get to the docks on the coast of Georgia. Simon and my dad talk in hushed tones through much of the ride while Chloe, Peregrine, and their mothers drink champagne and act like they're on vacation. Caleb stares out the window, and I try hard not to keep stealing glances at him.

During the drive, Simon, who sits in back with us as a lower-level sosyete member drives, plays tour guide as he tells us about the island my dad calls home.

"*Caouanne* is the French word for a loggerhead turtle," he tells us. "Turtles, which are abundant off the coast of Georgia, are as important and magical to andaba as snakes are to zandara."

Audowido hisses at this, and Peregrine makes a face as Simon continues. "Much like Carrefour, Caouanne Island is protected from outsiders by both geography and magic. We're out in the ocean, some three miles from the coast, so physically, we're isolated. But the island is also surrounded by charms so that boaters can't see it unless they're within one hundred yards of our shores. Otherwise, it's cloaked in mist and looks like a stormy area that should be avoided."

"Don't people sometimes run aground by accident anyhow?" Chloe says. "Like how people sometimes arrive at Carrefour's gate because they've taken a wrong turn?"

"Occasionally, although it's rare," Simon says. "But from the outskirts of the island, it looks uninhabited and overgrown. There are only a few narrow paths into town, and those are hard to find. Plus the protective charms around the outside of the island alert us anytime the perimeter is breached."

We drive through a deserted-looking marshy area and emerge at a wooden dock on an inlet. There's a state-of-the-art yacht glistening in the late afternoon sunshine ahead of us. The driver stops the car, and Simon motions for us all to get out. "The boat'll be a bit of a tight squeeze, since I didn't anticipate you bringing two months' worth of luggage," Simon says. "But we'll be all right. It'll take us just thirty minutes to get from here to the island. Everybody in."

We file into the boat, and the guy who was driving the Hummer, who Simon quickly introduces as Nick, slides into the captain's chair. Minutes later, we're pulling out of the inlet, into the wide-open Atlantic. Just like Simon said, I can't see anything that even remotely resembles land until we're almost upon it.

"Welcome to Caouanne Island," Simon says as the milky fog parts and a lush green forest seems to spring from the middle of the ocean in front of us. Nick navigates the yacht into a small channel among the trees and Simon leaps easily from the bow onto a dock to help pull the boat in and secure it. "Ladies first," he says once the boat has stopped moving. He offers Chloe a hand and helps her onto the dock.

I'm the last to disembark, and as Simon takes my hand and gives me a boost off the boat, I could swear I hear him say, "Welcome home."

There's another stretch Hummer waiting beyond the trees, and after the guys load up the luggage and we all climb in, we set off down a dirt road that seems to wind deeper into a darkening forest.

"I can see why people would think the island is uninhabited," I say as the branches and boughs of the trees scrape the windows and the roof.

"Just wait," Simon says, adding a moment later, "Here we are."

We all strain to see out the windows as we enter a small downtown area that looks like an upscale seaside fishing village. It's spotless, with pristine, old-fashioned storefronts, late Victorian architecture, and impeccably dressed people strolling down the street.

Soon we arrive at a stately southern mansion just on the other side of the town center. It's pale yellow with shiny white shutters, wrought iron balcony rails, and ivy creeping up the two broad columns that support the roof of the front porch. The lawn is bright green and perfectly trimmed, and the front garden is lined with maroon and white roses. I like it immediately; it's much more modern-looking than the sweeping Gothic mansions the Marceaus, the St. Pierres, and I live in.

We step through the front door, and I'm startled to feel an inexplicable sense of familiarity—not like I've been here before but like I somehow belong anyway. It's not until I turn to my left and see a huge painting of my mother holding me as an infant that I realize why. "This is your house?" I say, turning to my father.

He smiles sadly and nods at the painting. "Your mom had

that commissioned and sent to me as a gift a few months after you were born. It made me feel like you were nearby, even when the two of you were far away."

I turn back to the painting, and for a moment I feel an overwhelming sense of sorrow for my parents. My mother's eyes are mournful, even though she's smiling. I know without asking that she was grieving for the husband she'd had to part with for reasons beyond her control.

My father glances once more at the painting. "I'll show you around in a bit, but for now, my sosyete is waiting. Shall we go meet with them first?" Without waiting for an answer, he beckons us to follow him down a long hallway. Caleb falls back with Oscar and Patrick as Peregrine and Chloe link their arms through mine.

"So this place is kind of yours too," Peregrine says as we pass impressionist paintings in gilt frames and intricately etched bell-shaped vases on pedestals.

I shrug. "I guess."

"How lovely for you," Peregrine says flatly, exchanging glances with Chloe.

"I'm not abandoning you, if that's what you're worried about," I tell them, but Chloe doesn't seem to hear me, and Peregrine just shrugs and looks away.

The hallway spills us into a big, open room with soaring ceilings and arched windows that overlook a huge, sprawling garden in the backyard. Four people—one man and three women—are sitting around a long, rectangular wooden table with another dozen empty chairs set up around it. They rise when we walk in.

"Welcome back, Matthias," says one of the women, who's tall, slender, and beautiful with chestnut hair and high cheekbones. Her eyes rest on him before she turns to the rest of us and says, "And welcome, all of you, to Caouanne Island. Please, make yourselves comfortable. We're so happy to have you."

My father quickly introduces the group to us. The woman who stood to greet us is Diane; the other two are Shelly and Veronica. The man, who's lanky and stern-looking, is George, the third king in my dad's generation, and he shakes hands firmly with my dad and Simon before turning to us and echoing Diane's greeting. As we go around the room quickly introducing ourselves, I begin to feel uneasy. They're all looking at me like a bug under a microscope.

"So you're Eveny," Diane says as we settle around the table. "We've all heard so much about you. It's fascinating to finally meet you."

"It's nice to meet all of you too," I say, but I'm feeling weird, because they're still staring. "Um, and thank you for having us here," I add.

"Well, it's your island too, isn't it?" Diane says, and I don't think I'm imagining the edge to her voice.

My father shoots Diane a look and takes over smoothly. "You've been called here today because our sosyete is very concerned about yesterday's attack against Eveny and has some important information they want to share with us. George will explain what we know."

George stands, and although his expression is grave, his eyes are kind. He's about my father's age, with close-cropped salt-and-pepper hair and a neatly trimmed goatee.

"We made contact with a Main de Lumière defector, who informed us that there are at least two other undercover operatives already embedded in Carrefour, and that they're townspeople you trust," he explains quickly. "That's in addition to Drew Grady. We believe they're ready to move against you—and that they've been instrumental in helping Main de Lumière disable your protective gate."

"Wait, that's impossible!" Peregrine's mother says. "Our gate has worked for more than a hundred years. There's no way it could be disabled by anyone who isn't magical."

"Then how do you explain what happened to me?" I ask. "The man who attacked me, he wasn't from Carrefour. Sure, he could have gotten in with one of the townspeople's keys, but if the charm on the gate was working, he wouldn't have been able to harm me."

"I'm sure there's an explanation," Peregrine's mother says firmly, but I can read uncertainty in her eyes.

"Which is why we need to hear George out," I say, looking at my father's brother king, who nods at me gratefully.

Peregrine stands suddenly before George can continue. "How do we know this source of yours even defected? Maybe he's just lying on their behalf."

George shakes his head. "I wish that were the case," he says. "But within twenty-four hours of him giving us this information, he was found dead."

"Dead?" Chloe repeats as Peregrine slumps back into her seat.

George's mouth compresses into a thin line. "He was dumped on our shores, which means Main de Lumière has discovered our location too. They must have tortured him until he talked. The last thing he said to us is that Main de Lumière is planning to destroy both andaba and zandara by eliminating the one person who's essential to both magical traditions. That can mean only one thing." He closes his eyes, as if the rest is too painful to ponder. There's suddenly a sour taste in my mouth, and I brace myself for what I know is coming next.

Diane stands. "If we don't do something about it," she says, looking directly at me, "we believe that Eveny will be dead within a matter of days."

4

"*I*t's exactly like Drew said before he died," I say twenty minutes later, as we break for a meal and tuxedoed waiters bring us roasted chicken, grilled peaches, pecan green beans, and truffled mashed potatoes on huge gold platters. "I wish they could understand that I'm still new at all this. I'm no more powerful than anyone else."

"But that's not true, now, Eveny, is it?" Diane asks. "You're quite different from all of us."

Simon gives her a look before turning to me. "What Diane means to say, Eveny, is that you're still a bit of an unknown. You've only just begun to tap into your zandara abilities, but we don't yet know the extent of your andaba powers, and that's what Main de Lumière is apparently concerned about."

"My andaba powers?" I ask, looking from Simon to my father in confusion. It was only a couple of weeks ago that I learned my father was an andaba king, but I had assumed that my andaba blood would merely strengthen my skill in zandara.

It's Diane who finally begins to explain. "As you may know, andaba is based around a patriarchy, the same way zandara is centered around a matriarchy. Power here is passed from father to son. So while women have always been respected, we've never been the ones with the true power, just as the men in your magical tradition take a backseat to the queens.

"But for the first time in Caouanne Island history," she continues, glancing at my father, "we have a female heir, which creates a very . . . unique situation."

It takes me a split second to realize exactly what Diane means, and when I do, I feel like I've swallowed a jagged piece of glass. "Me?" I ask. "You're saying I'm an andaba ruler?"

Diane nods. "Of course this is because your father, our most powerful king, had a child with the heir to a matriarchal structure: your mother. If he'd simply stayed on the island and had a child here, as he was intended to, his firstborn would have been a boy, just like every other firstborn in the history of andaba.

"So while you're obviously a Queen of Carrefour, Eveny, you're also a Queen of Caouanne Island," Diane continues. "We're quite fascinated by what this might mean for the future of andaba. But we're also very aware that if Main de Lumière gets to you, they'll be able to destroy not just the zandara bloodline in Carrefour, but also the future of andaba on Caouanne Island. That's what makes you such an appealing target. Of course Peregrine, Chloe, and their mothers are targets too—as are the kings here on Caouanne Island—but you're unique, and they have their eyes on you."

George picks up her explanation. "Eveny, they know that eliminating you before you give birth to an heir would effectively cripple both andaba and zandara, because your bloodline would be destroyed."

My head spinning, I turn to my dad. "Why didn't you tell me this?"

He hesitates. "Honey, you've had so many revelations lately that I didn't want to overwhelm you. The truth is, you're not just a part of our sosyete; you're the leader, since it was our ancestors who founded the sect. When you turned seventeen, that authority fell naturally to you."

Suddenly, I realize something. "Wait, is that why you came back?" I ask. "Because the future of Caouanne Island rides on me? Because you wanted to bring me here to assume my rightful place or something?"

My father looks startled. "Of course not, Eveny. I came back after Main de Lumière's attack on you because you were in great danger. I couldn't live with losing you."

I turn to Caleb. "Did you know about this?" I ask. "That I'm an andaba queen too?"

"No," he says. He glances at my father. "I would never have kept something like this from you. It changes everything."

Peregrine, who managed to clean her plate while we were

discussing the possibility of my imminent death, holds up a fork. "Clearly, for Eveny's protection, we should all return to Carrefour immediately," she says.

Diane looks like her eyes are going to pop out of her head. "Why on earth would that be the preferable situation? Am I incorrect in recalling that just yesterday, Eveny was attacked inside your walls?"

"We'll work on that," Peregrine says. "Besides, Caleb is better able to protect her there. Inside Carrefour's walls, he's able to sense when she's in danger."

"When his abilities aren't being disrupted by his lust for Eveny," Diane shoots back. I can feel my cheeks burning as she adds, "You know as well as I do that he's compromised, and his abilities are lessened because of it."

"It's over between us," I say, swallowing the lump in my throat as I wonder how she knows about Caleb. My father must have told her, which makes me feel betrayed. "His feelings are no longer an issue."

Diane gives me a withering look. "And I suppose you feel you'd be safer in a place where we know there are at least two Main de Lumière operatives lurking?"

"You have Main de Lumière informants washing up dead on your beaches, so I'd say your little island here is just as exposed," Peregrine says before I can answer. "At least in Carrefour, Eveny is at home. And she already knows how to use her zandara abilities, which are stronger there."

"All the more reason she should stay here, to begin

learning about andaba," Diane says.

The conversation disintegrates from there. Chloe's and Peregrine's mothers jump into the fray on Carrefour's side, as Simon and Shelly both speak up in favor of me staying on Caouanne Island. I can barely differentiate the voices that echo rapid-fire around the room.

"We have a protective wall!"

"We're isolated from the mainland!"

"Eveny's been one of us for months now!"

"Yes, and you've been keeping her from her rightful role here!"

"Stop, everyone!" I say, interrupting the volley of accusations. "Fighting isn't getting us anywhere. Look, why don't I just disappear for a while? If I hide out somewhere else, maybe they won't find me."

"That's a terrible idea," Diane says.

"You know, I'm really starting to dislike you," I say, which earns me a glare from her and a stifled laugh from Caleb.

"Diane means that you'll always be safer in a town protected by magic," Simon says. "We'll still have the upper hand. And frankly, if you're here on Caouanne Island, we'll be able to fight Main de Lumière off much more effectively with the addition of your power."

"Which is exactly why we need her in Carrefour," Peregrine's mother says. "Because of her power."

That's when it dawns on me that the sosyetes aren't just trying to protect me. They're fighting over who gets to keep me to enhance their own magical abilities. The realization hurts. "Look," I say, "it's my life you're arguing about. Shouldn't I be the one to decide where I go?"

"You're a child," Diane says.

"She's a queen," Caleb says immediately, "of both towns."

I'm grateful for Caleb's intervention, but the weight on my shoulders feels suddenly immense. Whichever town I choose, I'll be putting the sosyete there in grave danger, because the town will be a bull's-eye for Main de Lumière. On the other hand, I'll bring more protection to the town I'm in simply by being there and contributing my power. It's an impossible choice.

"What do you think?" I ask Caleb.

"I think," he says, "that it's up to you. And I'll be behind you, one hundred percent, whatever you choose."

As I look around me, I see people who, for all their faults, are my family. I may not always approve of Peregrine and Chloe, but they're my sisters. On the other side stands a group I hardly know but whose strongest king is my only living parent, a man who loved my mother enough to defy tradition and marry her. I can't believe he would lead me astray either.

Finally, I turn to Diane. "I'm sorry," I say. "I have to go back to Carrefour for now." I look at my dad and add, "You only just came back for me. Mom's family, well, they've always been a part of my life. I have to stay and fight with them."

"That's a terribly shortsighted decision," Diane says.

"That's enough, Diane," my father says quickly. "She's

your queen." He turns to the rest of the group and adds, "She's a queen to all of you, and she deserves your respect, whether you agree with her or not. We all need to support her now. Our future is in her hands."

Instead of soothing me, the words make me feel queasy. It's not a responsibility I've asked for, and it scares me to know that so many people depend on me. I wonder if I'll ever feel like the leader they expect me to be.

"Fine, then, it's decided," Diane says, looking back to me. "Eveny will return to Carrefour. In the meantime, we'll cast as much protection as we can over both towns and Eveny herself."

"What do you want us to do?" Chloe's mother asks.

"Meet us in the ceremonial room here in Matthias's house at midnight," George says. "We'd like you to sit in on our ceremony. Although you can't cast with us, we feel your presence might strengthen our influence with the spirits. We work with different spirits than you do, but they all live in the nether, and they may be able to communicate with each other. If that's the case, having them know we're allied is important. So it's best to spend the next few hours getting some rest."

"Or doing your hair. Or shopping. Or whatever it is you queens do," Diane says, smirking at the Carrefour contingent. "Because goodness knows, the way you look is far more important than saving lives, right?"

"That's enough, Diane," my father says.

A shadow crosses her face, and then she stands up, slams her hands on the table, and strides out of the room.

My father takes us all to our rooms and tells us to make ourselves at home while we wait for the evening ceremony. "We'll show all of you around tomorrow," he adds. "It's important to me that you get to know the island. But for now, you must rest. All of you."

Peregrine eyes the bathroom at the end of the hall. "Does this house of yours have a Jacuzzi tub? I'm in desperate need of a long soak after that hideous experience flying coach."

My father gives me a look and forces a pleasant expression. "Yes, Peregrine, I think you'll find the accommodations here very comfortable."

Right away, Peregrine, Chloe, and their mothers begin chattering about how they'll pamper themselves for the next few hours. Caleb and the other protectors stand off to the side, whispering to each other.

"Don't you think we should be coming up with a plan or something?" I say. "Considering that the whole reason we're here is that our lives are in danger?"

"Eveny, dear," Chloe's mother says, "nothing's going to happen to us this evening. Your father said it himself; this is a safe place. So we might as well enjoy our vacation, don't you think?"

"This isn't a vacation," I say, but my words are lost in their resumed babble about baths and facials and blow-outs.

"You doing okay?" Caleb asks, coming up beside me and putting a hand on the small of my back. His touch makes me shiver, and noticing my reaction, he quickly pulls away. "I mean, if you want to talk about what happened downstairs . . ."

"No, I'm fine," I say quickly. "I think I'm going to go explore the garden I saw out back."

"I can come with you."

"I'd rather go alone." I don't meet his eyes as I say the words, because they're not true. I want to be with him. But I know he'll only act cold and distant, and I'm so overwhelmed right now, I don't think I can handle that. I feel him stiffen, and he takes a step back.

"No problem," he says. "Just don't leave your dad's property, okay? Since we're not in Carrefour, I won't be able to sense it if you're in danger."

"I'll be fine," I tell him, and head downstairs alone before he can say anything else.

5

My father's garden is much sparser than the one outside our house in Carrefour, which makes sense, I suppose. Andaba isn't based on herb magic the way zandara is, so there's no need to have a yard full of plants and flowers. Still, there's a rose garden on the left side of the house, and that's where my feet carry me now, led by the familiar, comforting scent that always reminds me of my mother.

"Hello." I'm startled to hear my father's deep voice from among the roses as I round the corner.

"I didn't expect to find you out here," I say, joining him in a small, circular clearing surrounded by pale pink New Dawn roses.

He glances at me. "This is where I come when I need to be alone with my thoughts."

I hesitate. "Do you want me to leave?"

"No, no, that's not what I meant," he says quickly. "I'm glad you're here. This garden, it always reminds me of your mother. It's nice to have you share it with me."

"Mom would have loved it," I agree, relaxing a little as I look around at the dozens of rose varieties, many of them similar to the ones growing in my garden in Carrefour.

"She planted it herself, actually," he says softly. "Back when we were still crazy enough to believe in a future where we could spend time here as well as in Carrefour. It seems silly now that we ever thought either of our sosyetes would accept the relationship between us. There was even a time when we dreamed of bringing herb magic to Caouanne Island. We thought there might be a way to blend andaba with zandara to strengthen both."

"Turns out there was a way," I say, looking away. "Me."

"That's not what I meant. You were always something separate from that."

"Except I'm not, am I?" I say. "I'm some strange blend of both forms of magic. And I hardly understand any of it."

He studies me, then sighs. "Can I show you something, Eveny? I think it might help make things a little clearer."

I follow him down a path, through a small arch in a tall hedge wall, and into another area of his garden. I gasp as soon as I realize what I'm seeing.

"Wait, these are Mom's hybrid roses," I say. "The Rose of Life." Indeed, this whole section of the garden is filled with the familiar purple roses with gold-flecked edges, the ones that I thought only grew in my family's garden in Carrefour. A small jolt of electricity shoots through me as I touch one. "You grow them here too?"

"The last time I saw your mother, when you were just a little girl, she gave me one of the Rose of Life bushes to plant on Caouanne Island. She said that as long as it grew here, we would be connected. Over the years, I've planted a whole garden from it."

I bend and smell the roses, and when I close my eyes, I can almost see my mother reaching out for me.

"Did you know we actually developed the Rose of Life together?" he asks after a pause.

"Wait, what?"

"It's a hybrid. Magic had nothing to do with it. It was all science, cross-pollination." A faraway expression sweeps across his features. "I first came to Carrefour as a botany student, you know. I had no idea the town was magical. I'd only ever known andaba. I took an internship working under Boniface, who ran a botany center at the time."

"Boniface ran a botany center?" I'm struck by how little I actually know about the history of the people I'm closest to.

My father chuckles. "He's retired now, of course, but there was a time when he and your mother believed that zandara could be enhanced by engineering the very plants themselves. In other words, if plants with different zandara uses were bred together, the resulting plant could be used differently in charms. It was the first time I know of that science had been

used to tinker with magic. They were on the cusp of something very important, I think, but much of that died with your
mother."

I swallow the lump in my throat. "So they knew you had
magical blood too when they hired you as an intern?"

He laughs. "Oh no, absolutely not. They thought I was
merely an earnest botany student from Savannah, and I
believed Boniface and your mother were just two very intel-
ligent plant enthusiasts. Once I discovered what your mother
was, I realized I was unwittingly working on hybrids that
would enhance her sosyete's magic.

"You could say the Rose of Life is what drew us together
in the first place, actually," my father continues, reaching out
and touching one of the rosebuds. "At first, I thought your
mom's goal was just to create a hardy rose that could with-
stand the winter. But when I learned about zandara, I realized it was something else entirely. She was trying to breed
plants that, for a variety of scientific reasons I won't bore you
with, shouldn't have been able to mate. But then she told me
one night that she'd already managed to merge a wingtip rose
with red clover."

"Love, luck, and protection," I say.

"Very good," he says. "She called it a Happiness Rose. I
was very impressed with what she'd done. She told me then
that she was trying to breed that rose with acacia."

"Acacia? For immortality and to communicate with
spirits?"

He nods. "Exactly. I didn't understand it at the time. But what she was trying to do was to create a rose that was capable of bringing people back from the dead."

My breath catches in my throat. For a moment, all I can think about is what might have been. If my mother had succeeded, perhaps she could have had a chance at returning to us. "But it didn't work, did it?"

His face falls. "I wish to God it had. But it's impossible. We managed to crossbreed the plants, but the magic never worked. The dead just aren't meant to return to life."

My heart aches, and I can't find the words to reply right away. "So when did you tell my mom that you knew about zandara?" I finally ask. "And that you were magic too?"

He looks lost in thought. "I'd been in town for a month. We were in the garden at night, cutting roses, and Boniface had gone to bed. There was a full moon, and when she turned to me to say something, the way the moonlight lit her face made her look like she was glowing. Without even thinking about it, I leaned forward and kissed her, and it felt completely different from any kiss I'd ever had before, like there was an electrical current running between us. I'd never felt so alive, and I knew she felt it too. I was the one who pulled away, because I had a secret. I couldn't kiss her again until I'd come clean."

"So you told her? About andaba?"

He laughs. "The words just fell out of my mouth in a jumble. I don't think she believed me at first, but when she finally did, she looked scared. I had to reassure her that I'd had absolutely no idea when I came to Carrefour that there was magic in the town. I only realized when I saw her performing a ceremony with Scarlett St. Pierre and Annabelle Marceau one night.

"She thought we should tell her sister queens that I had magical abilities too, but I told her it was a bad idea," he continues. "They would have believed I was there for the wrong reasons. I would have been thrown out of Carrefour, and I would never have seen your mother again."

"But why?"

"Different magical groups don't usually trust each other, Eveny," my father says. "Zandara and andaba both originated with practitioners of voodoo, but a century down the line, they're as different as night and day. I'd been raised to distrust anyone who practiced magic outside of andaba. And your mom had been raised with the same feelings about zandara."

"It's why Peregrine, Chloe, and their moms seem to have a grudge against andaba, isn't it?" I ask. "It's the same now as it was when you were younger."

"I'm afraid so. That's why your mother and I started dating in secret," my dad replies. "Boniface was the only one who knew about us. I was surprised he didn't seem to mind, so I asked him why. He told me that rules shouldn't stand in the way of what two people feel."

Heat floods my face as I think about Caleb. I wonder if Boniface would have the same kind of advice for us. "So Mom was in love with you from the start too?" I ask.

"I've never felt so loved by someone in my life." He blinks a few times, like he's trying to get ahold of himself. "I didn't know love could feel that powerful. Until you came along, that is."

"But you weren't there." I can't help sounding as hurt as I feel. "With me, I mean."

"That's what we wanted everyone to believe," he says. "It was safer that way. By the time you were born, your aunt and your mother's sister queens knew my secret. We trusted them, but if anyone outside that circle found out that your mother and I had created a child together, you could have been in terrible danger. So I had to go."

"I know," I say softly. "I can't blame you for that. But it's hard for me to believe that you loved me as powerfully as you say. How could someone feel that way and leave?"

"That's exactly why I couldn't stay away, honey. The first time I came back was the day after your birth. I held you in my arms, and I couldn't believe how tiny and perfect you were. Your mom and I just kept saying, 'We made this.' The love you feel holding your own child in your hands, well, it's a whole different kind of love, bigger than I could have imagined."

"You felt like that about me?" I ask, suddenly choked up.

"Of course. The second time I returned was just before your first birthday. I know you don't remember, but your mom, Boniface, and I had a little birthday party for you in the back garden. You got frosting in your hair." He smiles. "You can ask Boniface."

I'm so shaken by what he's telling me that the only thing I can think to ask is, "Where was Aunt Bea?"

His smile wavers. "Your mother didn't want her to know I was there. She was very much against my presence in your mother's life."

"Did you come back again?"

The smile vanishes from his face. "The third time I came to see you was four days before your mother died. Your aunt has believed since then that I was followed to Carrefour by someone powerful enough to temporarily disable Carrefour's protective charm. To this day, I believe that's impossible."

"But she's always blamed you anyhow," I say, thinking of all the times I asked about my father when I was younger, only to see Aunt Bea's expression grow stony and closed off.

"Yes." He's silent for a moment. "But since the day your mother died, I've had only two things driving me. One is the need to protect you, not only because you're my child, but because your mother and I created a dangerous situation for you simply by conceiving you. It's my fault that you're in harm's way."

"What's the second thing?" I ask.

My father takes a deep breath. "My work on this earth won't be done until I find out who killed your mother," he says. "And until I put that person in the ground."

A shiver goes through me as he pulls out a pocketknife and swiftly cuts one of the Rose of Life stems. "Here," he says, holding out a bloom for me. "Your mom always told me to carry one with me whenever I missed her. She said it would make me feel like she was here with me. Maybe it was just the power of suggestion, but holding on to one of these always did make me feel a little better. This one's for you."

He tucks it behind my ear and kisses me on the cheek, and then he's gone. I stand in the garden for a long time, surrounded by the scent of my mother's roses and by a swirling cloud of facts about a past I'm realizing I never really knew at all.

6

*W*hen I eventually head back to the house to get ready for tonight's ceremony, I run into Caleb upstairs.

"Hey," he says, shifting awkwardly.

"Hey."

We stand there for a moment, just staring at each other, before we both begin speaking at once.

"You first," he says with an uneasy laugh.

I hesitate. "I just talked to my dad."

He blinks a few times. "He told you the story?"

"What story?"

He sighs. "About my dad and how he failed your mom."

"No, of course not," I reply. Caleb has told me before that his father always blamed himself for letting my mother die, since he was charged with protecting her. "Why would you think he was telling me that?"

He looks away. "It's what your dad wanted to talk to me about yesterday, just before you were attacked." He draws a deep breath. "He blames my family, Eveny, and he hates me because of it. Maybe you should too."

"My dad doesn't hate you," I say, although instantly, I wonder if I'm right. "And whatever happened with our parents, that shouldn't have anything to do with me and you."

Caleb is silent for a long time. "Eveny, my dad broke the rules fourteen years ago, and your mom wound up dead because of it," he says finally. "She was murdered because my dad wasn't there to protect her, whether you want to admit that or not. And within a year, he was dead too—because of the curse that hangs over the head of every protector if he lets his queen die. That's why we can't break the rules, Eveny. That's why it was so stupid of me to kiss you or to think we could ever be together. That's why it doesn't matter what I feel for you and what you feel for me. You want to wind up dead like them? Because I don't."

"They're not dead because they broke the rules," I say, trying to keep my voice calm.

"How can you say that?" Caleb replies immediately. "My dad was supposed to be keeping guard outside your house the night your mom died, okay? But he wasn't there."

"It's not his fault," I say, trying to cut the story off.

But Caleb shakes his head vigorously and continues. "Yes, it was. And it was mine too. I was really sick that night. I had a high fever, and my dad was worried about me, so his mind wasn't on his responsibilities. Before your mom performed the ceremony with Peregrine's and Chloe's moms, she insisted that my dad go home. She told him to go be with his family, to go care for his son."

"Caleb—" I say, but he just keeps talking.

"By the time my dad got home, my fever had spiked to a hundred and five. My mother had also gotten very sick and was too delirious to realize that I needed to go to the hospital. I would have died if my father hadn't come home when he did."

"So he saved your life."

"Maybe, but because he came back for me, he wasn't there to protect your mother. I lived, but your mother died."

I swallow the lump in my throat. "That wasn't your dad's fault. And it definitely wasn't yours."

He turns to me with a desperate look in his eyes. "But it was. There's no escaping that. I'm so sorry, Eveny. So sorry." Caleb shakes his head. "He left Carrefour in shame because he couldn't live with what he'd done."

"I'm sorry about your dad," I say, reaching out to touch Caleb's arm. "But you and me, it's not the same."

"Of course it is! Don't you see? My dad put love—love for me and my mom—before his duties. He ruined his own life and your mother's because of one selfish decision. I'm not going to put you in the same kind of danger my dad put your mom in. Ever."

"But it's different, Caleb," I say. "He couldn't have known what was about to happen."

Caleb pulls away from me. "Try to understand where

I'm coming from. You're in danger, and all I care about right now is keeping you safe. Whatever happened between us—whatever feelings we have for one another—it has to be over. All of it. Your dad's right."

"No, he's not," I protest. "You want to know what I was out there talking to him about? It was about how he and my mom broke all the rules to fall in love. They were never supposed to be together either."

Caleb stares at me for a long time, and when he folds his hands over mine, I'm sure he's going to say that he sees my point of view. He leans forward and kisses me softly on the lips, but when he pulls back, his eyes are filled with sadness. "I can't. It doesn't matter how I feel. What matters is you staying alive. I'm sorry."

He walks away without looking back.

That evening, I avoid Caleb's gaze as we all follow Diane and my father down a long hall and into a large ceremonial room that reminds me of the parlor where my mother used to perform zandara in my house. Even though I know Caleb's heart is in the right place, I still feel rejected. Knowing I'm apparently so easy to stop caring about hurts.

As we enter the room, Diane touches my father's arm and says something in his ear. He smiles and whispers back, and I'm struck again by the easy familiarity between the two of them.

"Want to light the candles while I get the fireplace going,

Eveny?" Simon asks, appearing at my elbow and smiling kindly at me.

"Sure," I say, taking a long, antique-looking tinder lighter from him. I move around the room quickly until all the candles are flickering, and then I rejoin the group.

My father is in the midst of apologetically telling Caleb, Oscar, Patrick, and their fathers that they'll need to step out of the room, along with Diane, Shelly, and Veronica. "We feel our collective presence will be stronger if the only people in the room are those with magical abilities," he says.

Caleb shoots me a look before ducking out, followed by the other protectors. Shelly and Veronica trail behind them, and Diane rolls her eyes dramatically as she strides out of the room. The door closes heavily.

"Now," my father says, "shall we get started?"

"Wait," Peregrine's mother says. "How exactly do you plan to execute this charm? I don't see what good we'll do here."

"You're right," my father says. "But Eveny's going to need your moral support. This will be her first time working with andaba, and knowing you're behind her will help, I think."

I feel even more uncomfortable than I did before, but my dad's right. It's hard to focus when I feel like the two sides of my heritage are at odds.

"Fine," Peregrine's mother mutters. "But let's make this quick."

"Good luck," Chloe says, giving me a small smile as she, Peregrine, and their mothers take seats along the wall.

"Thanks," I say as my father, Simon, George, and I form a circle.

"Just follow along," my father says, squeezing my hand. "Trust me." He takes a deep breath and says, *"Guardabarrera, ¿está usted ahí?"*

The other two men chant, *"Dejarnos entrar, señor. Dejarnos entrar."*

As soon as they're done speaking, there's a whoosh of wind, and the air changes in the room. I'm accustomed to the air pressure feeling heavier with the presence of a spirit, but this time, it seems to get lighter and crisper.

"Okay, Eveny," my father says. "Try to focus your energies toward the center of the room." He takes a bowl from the table and approaches the fire and begins to chant.

"Oh lonely warriors, spirits of the sea,
Hear our cry, accept our plea.
With grave dirt and muerte dust our passage fee;
With the strength of our hearts, we call out to thee."

He throws a handful of dark dust from the bowl into the fireplace, and as Simon and George repeat his words, he raises the bowl to his mouth and blows the rest of the dust into the flames. He steps back just as the room begins filling with sweet-smelling white smoke.

"What's happening?" Chloe asks from behind me, her voice sounding very far away.

I don't know the answer, but I realize I'm not frightened. There's something about the smoke that comforts me, as if from a long-lost memory.

But I'm completely unprepared for what happens next. The kings step forward and, using small pocketknives, each of them pricks his own index finger and squeezes a drop of blood into the fire. The smoke swirls more and more quickly until it's collected in the center of the room. It takes on the shape of a small tornado at first, but as it whirls, it begins to develop features that look human. Soon, I can make out the faintest outline of a man's face in the spinning smoke. "I am here," a male voice with a strong accent hisses from the cloud.

Peregrine screams, and George says quietly, "It's okay. It's a friendly spirit we deal with often."

"Captain Cabrillo, commander of the *Nuestra Mujer del Mar*," my father begins in a booming voice. "We reach out to you to ask for your protection and your intervention on our behalf."

"Matthiassssssssss," the voice hisses. I can see the lips of the foggy figure moving slowly. "We receive your *súplica*, your *petición*. On whose behalf do you make this plea?"

"On behalf of my sosyete, and the sosyetes of Carrefour."

"Carrefour?" The cloud swirls before the voice adds, "Your daughter. She is here?"

"Yes, Captain Cabrillo, she is here." My father nods at me, and I take a half step forward. I hold my breath as the face of the spirit materializes in front of me.

"Eveny," the spirit says. "*Gusto en conocerla.* It is nice to meet you after so many years of *su padre* talking of you."

"I—it's nice to meet you too," I say, trying not to sound as freaked out as I feel.

"I understand you are in need of my assistance," he says.

"Yes, sir," I reply. I draw a shaky breath. "Main de Lumière is after me, as well as my sister queens and my brother kings. We need as much protection as we can get right now. Please, sir, we'd appreciate anything you can do to help us."

The cyclonic mist shakes a little, and it takes me a moment to realize the spirit is laughing. "Such a humble request," he says. "Very well, Eveny. I am sure you know the limitations of those of us in the spirit world. We can intervene in human affairs, but only to a small degree. So we will look after you and your friends to the best of our abilities. But our protection can only buy you time. Do you understand me?"

"Yes, sir," I say.

"*Muy bien,*" the spirit says. "Matthias, you are here?"

"I am here, Captain," my father says right away.

"I will leave you the doubloons for José de Mateo, on your shore at dawn. I trust you will see him through?" The mist moves in my father's direction.

"Yes, Captain," my father says. "It shall be done."

"*Muy bien.* Then I wish you *buenas noches* and *sueños del cielo,* dreams of heaven."

"And to you, Captain," my father says.

"Dreams of heaven . . . to me?" the spirit asks. The swirling cloud turns darker as he hisses, "But surely you know I am headed to hell."

And with that, the smoke and the sound of his laughter whisk toward the fireplace and up the chimney. He's gone before I can blink, and then the candles all flicker out at once and the air pressure in the room returns to normal.

"What the—?" Peregrine's voice sounds terrified in the darkness. "What was that?"

There's the sound of a match striking, and my father's face appears behind the dancing light of a flame.

"That," he says, "was Captain Cabrillo, the commander of a Spanish galleon that sank off the Georgia coast in 1622. Fifty-six of the crew members aboard were trapped in the nether. When andaba was founded, the spirits our ancestors reached out to were all buried in watery graves, like the crew of *Nuestra Mujer del Mar*, Captain Cabrillo's ship. Most of the spirits we've dealt with over the years are of Spanish descent, so our charms have evolved with Spanish words and phrases. For a very long time now, Cabrillo has been assisting us, in exchange for our helping his crew cross over from the nether to a true afterlife."

I exchange looks with the others. "So that was really the ghost of Cabrillo?" Chloe asks.

My father nods. "I know that in zandara, spirits can only talk through humans, in possession ceremonies. But because andaba uses grave dirt, we're able to reach a bit further into the nether and get the spirits to actually materialize."

"What was the other kind of dust you threw into the fire?" I ask.

"Muerte dust," my father says. "Ashes and several other ingredients mixed with the ground bones of sea turtles. They help us to cross the line between land and ocean, life and death."

"Turtle bones?" Peregrine says.

My father is quick to clarify, "We respect turtles as much as you respect snakes, I promise. We only harvest their bones once they're dead. In andaba, we see it as their final spiritual gift to us."

"Ew," Peregrine says. "It's still gross."

My father shrugs. "Every magical tradition uses different elements, Peregrine. Some might say your reliance on a snake is disturbing." He glances at Audowido before turning to me. "And now we must pay the price for Cabrillo's help. We must assist his sailor José de Mateo in crossing out of the nether."

"How do we do that?" I ask.

"Cabrillo leaves us doubloons from his sunken ship, and we use it to pay other spiritual gatekeepers," he says. He glances at me. "But leave that to us. Perhaps it's time for you to get some rest."

I suddenly realize that I'm exhausted. "I feel like I'm about to collapse."

My father smiles, but there's sadness in his eyes. "It's because it was your first time communicating with the spirit world using andaba," he says. "The first time is always the hardest on your system. And you did very well, Eveny. You've proven what I long suspected: your andaba abilities are strong.

"Unfortunately, that means that Main de Lumière's fears are true," my father concludes, looking at me with a strange blend of fear and pride. "You could be the most powerful queen the world has ever known."

7

That night I dream of shipwrecks and storms, of gold coins washing up on deserted beaches, and of the bones of sailors who died centuries ago.

When I awaken, I realize that Peregrine, who's sharing a bed with me, is already up, staring at the ceiling. Chloe is still fast asleep on an air mattress on the floor.

"Morning," Peregrine says without looking at me. "Bad dream?"

"How did you know?"

"You were thrashing around like a mental patient."

I apologize for waking her, but she waves me off. "It wasn't you. I woke up on my own. I've got to say, I'm pretty freaked out by everything here. That andaba ceremony . . . it just wasn't right."

"Because they got the ghost of the captain to actually appear to us?"

"I guess. It just feels strange. I always thought we were running a big risk by inviting spirits to take over our bodies in zandara. But at least we have some control over the situation."

I shrug and wait for her to go on. I'm surprised to hear her expressing any kind of concern about zandara, which she has, so far, seemed to adore wholeheartedly.

"But in andaba," she says, "the way they actually bring the spirit back, well, it's weird. I mean, spirits aren't supposed to be able to bring their physical forms back from the dead with them, are they?"

I roll onto my back and stare at the ceiling. "Just because we don't do it in zandara doesn't mean it's wrong. Maybe we can learn something from andaba about what's possible."

"But doesn't it make you uneasy?"

"Not exactly. It makes me wonder what else I don't know yet."

Peregrine goes to take a shower, so I step over Chloe and head downstairs to the kitchen in my T-shirt and pajama pants. My father is standing at the stove flipping pancakes when I walk in. "Hi, honey," he says. "I thought I'd get some breakfast started. How are you doing?"

I shrug.

"The ceremony last night worried you a bit, didn't it?" he asks. When I nod, he adds, "You know, that's the first time we've seen Captain Cabrillo so clearly in a very long time."

"Really? How come?"

"The more kings we have performing a ceremony, the

stronger we are. For a long time now, it has just been Simon, George, and me, and occasionally Simon's son. With you here too, we were able to call on Captain Cabrillo much more effectively."

"What about the other kings in my generation?"

"George's son won't be seventeen until next month, so he's not casting with us yet. And Simon's son, well, he was getting ready for a trip yesterday. But you'll meet him today." He pauses, and a shadow crosses his face. "There's one more andaba king alive right now. My father."

"Wait," I say, my heart suddenly thudding. "Your father is still alive? I have a grandfather?" All these years, it was just Aunt Bea and me. Now, with my father's return and the revelation that I have a living grandparent, I've effectively doubled my family in less than three weeks.

My father nods. "Up until about a year ago, he was here with us, which made us much stronger, since he's a very powerful king."

"So where did he go? Will I get to meet him soon?"

"He was diagnosed with lung cancer last year," my father says. "Just like zandara, andaba has very strict rules about kings not extending their own lives. The only possibility of real treatment was for him to move to the mainland, see an oncologist, and begin chemotherapy."

"So he's in a hospital somewhere?"

My father frowns. "It's been a long time since anyone here on Caouanne Island has heard from him. He kept us updated through the first two rounds of chemo, and then he stopped calling about six months ago. Last I heard, he was trying to track down a few leads on Main de Lumière."

"You don't think he died, do you?" I ask, my heart plummeting.

"No," he says firmly. "In andaba, we always know when a king has perished. The sky turns black on the day of his death, and the leaves all fall from the island's trees."

"So why hasn't he been in touch with you?" I ask.

A muscle in my father's jaw twitches. "After I married your mother, everything changed between us. I think he felt like I'd betrayed him by leaving. Unfortunately, our relationship has been strained since then."

I stare at my dad, feeling suddenly guilty. "Was he mad at you because you had a child with someone outside of Caouanne Island?"

"Honey, it had nothing to do with that. It had to do with me following my heart over tradition. He felt like I was abandoning my responsibilities here."

"But you came back," I say. "You left Mom and me and returned here."

"But I did that in order to protect you, not because I was choosing andaba over my family. My father knew that and resented it."

"Have you tried talking to him?" I ask. "Before he disappeared, I mean?"

My father sighs. "It's more complicated than that,

unfortunately. My father's very obstinate once he makes up his mind."

I pause as it sinks in just how much my father gave up. I take a deep breath. "I'm lucky to have you back in my life. I don't think I've been giving you enough credit for that. You know, in zandara, queens don't usually know their fathers." Peregrine and Chloe had filled me in a couple of months ago about the strange tradition in Carrefour of zandara queens having one-night stands with men for the sole purpose of getting pregnant, and then casting charms to erase the men's memories.

My father makes a face. "I never did understand that part of zandara. I've always thought it's important to know where you come from. Then again, I'm not sure the system on Caouanne Island is a great idea either."

"Why? What do they do here?"

He hesitates. "When a future king is a child, the current kings get together and choose a future wife for him."

"Like an arranged marriage?" I ask.

"Sort of," he says. "They base the decision on a few things: compatibility, friendships between the parents, and of course, power."

I think about this for a moment before what he's saying really hits me. "So you had someone you were supposed to marry?"

"That's in the past," he says quickly.

I study his face before realization dawns. "Diane," I say.

"Diane was who you were paired with, wasn't she? That's why she's been so cold to me."

"It doesn't matter, Eveny. I fell in love with your mother." He pauses. "I remember my father in a rage, telling me that I was shaking the very balance of andaba with my decision, undermining decades of alliances between families."

"But you chose love," I say.

My father nods. "I chose love."

"Wait," I say after a pause. "Do *I* have someone I'm supposed to marry? Since I'm an andaba queen?"

My father hesitates. "It's different with you. We've never had a queen before. But I promise, I have no intention of trying to force anyone on you. You should be able to choose for yourself."

"Good morning." A deep, sleepy voice from the doorway cuts our conversation short, and we look up to see Caleb standing there in sweatpants and a Ron Jon T-shirt. "I hope I'm not interrupting."

My father and I exchange looks, and I wonder if he's thinking, as I am, about the timing of Caleb's arrival. If I truly have a choice about who to love, I wouldn't think twice.

"No, Caleb," I say. "You're not interrupting at all."

The mothers sleep in while the rest of us grab pancakes and orange juice. By eleven, everyone's up and ready for the day.

"We don't have to leave for the airport until four," my dad says. "Does anyone feel like a tour of the town?"

The mothers and their protectors decline, but Peregrine and Chloe say they'll come. Simon arrives a few minutes later, and we pile with our protectors into his car and my dad's for the short ride into town. They parallel park on Rue Vert, the main road through Caouanne Island, and we step out onto a brick street. American flags snap in the breeze, and wind chimes sound from many of the doorways.

"Caouanne Island was built around the same time as Carrefour," my father explains as we walk. "There's a canal over to the left that cuts the island in half. It's spanned by a bunch of little bridges—which we'll see in a bit—so some of the townspeople joke that we're the secret Venice of the South."

Simon chuckles and adds, "Our ancestors came from New Orleans, just like yours did. The difference is that when they moved here, they cut ties almost completely with that part of their history. That's why Caouanne Island doesn't feel as reminiscent of New Orleans as Carrefour does."

We take a left off Rue Vert. Ahead of us, I can see a small arched bridge spanning a twinkling canal. "Because everyone in town knows about andaba," Simon continues, "it's been much easier for us to keep up the town than I imagine it is for you. Unlike you, we don't have to hide our powers. The residents here have everything they want and need."

"But who works for you?" Peregrine asks. "In Carrefour, we have the Périphérie. You know, the poor people who aren't in on the Secret of Carrefour. That's who works in our stores and restaurants."

I give her a look.

"Here on Caouanne Island, we don't see a reason to divide the haves and the have-nots." Simon looks straight ahead as he speaks, and I have the distinct feeling he's judging us. "Everyone in town has a job. Everyone benefits equally."

"Like communism?" Peregrine asks.

Simon looks at her like she's crazy. "Of course not. Simply like a utopian society."

She shrugs. "Sounds like a lot of work."

"Hard work is the backbone of every successful society," Simon says. "For example, take me: I'm a king, but I act as a boat captain when I'm needed, and I use my carpentry skills to beautify the town and keep up everyone's homes. In fact, I built this bridge." He gestures ahead of us to the wooden footbridge that arches over the canal. "It took me two years," he adds, "but it's my masterpiece."

"It's nice and all," Peregrine says, "but I thought you said you could use your magic out in the open here. Why would you do things by hand?"

"Because," my father answers, "we believe that magic should be used in moderation and that we should never take the spirits' generosity for granted, because it always comes at a price."

Peregrine makes a harrumphing noise, but she drops the subject. "So anyway, when's lunch?" she asks. "I want to have some time to go shopping before we go home."

Caleb and I stay behind with Simon to admire the bridge he built while my dad takes the others back toward Rue Vert to grab a table at the diner. Simon beams as he explains how he constructed an arch over the water tall enough to let canoes and kayaks through but with a low enough incline that it's easy for pedestrians to cross.

"It's modeled after the Kapellbrücke bridge in Lucerne, Switzerland," he says as he leads us onto the bridge. I notice that the wooden trusses all feature paintings, and I lean closer to see them as Simon continues. "The Kapellbrücke is full of landscapes and portraits, but I'm a lousy artist, so I was never able to do that here. But as it turned out, my son is a very talented painter. When he was fourteen, he started working on this bridge. So now, it's not only my masterpiece, but his too."

"Your son's really talented," I say as I stare at the images of shipwrecks, dark storms, and the early days of the town.

Simon smiles. "I'm very glad you think so."

"Eveny?" Caleb asks. He's farther down the bridge, almost at the other side of the canal, studying a painting closely. "This one looks just like you."

I walk over to see what he's looking at, and I'm surprised to see my own eyes looking back at me from a painted image. The girl's red hair flows in the breeze, and the white dress she's wearing billows out behind her. She's standing on a beach somewhere, and above her head, in the clouds, hovers a crown.

"It *is* Eveny," Simon says, coming up behind us.

"Your son painted this?" I ask. "How did he know what I look like?"

"He said the image came to him in a dream."

I blink a few times. "Your son dreamed about me?"

"Not only did he dream of you," Simon says, "but he dreamed of your coronation as queen. He knew you'd be back here someday."

I bend down to look at the painting again. It's beyond strange to see such an accurate depiction of me in a place I've never been, painted by an artist I've never met. As we walk back across the bridge and toward Rue Vert, I can't shake the strange feeling that the residents of Caouanne Island seem to have laid out the pieces of my life long before I got here.

"It's like they're already expecting you to return," Caleb says softly as Simon strides ahead of us.

"It's more than that," I reply. "I'm already part of their story, whether I like it or not."

After a huge lunch of fried green tomatoes, corn bread, and Brunswick stew—a thick, sweet, and smoky regional specialty with tomatoes, lima beans, okra, corn, onions, beef, and chicken—we finish up with piping-hot peach cobbler and homemade vanilla ice cream at the diner. Peregrine and Chloe head off to shop, with their protectors in tow and Simon escorting them, while Caleb and I return with my dad to his house.

"Caleb, do you think you could give me a hand with something in the garden?" my father asks when we pull into the driveway. I notice that there's another car in front of the house, a beige Lexus with tinted windows.

Caleb glances at the car, then at me. "Sure, Mr. Desjardins. Eveny, you okay?"

"She'll be fine," my father says before I can answer. He avoids meeting my eye as he adds, "There's someone here to see you, Eveny. Why don't you head in?"

Caleb and I exchange looks. I shrug, and he follows my father around the side of the house while I head inside.

As I round the corner into the living room, I see a guy my age with slightly overgrown blondish hair, long eyelashes, deep dimples, and broad shoulders. "Hi there." His voice is deep, warm, and tinged with a Georgia accent. I feel vaguely disloyal to Caleb for the unexpected surge of attraction that shoots through me.

"Hey," I say, staring at him.

"You're Eveny," he says with a smile as he steps forward. He takes my hand gently, and the second we make contact, all the hair on my arm stands on end. "I'm Bram, your brother king."

"Bram," I repeat in a whisper, and as he continues to smile warmly at me, I suddenly feel safe. I wonder if it's because of the magical connection between us, the fact that we're two leaders in the same sosyete. "It's, um, nice to meet you."

"And you." He's still shaking my hand, and when he finally stops, it takes him a moment to actually let go.

"So," I say.

"So." He waits for me to speak.

"You're Simon's son?"

"Yes."

"You painted me. On the bridge." I feel foolish the moment the words are out of my mouth, but Bram looks amused.

"You spotted that," he says, smiling at me. "I'm relieved to see I captured you accurately."

"Your dad said you dreamed of me?" I can feel my cheeks heating up; it's weird to imagine this hot guy lying in bed at night thinking about me. "How?"

"Andaba connects us. Maybe you've dreamed of me too and didn't even realize it. Do I seem familiar to you?"

I nod slowly. The way he's looking at me—warmly, like we're already old friends—is both comforting and disconcerting at the same time. "You're a king?"

He chuckles, the sound rising up from somewhere deep in his chest. "Since November, when I turned seventeen. It takes some getting used to, doesn't it?"

"Understatement of the year."

"I'd imagine it's even more unsettling for you. After all, I grew up with this. To you, it's all new." His expression is pleasant, his eyes full of compassion.

"Yeah. You're right." I finally relax a little. "It's nice to meet someone who finally understands that."

His brow creases. "Your sister queens in Carrefour don't?"

"I think they're too busy worrying about their hair." I half intend it as a joke, so I feel a bit guilty when he frowns.

"That's got to be really frustrating," he says.

"They mean well," I hurry to add. "Honestly. They're not so bad."

"Well," he says after a pause. "I suppose I'll find out for myself soon enough. They're here with you, aren't they?"

I nod just as my father and Caleb come in through the back door. I suddenly feel as if I'm betraying Caleb in some way and take a big step back from Bram. As Caleb stares Bram down, the air between them seems to crackle with tension.

"Well," my father says after a moment, clearing his throat and glancing at me. "Caleb, allow me to introduce Eveny's brother king, Bram Saxon."

He reluctantly reaches out to shake hands with Bram. "So you painted that bridge?" Caleb asks.

"Sure did."

"Weird that you're dreaming of Eveny," Caleb says. He walks away before Bram can reply.

Bram turns to me. "Is he always so polite?"

"That's just Caleb. Don't worry. He's . . . protective."

Bram's eyes bore into mine until I can feel my cheeks flaming. "Yeah, well, so am I."

"Eveny," my father says, interrupting the sizzling silence between us. "I have some news for you. Bram here," he says, then pauses. "Well, he'll be moving to Carrefour immediately."

"Wait, what?" I stare at him, then at Bram.

"Simon, George, and I believe it's for the best, and Peregrine's and Chloe's mothers have agreed to open the gate to allow Bram and his uncle Bill into town."

"But . . . why?" I ask, baffled.

My father sighs. "Caleb's judgment is compromised," he says, glancing toward the stairway. "Because Bram has andaba powers too, you and he can be very powerful together. Simon is needed here, so Bram will come with his uncle as his guardian instead. It will be helpful to have him with you to protect you."

"But I don't need protecting," I say. "And Caleb is doing just fine. I don't need Bram." I glance up at Bram, who's staring at me now. "No offense or anything."

"None taken." He gives me another small smile, and I'm startled to feel my pulse quicken immediately in response.

"The decision has already been made," my father says. "He'll relocate this weekend and will start school with you on Monday."

"But—" I begin.

"Eveny, you need to trust that this is for the best," my father says, cutting me off. He turns to Bram and says, "Your father asked me to tell you he's expecting you at home."

Bram nods and turns to me. His eyes hold mine for what seems like a full minute. I feel pinned by his gaze, and I wonder fleetingly if he's using some sort of magic on me. "Eveny," he says finally, his voice smooth and deep, like dark molasses. "I look forward to getting to know you better."

He nods at my father, and I stare after him, perplexed and shaken, as he disappears out the front door.

8

*A*head to Pointe Laveau Academy on Monday with my heart racing. I barely spoke to Caleb on the return trip from Caouanne Island, and I have the feeling that like me, he's wondering how Bram's arrival will change the dynamic here in Carrefour.

My father assured me Bram would be in school today, so I'm surprised when I don't see him all morning and when he doesn't join us in the Hickories for lunch, despite Peregrine's grudging invitation before we left the island. Caleb doesn't say a word to me at lunch, and Peregrine and Chloe are uncharacteristically quiet as Arelia and Margaux hurriedly arrange a platter of crudités in the center of our cashmere picnic blanket.

"Gin and tonic?" Margaux asks, glancing nervously at Peregrine and then at Chloe. I can almost see her wheels turning as she tries to figure out where everyone vanished to all weekend without her. We promised our parents that we would keep our visit to Caouanne Island a secret for now. *You never know who you can trust*, my father had reminded us.

"Obviously," Peregrine says, rolling her eyes. But even her derision feels halfhearted today.

"Have you seen him yet?" Chloe whispers as she sits down beside me. "Bram, I mean?"

I shake my head.

"He's cute, don't you think?" she asks.

I shrug. "I don't know." The truth is, I feel like I'm being disloyal to Caleb if I say it out loud.

I finally encounter Bram in fifth period American history, the one class I share with Caleb. In fact, I'm so distracted with acting like Caleb's silent treatment isn't bothering me that I don't even notice Bram come into the room until Ms. Sargent asks for our attention. When I look up, he's standing there beside her, looking perfect in his standard-issue Pointe Laveau khakis and oxford, which he's wearing with boat shoes. His eyes fall on me, and he holds my gaze for a long moment before smiling slowly and looking away.

"Quiet down, folks," Ms. Sargent says, peering over the rims of her glasses, "and please help me welcome Pointe Laveau's newest student, Bram Saxon, who will be joining us for the remainder of the school year."

Bram half raises his hand in greeting. "Hey, y'all," he says, his voice deep and gravelly. I can feel Caleb's eyes on me, but I resist the urge to turn around.

"Bram, there's an empty seat beside Eveny Cheval there," Ms. Sargent says, gesturing to me. "Eveny, can you raise your hand so that Bram knows where to go?"

"Oh, I know who Eveny is," Bram says. As his eyes lock with mine again, he smiles steadily. He doesn't break eye contact until he sits down beside me.

"Hey, you," he says in a low voice a moment later, once Ms. Sargent has started lecturing on the Great Depression.

I give him a smile. "Hey. And, um, welcome."

"Thanks, Eveny." His eyes, I realize a bit distractedly as he blinks at me, are the exact color of New York's Hudson River during a storm: deep gray with tiny flecks of blue. "That school uniform suits you, you know. You look really pretty."

"Oh. Thanks."

"Listen," he says a moment later as Ms. Sargent drones on in the front of the room. "Are you and I cool?"

I just look at him. I want to tell him that we're the opposite of "cool," because my cheeks feel warm, and my heart is racing, which I can't understand. But I have the feeling that's not what he's asking about.

"Me being forced on you like this . . . ," he continues, his voice trailing off. He shakes his head. "Well, if I were in your shoes, I'd be kind of upset. But I hope you know there's nothing I'm trying to do here except protect you."

"I'm not upset," I manage. "But I really don't need protecting." I glance over at Caleb, and this time, I catch him looking right at me. I shoot him a small, tentative smile, and although he looks guilty to have been caught staring, he gives me a slight smile in return before eyeing Bram and then turning away. Again, I can almost feel the chill in the air between them, and it unsettles me.

"I know you have Caleb to look out for you," Bram says a moment later. "But I want to help. If I can play even a small role in making sure you're safe, I'll be happy. So we're okay, you and me?"

"You and me?" I say, flustered. "Yeah, of course."

After class, Caleb hurries out without a glance, so I sigh and begin packing up my bag. When I look up, Bram is standing beside my desk. "What's your next class?" he asks.

Something flutters in my stomach. "Physics."

He looks at his schedule. "I'm headed to trig in room 114. Any chance that's the direction you're headed?"

"Um, yeah, I'm actually right across the hall."

"In that case," he says with a smile, "can I walk you to class?"

Bram falls into step beside me, and I can't help comparing him to Caleb as we make our way down the hall. He's about the same height, with the same broad shoulders. But other than that, he's the physical opposite of Caleb. Caleb's hair is close-cropped and black, while Bram's is longer and lighter. Caleb's eyes are the blue of a sunny sky, while Bram's are the gray of a stormy one. And Bram's pale, slightly freckled skin, which looks a lot like mine, is a sharp contrast to the brown smoothness of Caleb's skin.

"So," I begin, in an attempt to think about something—anything—other than Caleb, "where were you at lunch, by the way? You can eat with us, you know. If you want."

"No offense, but those girls you hang out with, well, let's just say they're not my cup of tea."

I smile at his old-fashioned choice of words. "Mine either, I guess. But you'll get used to them."

"Maybe. Anyhow, I'll think about joining you for lunch. Thanks for the invitation."

"Well," I say with faux brightness as we arrive outside the classroom, "your trig class is right in there." I nod toward the door.

"Thanks, Eveny," Bram says, and the way his voice rumbles does something strange to me. "See you later."

"Sure."

"Oh wait!" He pauses at the door, digs in his pocket for a second, and pulls out a folded piece of paper. "I drew this last period. It's for you."

I take it from him and he disappears into the classroom without another word. I unfold the piece of paper after he's gone, and I see that he's drawn a beautiful sketch of me, my chin propped on my hand as I study my textbook intently.

That evening, Aunt Bea is working late, and my father and Boniface are nowhere to be found, so I grab a Lean Cuisine meal from the freezer, microwave it, and settle in to eat by myself while reviewing for the French test I have on Wednesday. I've just taken the first bite when I hear the front door open.

"Eveny?" my father calls from the front hall.

"In the kitchen!"

He rounds the corner a moment later, and I'm about to ask if he wants me to make some spaghetti or something when Caleb appears behind him, looking exhausted and unsettled.

"What are you doing here?" I blurt out, then immediately turn red. I can feel my cheeks flaming.

Caleb opens his mouth to answer, but my father cuts in. "He'll be staying with us for a while."

"Staying with us?" I repeat. "Like in our house?"

"That's right," my father says. "Oscar and Patrick will be doing the same for Chloe and Peregrine. After the attack on you on Thursday, the mothers and their sosyete have decided it's best not to put anyone at further risk, which means taking every precaution available. I don't necessarily agree, but Caleb is one of those precautions."

Caleb looks up, then clears his throat and glances away again.

"But . . . what about his mom?" I ask. "Won't she be alone? Is that safe?"

"She'll be fine," my dad says. "She's not a target for Main de Lumière. And the mothers have promised to arrange a protective charm around her house."

"Well," Aunt Bea interjects from the doorway. I didn't

hear her come in. "I'm so pleased you've worked all of this out without consulting the rest of us, Matthias." She's glaring at my dad, and my stomach swims uncomfortably.

"This wasn't my idea," my father says, glancing at Caleb, who looks at the ground. "But it's what we're going to do."

"And you're in a position to be making decisions for Eveny now?" she shoots back.

"I'm just trying to do what's best for her," my father says.

"Are you? Are you really?" Aunt Bea says. "Because it seems to me that everything bad that's happened to this family revolves around *you*, Matthias."

"Aunt Bea!" I say sharply. I know she doesn't like my dad, but she's been quiet about it up until now. Having her snapping at him in the kitchen like this, especially in front of Caleb, makes me uneasy. "Can we talk about this later?" I add.

"When, Eveny?" she asks, turning toward me, her eyes flashing. "After he's ruined our lives too? After he's once again brought the enemy right to us?"

"What are you talking about, Bea?" my father says. I'm surprised to hear sadness in his tone instead of anger. "You're not being reasonable."

"Aren't I? And I suppose it's just coincidence that mere weeks after you show up, Main de Lumière is sending its henchmen after Eveny again?" she snaps. "Feels an awful lot like déjà vu, if you ask me."

My father flinches. "I didn't have anything to do with that."

"Aunt Bea, I agree with him," I say, and she gives me a look so mournful that I feel instantly like I'm betraying her. I take a deep breath and add, "I'm sorry, but what you're saying isn't fair."

"Isn't it?" she says, the venom in her voice growing as she turns back to my dad. "Don't you see? We were doing just fine in Carrefour before your father came along twenty years ago. Then he broke your mother's heart and left us defenseless after leading Main de Lumière to our doorsteps."

"You can't keep blaming me for that, Bea!" my father protests. I'm surprised to see tears glistening in his eyes. "No one was more devastated by Sandrine's death than I was."

"That's not true," Aunt Bea says, her voice suddenly dangerously soft. She turns to look at me. "Sandrine's daughter was. *Your* daughter, Matthias. Her mother is dead, and all you can think about all these years later is how it impacted you."

I open my mouth to respond, but Aunt Bea silences me with a look. "Stay out of it, Eveny," she says. "This is between me and your father."

Caleb moves over to where I'm standing and surprises me by placing a hand on my shoulder. It's not until he touches me that I realize my heart is racing a mile a minute.

"I *know* Eveny was devastated," my father says. "And I'll never be able to make that up to her. But what do you expect me to do? I would have given anything to be there to see my daughter grow up, Bea. But Sandrine asked me to leave. She said that Eveny would never have a normal childhood as long as I was around, and I agreed. Main de Lumière would have realized much sooner that Eveny was the child of two magical traditions."

"But they realized anyhow, didn't they?" Aunt Bea says. "And I'm the one who kept her safe. But it wasn't enough, was it? You had to come back and screw it all up again."

"*I'm* the one who screwed it up?" my dad says. "Maybe you could have raised her with *some* concept about her background, so she wouldn't be so defenseless now!"

"Well, maybe if you hadn't been so busy gallivanting around the world, you could have taught her about her heritage yourself." Aunt Bea crosses her arms.

"Guys—" I say, trying to step between them. But it's like I haven't spoken. I'm not even sure they're aware I'm in the room anymore.

"For God's sake, Bea, I wasn't gallivanting!" my father says. "I was trying to find a solution to the Main de Lumière problem. My whole *life* has been about protecting my daughter."

"No one asked you to do that," Aunt Bea snaps.

"Sandrine did! Not that she had to. Eveny's my child, Bea. There's nothing in the world more important to me than keeping her safe."

"If only you'd felt that way about my sister too," Aunt Bea shoots back. "Maybe she'd still be alive."

"Stop it, you guys!" I cry. My father and Aunt Bea both turn to look at me in surprise. "Just stop! What's happened has happened, okay? You can't keep blaming each other for it. My childhood was fine, but it's over now. It doesn't matter who did what."

"Eveny—" my father begins, but I cut him off. I can't hear any more of this.

"Enough!" I say. "You're my father, and I owe you some respect for that." I turn to Aunt Bea. "And you're the one who raised me, which I'll never be able to repay you for. I love you both. But this is *my* fight. This is *my* town. And if you want to do what's right for me, you'll stop arguing with each other and help me figure out how to save it."

They both stare at me as I turn and stride out of the room. It's not until I've slammed the door to my bedroom that I realize I can barely breathe.

9

Forty-five minutes later, I head out to the garden to clear my head. I haven't been out there for long when I hear the back door open and close. A moment later, Aunt Bea joins me on the stone bench by my mom's roses.

"Your mother always used to come out here when life was getting difficult," she says. She looks at me, and I can see that she's been crying.

"You all right?" I ask.

She nods, wiping a tear away.

"Look, if this is about the attack on Thursday, it's under control, okay? My dad's right; we've been coming up with a plan, and—"

"No." She puts a hand on my leg to stop me and takes a deep breath. "This is about me and the decisions I need to make for myself now. I've spent too long living the life your mom picked out for me."

"Oh." Her words and the bitterness in her tone cut into me. "You mean a life raising me."

"No. I never regretted raising you. When we were in New York and things were normal for a while, being your guardian was the best thing in the world." She hesitates. "But things are changing. You know that as well as I do. I've never liked zandara, and now it's stealing you away from me just like it stole your mom."

"I'm not being stolen," I say, squeezing her hands, "and we'll get things under control soon. Then we can try to go back to normal."

She surprises me by pulling away. "Eveny, things are never going to be normal here. You know that." She pauses and adds, "That's why I have to leave."

I blink at her. "Leave?"

"You know how much I love you, Eveny. But it's time I start looking out for myself. Your father's here now, and although I feel he's not being entirely honest, I do believe him when he says he'll keep you safe." Her tone is bitter as she adds, "It's in his best interest, after all, and he's always done what's in his best interest. At least we can rely on that."

"Aunt Bea—" I begin, but she cuts me off.

"Let me finish. Regardless of his motives, his powers will allow him to protect you in ways I never can. I have to trust he'll look out for you. But I can't be here with him. And I can't watch your life be taken over by magic. I don't have powers to save you, Eveny, and I'm not trained to protect you the way

Caleb is. All I have is the power of my heart, and for the last fourteen years, that was enough. But it's not anymore."

I can feel tears in my eyes. "You're really leaving?"

"I have to, Eveny."

"But you don't!" I shoot back. "We can figure something out. I can talk to my dad. . . ." My voice trails off, and I look at her sadly, knowing she's already made up her mind. I realize her feelings about my father have been festering for years, and I understand why she can't live under the same roof as him. But the fact that she's so easily abandoning me—after all we've been through together—is crushing.

Her face softens. "I'll stay in Carrefour, but I can't be around the sosyete anymore. I'll be at the bakery if you need me, but I think it's best for now if you and I have some distance."

"Best for who? You or me?"

She sighs. "Me. It's what's best for *me*. I'm finally doing something for myself. I'll always love you, just as I have since the day you were born, but it's time I find my own path and trust you to find yours. It's clear that you've already made your choice."

I shake my head vehemently. "But this is who I am. I didn't *have* a choice. Don't you see that?"

"But you *did* have a choice," she says softly. "You *still* do. You could walk away. If you don't, zandara will destroy you, Eveny, the same way it destroyed your mother."

"But—" I say, but she interrupts.

"You're making your own decisions now, and decisions always come with consequences. You've chosen your mother's lifestyle over mine, and that's okay. But I'm under no obligation to stay here and watch you destroy your future. I'm already packed. I just wanted to tell you in person."

"Please don't go," I say, my throat tightening. "Please. Aunt Bea?"

She stands up and puts a hand on my shoulder. "It's already done, Eveny." She walks away before I can say another word.

Save yourself. The whisper comes again as I sit here trying to stop the tears from flowing. I'm not sure if it's in my head or whether there are actually spirits speaking to me through the leaves of the rosebushes.

"What if I don't know how?" I finally say.

The only reply is silence.

The house is dark by the time I walk back inside; my father and Caleb have both gone to bed. Aunt Bea's door is open, and when I peer inside, I see that her room is empty. She's gone.

Tears cloud my vision as I walk into my own bedroom and pull the door closed behind me. The person who raised me, my one constant through everything, has walked out of my life. I've never felt more alone.

I'm sitting on my bed, my knees pulled up to my chest, when my door opens a crack. I look up, thinking it's my dad. Instead, it's Caleb.

"I heard you crying," he says. I just stare at him as he clears his throat. "I knocked, but you didn't answer. What's wrong?"

"Nothing," I mumble, picking at my comforter.

"It's not nothing, Eveny," he says. "You're upset."

"Why would you care?" I know I'm misdirecting my frustration, but he's let me down too. I'm sick of people hurting me.

"You know why."

I look up at him uncertainly, expecting to see his stony expression, the one that says everything about him is closed off to me. But instead, there's warmth in his eyes. "What is it?" he asks.

I hesitate. "How can I be this strong zandara queen," I say after a moment, "but also this needy little girl who doesn't want people to leave her?"

"You're not needy," Caleb says. "Who left you?"

I recap my conversation with Aunt Bea. "She was the one person I could always believe in, Caleb," I say. "How could she have walked out on me so easily?"

Caleb sits down on the bed next to me. Right away, I can feel the heat rising to my cheeks. There's something about being with him that always creates an electric charge in the room, and I can't figure out if it's the magic that binds him to me as my protector, or simple attraction.

He begins to rub my back, and my whole body suddenly feels warm. I know I'm blushing, and I hope he doesn't notice. "It's not like she's walking away forever," he says.

I shake my head. "You don't know that."

"Eveny, she's just moving out. It sounds like she wants her own life."

I wipe my tears away and sniffle. "How come I'm not worth staying for?" I ask in a voice so small I can barely hear it. My father left. My mother left. Now Aunt Bea. Maybe I'm feeling sorry for myself, but it's true: the people who mean the most to me all disappear when I need them. "Everyone leaves, Caleb."

Caleb stops rubbing my back and waits for me to look up at him. "I won't leave."

"Yeah, well, that doesn't count. You have to be here."

"No, I have to protect you," he corrects me. "I don't have to be here in your life. I could choose to be like Oscar and Patrick."

I laugh a little, despite myself, and wipe my tears away. "You don't seem like you'd be very good at chewing tobacco and lurking in the shadows."

"It's true. I'm partial to Trident and daylight," he says with a straight face.

I crack a small smile, and Caleb begins gently stroking my back again. His fingers are so warm I can feel them through the thin cotton of my sundress. It's like his heat is radiating through me.

I draw a deep breath. "The thing is, I don't know who to trust anymore." I can feel the tears running down my cheeks again, but this time, I don't try to stop them. "Maybe my dad has my best interests at heart, but the way my aunt Bea hates him, it makes me feel so confused. I mean, she's right to be wary, isn't she? Why has he suddenly come back? If it was just about protecting me, wouldn't he have been here sooner? I feel like there's so much more to the situation that I'm not understanding."

"But maybe there's not," Caleb says. "He changed everything when he came into your mom's life. I think that all your aunt can see is that he created problems. She's reacting to that."

"Maybe."

He pauses. "But sometimes, the people who bring the biggest complications into our lives are also the ones who make our lives complete." He pulls me toward him, and after my head is against his chest and I can hear his heartbeat, he adds, "Sometimes, they're the ones who make you feel whole."

I tilt my chin to look up at him, and for a long moment, we just stare at each other.

I know he's going to kiss me a millisecond before he does, but I'm still not prepared for how right it will feel. As his lips touch mine and his arms snake around me, pulling us together like a jigsaw puzzle, it feels like finally coming home after a long journey.

I kiss back, and then, it's something more.

"We shouldn't be doing this," Caleb murmurs between kisses, but his words are lost in our heavy breathing as the sheets wind around us, tangling us closer together. I kiss back hungrily.

"Eveny," he whispers, and then my hands are under his

T-shirt, on the flat plane of his abs, the bulge of his muscles, the smoothness of his skin. My own body takes over, and before I can think about it, I'm pulling his shirt over his head and falling back into his arms. He makes a low, guttural noise as he pulls my dress over my head too, and then he fumbles with my bra and pulls me to him, so that we're pressed together, skin to skin.

I try to remember to breathe as he moves his weight on top of me. His lips break from mine long enough for him to stare into my eyes for a moment. Then, he's kissing me again, and his hands are on my body, touching me everywhere.

Suddenly, he pulls away, his breath coming in ragged gasps. "We can't."

"I know," I whisper. "I know."

He reaches over me to grab my dress from the floor, hands it to me, and rolls away to pull his own shirt back on. Then he flops onto his back, his jaw glistening with sweat, his eyes wild. I shimmy my dress over my head and lie down beside him.

"Don't leave," I say after a minute. "Please."

"I won't." We lie there in silence, and after a while, I turn onto my side, facing away from him so he can't see my tears. He rubs my back again, his hands moving in slow, gentle circles, until I finally drift off to sleep.

When I awaken several hours later, it's pitch-black in my room, and at first, I think I've imagined everything. But then I realize I'm still in Caleb's arms. We're lying on top of the covers, and he's curled around me, his chest rising and falling slowly, creating a rhythm for my own heartbeat to follow. I'm careful not to move, because I don't want to wake him and ruin this moment.

I lie there in the darkness and let myself imagine what it would be like to have a life like this, a life where Caleb and I could be together. "I love you, you know," I whisper, and he stirs, but only a little. I finally drift back into a peaceful sleep.

When I wake up the next morning, he's gone, and the space he's left behind is cold and empty, almost like he was never there at all.

10

Breakfast the next morning is awkward and mostly silent. I'm worried that my father is being so quiet because he knows what happened last night with Caleb, but if he does, he gives no sign of it. The only thing he says is, "I'm sorry to hear about your aunt Bea moving out."

I just nod stiffly. I'm annoyed at my father, although I know that's not fair. He didn't make Aunt Bea leave. But then again, if he hadn't come back, she'd still be here.

All my nerves are on edge as I wait for Caleb to appear, but he never does. Instead, I hear footsteps on the stairs and then the front door opening and closing. My father stands and says, "Caleb will be driving you to school from now on. You should go join him."

On cue, I hear a car horn honk outside, and I jump. My father raises an eyebrow at me as I grab my backpack and head out the front door. Caleb is behind the wheel of his Jeep, staring at me, but as soon as our eyes lock, he looks away. He starts the engine without a word once I've climbed in.

"So," I say after we've made our way down the driveway in silence.

He glances at me but doesn't say anything.

"About last night . . . ," I begin, trailing off as the image of Caleb curled around me in my bed flashes through my mind.

"I shouldn't have done that," he says. "I'm sorry."

"But . . . it was wonderful."

"Don't you understand? That's why it can't happen. This, all of this, is wrong." He gestures back and forth between himself and me. "It's against the rules, and it's just not smart."

I blink a few times, pushing back the tears I can feel pressing at the back of my eyes. So we're here again. "The rules are stupid, Caleb," I say, unable to keep the weary sadness out of my tone. "They were written more than a hundred years ago. Maybe it's time we make some changes."

"Eveny, we can't!"

"But—"

"I'm done," he cuts me off. "We've talked about this a million times, Eveny. And I'm really sorry for my lapse in judgment. But you need to move on. I do too."

The words cut deep. I'm silent for the rest of the drive to school, and when Caleb parks, we look at each other for another moment. "I know you don't understand," he says. "But I don't have a choice."

"Of course you do," I say. "You always do. But I see you've already chosen." I get out of the Jeep, slamming the door behind me, and walk away before he can say another word.

I'm at my locker pulling books for first and second period when Liv appears out of nowhere. "Can we talk?" she asks, putting a hand on my arm.

My heart sinks; she has refused to speak to me since Drew's funeral, because she thinks I know more than I'm telling her about his death. The last thing he'd told her that night was that he was going to New Orleans to find me. I've lied and said I never saw him, but she doesn't seem to believe me. I miss her friendship, but I just can't handle any more heartache today.

"Look, I'm sorry that you're hurting," I say, "and I know you think I'm an awful person, but I'm having a really crappy morning, and I have the worst headache in the entire world, so can we just not argue today?"

"Please, listen to me," Liv says quickly as I start to turn away. "I want to apologize."

I stop and look at her. "You do?"

"I . . . I made a mistake, okay?" she goes on. "It's what I do. When I get hurt, I push everyone away."

"But you didn't just push me away," I say. "You blamed me for Drew's death. And you acted like I'd betrayed you."

The class bell rings, and around us, other students stream down the halls, disappearing into their first period class-rooms. But neither of us moves.

"I know," Liv says, looking down. "I was really upset, and I took it out on you. I'm sorry. Can you forgive me?"

A wave of guilt washes over me, because at the end of the day, Liv isn't exactly wrong: I was involved in Drew's death, although I know she'd never be able to understand it. "Of course I forgive you, Liv," I say. "And I'm sorry. About Drew, I mean. It's horrible to lose someone."

She nods and looks away. "I miss him."

"I do too." It's not a lie. He wasn't all evil; he just bought into what Main de Lumière told him—that everything wrong in Carrefour was the fault of magic, and that my sister queens and I had to die for balance to be restored. I think it was easier for him to blame me and the Dolls for his parents' divorce and financial situation than it would have been to admit that he and his family weren't perfect to start with.

"So you've been spending a lot of time lately with Peregrine and Chloe and the other Dolls," she says softly. The second bell rings, and we're alone in the hallway.

"Yeah," I say. "They're my friends."

"I still don't get that," she says. "You're so different from them."

I shrug. "Maybe not as much as you think." After all, even though my priorities might not always match theirs, all three of us are queens who want the best for this town. But there's no way to explain that to Liv either. "Anyway, you can join us whenever you want. In the Hickories, I mean. You guys have a standing invitation to eat with us."

She looks away. "I don't think Max wants to. After what happened with Justin and Chloe, it's just awkward."

"Right." If only she knew just how complicated it all was. Last year, Chloe cast a love charm on Justin without realizing that he was gay, so for months, he trailed around after her like a lost puppy, despite the fact that he was really in love with Liv's best friend, Max. Now that Chloe has reversed the charm, Max and Justin are inseparable and Justin—who is technically a member of our sosyete—wants nothing to do with the Dolls anymore.

"But maybe we could hang out sometime after school or something?" she asks.

"I'd like that."

She looks relieved as she begins to walk away. A second later, she turns back. "Hey, I didn't even ask. How are things going with Caleb?"

For an instant, I can almost feel his lips on mine, his body pressed against me. But just as quickly, I see his cold, distant expression this morning. I swallow hard. "Not so great."

She seems genuinely sad for me. "Don't give up. I know he loves you. You can see it in the way he looks at you."

As she hurries down the hall toward her first period, I stare after her. "I'm not sure that's enough."

That day Bram joins us in the Hickories for the first time, settling down beside me on the cashmere blanket and smiling at the others. I'm surprised to see him here, considering his feelings about the other Dolls.

"Hey, y'all," he says. "Sorry I didn't eat with you yesterday. Anyone want to join me in the cafeteria line? Looks like they've got soggy mac and cheese on the menu."

Margaux and Arelia exchange looks. Pascal laughs.

"We don't eat down there," Chloe says. "Margaux and Arelia bring lunch for us."

Bram looks confused as the girls begin pulling food out of a huge insulated picnic basket. "Really?" he asks, glancing at me, then at Margaux and Arelia. "Y'all bring lunch for everyone? Every day?"

"It's their job." Peregrine looks at me and then back at Bram. "But what are you doing sitting all the way over there?" Her tone has dropped to a low purr. "Why don't you come sit by me?"

I'm surprised by the tinge of jealousy I feel when Bram shrugs and scoots over to Peregrine's side, even though I know fully well that she's just trying to get under my skin. It's exactly what she did with Caleb the second she realized I was attracted to him. But it's not like I've said I like Bram. She begins rubbing his shoulders, and he turns a little pink.

"Where's Caleb, Eveny?" she asks, and from the smug expression on her face, I guess that she already knows he's deliberately avoiding me.

I just shrug and try to sound nonchalant. "Not my day to watch him."

Peregrine laughs while Chloe looks at me with concern.

"But I hear he moved into your house," Peregrine says. Bram looks up sharply, his eyes meeting mine.

I grit my teeth. "It's just like Patrick and his dad moving into your house and Oscar and his dad moving into Chloe's. Just a protector-protectee thing. You know that."

"Still, how cozy that must be for you two," she says. Bram is still staring at me.

"So, Bram," Chloe says quickly, before Peregrine can continue her torture. "How are you liking Carrefour so far?"

He holds my gaze for a long time before turning to Chloe. "I admit, it takes a bit of getting used to. I lived my whole life on the water, so it's pretty different being landlocked, you know? I like it here, though. The people seem real nice." He turns to me again, his eyes fixed on mine.

When I look back at Peregrine, she's staring right at me too. Finally, she shifts her attention to Bram. "We're very welcoming in Carrefour, Bram," she says. "I'd be happy to spend some time showing you around town. In fact, it would be a pleasure." As she emphasizes the last word, she raises an eyebrow at me like a challenge, and I'm surprised to realize that I actually feel a little defensive. "Interested?" she adds, batting her eyes at him.

"Sure, I guess," Bram says with a shrug. He glances back at me. "Maybe Eveny can come along too."

Peregrine makes a face. "Oh, I think Eveny has more than enough on her plate, what with the love of her life moving in with her. I'm sure they'll be spending lots of quality time together from now on. Isn't that right, Eveny?"

I glare at her, but she keeps right on stroking Bram's back, her hand getting lower and lower as she presses herself into him, leaving him no choice but to pay attention to her.

In sixth period, Liv is telling me a story about her trip to the mall in Baton Rouge with Max, but my mind can't stay focused.

I'm thinking about Bram, which is strange, because after last night, I should only be thinking of Caleb. But being on the love-hate merry-go-round with him again is making me dizzy. Bram, on the other hand, seems uncomplicated, like a fresh start. And even with Peregrine throwing herself at him, he was still staring my way. I can't explain it, but my insides feel like Jell-O each time he looks at me.

Then there's Peregrine's behavior, which is weirder than usual. Sure, she seems to get a lot of pleasure from being bitchy. But I thought that she and I were okay; she'd actually been pleasant to me until the last few days. I suspect she's worrying that now that I know I'm an andaba queen, I'll leave Carrefour behind, but I can't imagine she'd believe that after all we've been through.

"Don't you think?" Liv asks, nudging me and disrupting my train of thought.

"Um," I reply, buying time since I have absolutely no idea what she was talking about while my mind wandered.

Mr. Cronin, our teacher, saves me from answering by

interrupting us. "Think we could focus on the work here, ladies?" he asks, looking at me pointedly. "I know you don't feel that what we're doing here in class is especially important, but perhaps you could humor me."

"Sorry," Liv and I say.

Caleb's Jeep is gone by the time I head outside after school, making my heart sink with a feeling of finality. Even if he's trying to distance himself from me, it would just be common courtesy to offer a ride to the person you're living with. Especially when that person doesn't have her driver's license yet and has no other way home. Of course as my protector, he has to stick by me anyhow, which can only mean that he's out there somewhere, keeping an eye on me from afar, but that he doesn't want to be trapped in a car with me.

Great. Rejected again. I sigh and head back toward school to look for Chloe, who usually doesn't mind driving me, but I run into Bram first.

"Whoa, girl, you're headed in the wrong direction," he says, intercepting me at the front entrance. "School day's over."

I smile. "I was just looking for Chloe."

"She and Peregrine drove off a while ago." He pauses and scratches his head. "Boy, that Peregrine is a piece of work, isn't she?"

"Understatement of the year. Just be careful, okay? She tends to chew guys up and spit them out. I wouldn't get too involved."

He raises an eyebrow. "Who says I plan to get involved?"

I shrug, thinking of the way he turned red at lunch as she pressed herself into him. "You're a straight guy. You'll fall for her. Everyone does."

"But I'm not everyone, Eveny." He holds my gaze the way he did at lunch, and suddenly, I'm finding it hard to breathe.

He smiles and changes the subject. "So why were you looking for Chloe anyway?"

I'm about to respond when my cell starts ringing. It's the tone I've set for Chloe—the "Barbie Girl" song. "Speak of the devil," I say before answering.

"Eveny?" Her voice sounds hysterical.

"Chloe? What's wrong?"

Bram looks at me, concerned.

"It's my mom," she says quickly. "Something's happened. I need you to get here as soon as possible."

"You okay?" I ask.

"No." I can hear her choking back a sob. "Eveny, she's been attacked. It's . . . it's bad. We need to heal her. Please get here as fast as you can."

11

ram drives me to Chloe's house and insists on coming inside, in case we need his help. Chloe, Peregrine, and I are forbidden by the rules of zandara from involving outsiders in anything related to our sosyete, but I don't think Bram really qualifies as an outsider. The lines are getting more and more blurred by the day.

The front door is open, so we head inside the house without knocking. We find Chloe in the living room with Peregrine and Peregrine's mother. Chloe's mother is lying on the couch, apparently unconscious, with several slash wounds through her blood-drenched silk blouse.

"What happened?" I demand.

"Scarlett was attacked!" Peregrine's mom says. "Right in her own home!"

Chloe is crying, and I'm filled with horror as I turn to her.

"Is she . . . okay?" I ask.

"I don't know," Chloe says. "That's why we need you. To help us with a charm."

I nod. Queens from different sosyetes can't cast together, so Peregrine's mom couldn't do much to help her daughter and Chloe before I arrived. Now that I'm here, my sister queens and I should be able to cast powerfully enough to save Chloe's mom. "Has someone called my dad?" I ask. "He should know about this too."

"He's here with all the protectors," Peregrine says. "They're in the parlor with . . . the person who did this."

A chill runs through me. "Another Main de Lumière soldier?"

I'm thinking of the terrifying man who attacked me last week, so I'm surprised when Peregrine nods solemnly and says, "Yes. Mrs. Potter."

I blink at her, my lungs suddenly constricting. I'm sure I'm hearing her incorrectly. "Mrs. Potter? The sweet old lady who runs the library?"

Chloe chokes out a laugh. "Sweet? I'm not sure you'd call her that if you walked in on her slicing your mother to shreds." She begins to cry again.

"Girls, you can't waste any more time," Peregrine's mother says. "You have to help Scarlett before it's too late. We can deal with the Potter woman afterward."

I nod and join hands with Peregrine and Chloe.

"Who's Mrs. Potter?" I hear Bram whisper to Peregrine's

mother as I begin chanting with Peregrine and Chloe.

"Someone we've all known for years," she replies. "And someone I intend to destroy as soon as we're done here."

I call on Eloi Oke to open the gate, and Peregrine invokes white oak bark, althea, wormwood, and walnut leaf. As Chloe begs the spirits for help, we begin to tap our feet slowly in rhythm and sway to the beat. A wave of gratitude sweeps through me as I watch the wounds on Chloe's mother's chest close and some of the color return to her face. We stop dancing when her eyelids flutter open.

"Chloe?" she asks, her eyes rolling around frantically until she sees her daughter.

"*Mesi, zanset,*" Chloe says, her voice thick with relief as she thanks the spirits.

"*Mesi, zanset. Mesi, zanset,*" all three of us say in unison, ending the charm.

Chloe releases our hands and rushes over to her mother. She throws her arms around her and cries, "I thought you were going to die!"

"What happened?" her mother asks, looking around at all of us.

"That's what we're about to find out," Peregrine says, her voice heavy with anger as she leads the way into the parlor.

Mrs. Potter is sitting on the floor in the corner of the room, her feet bound so she can't run away. Oscar's father, Anton, and Patrick's father, Benjamin, stand watch over her while my father speaks to Caleb, Oscar, and Patrick on the other side of the room. Caleb's eyes lock with mine as soon as I walk in, but then he sees Bram beside me and quickly looks away.

"Scarlett," my father says, staring at Chloe's mother. "You're okay."

She nods weakly and glances at Anton, who looks like he's about to cry.

"I'm so sorry, ma'am," he says, his voice choked. "I would never be able to forgive myself if she had succeeded in . . ." He can't finish the words.

"But she didn't," Chloe's mom says right away. "And you didn't do anything wrong."

But he doesn't look any less miserable, and when I glance back at Caleb, he's looking right at me again.

"You really think this is the only attempt that will be made on your life?" Mrs. Potter surprises us by asking from the corner, her tone full of venom. "You fools! The end is near for you evildoers!"

Her words and the way her normally docile eyes are blazing trigger a wave of fear in me. I glance at Peregrine and Chloe, who look as worried as I feel.

"Nonsense," Peregrine's mother shoots back. "You're just a crazy old hag. Who would recruit someone your age to act as an attacker? You practically have one foot in the grave already."

"Annabelle," she says in the sweet, high-pitched voice I'm accustomed to, "how you've underestimated me." She laughs and adds, "Or are you not bright enough to have realized by now that the biggest threat always comes from the people you least expect?"

"Whatever," Peregrine speaks up. "Main de Lumière is getting desperate. If you're the best they could do, we have nothing to worry about."

"Oh, Peregrine," Mrs. Potter replies. "Stupid, stupid Peregrine, who believes the world revolves around her. Don't you see that this is all part of the bigger plan? Your magic is the work of the devil. All of you. But I, dear friends, am a messenger of God."

She turns her fake smile on me, and I shudder.

"And Eveny Cheval," she goes on. "How naive you are. This is all about you. Don't you see that? You hold the key to everything, and that's why you must die. But first, all those who support you will be sacrificed to atone for their sins and yours. And in the end, you'll be struck down in a field littered with the bodies of your family and friends. How I wish I could stick around for the show."

I can feel myself shaking. The venom in her voice fills the air like poison gas.

Bram puts a hand on my back and steps forward. "How dare you try to scare Eveny with empty threats?"

"Empty?" she laughs. "Oh no, young man. Main de Lumière will prevail, bringing with it the dawn of a new era, an era free from your evil, free from your filth and your destruction. I'm merely the opening act. Rest assured, the next time we come after you, the job will be complete. Peregrine, Chloe, you might as well say good-bye to your mommies now. Their end is coming soon."

"Bitch," Peregrine says as Chloe chokes back a sob and

hugs her mother tightly, as if by holding on, she can protect her against Mrs. Potter's words.

"Sadly, I must go now," Mrs. Potter says, her tone suddenly eerily calm. I look at her in confusion as she focuses on me and says sweetly, "I would say I'd see you in heaven, but we all know *you're* not going there, devil-child."

Before anyone can make a move toward her, she flings herself forward, smashing her necklace hard on the floor, shattering the glass beads. In less than a second, her tongue flicks out, picking up a small pill that must have been inside one of the beads. She swallows quickly and smiles at us. "Cyanide, you see," she says before her words dissolve into choking and foam pools at the corner of her mouth. She doubles over, writhes for a moment, and then goes still.

Anton steps forward and puts a hand on her wrist. "Dead," he says. "What the hell? Why would she commit suicide?"

"Because she knew you'd kill her," I say, glancing at Caleb, who looks upset. "She'd delivered her warning, and she didn't want you to get any information out of her that she wasn't supposed to give."

"Eveny, the things she said," my father says after a moment of stunned silence. "She's wrong. Nothing's going to happen to you. I won't let it."

"Me neither," Bram says. His hand is on my shoulder again, and I try not to notice Caleb glaring at him.

"But what if her threats weren't empty?" Chloe asks. "She managed to get past Anton and Oscar to my mom, didn't she? And if someone like her could be allied with Main de Lumière, who knows who else has been compromised? They told us on Caouanne Island that there were at least *two* operatives here."

We all stare at the crumpled body of Mrs. Potter.

"How do we stop this?" Chloe finally asks in a near whisper. "How do we prevent Main de Lumière from coming after us?"

"We don't," I say after a pause. All eyes turn to me as I add, "We learn to fight back before it's too late."

I say good-bye to Bram and my sister queens, and then my father, Caleb, and I drive home together, the silence heavy around us. I don't know what they're thinking about, but I can't stop replaying Mrs. Potter's death, the way her body thrashed around violently and then suddenly went still.

What would make someone so convinced of a cause's righteousness that she'd willingly die for it? What would make someone buy into something so dark and malicious?

Caleb pulls into our driveway and cuts the ignition. None of us moves for a moment, and the quiet suddenly feels loaded.

"You're going to be okay, Eveny," my father finally says. "We won't let anything happen to you. I promise."

"I promise too," Caleb says, his eyes flicking to mine in the rearview mirror.

"But you can't know that for sure," I say. "Main de Lumière wants me dead. They want all of us dead. There's no guarantee that we'll be able to fight them off."

No one says anything, so I speak up again. "Look, everyone's fine for now. Let's just stay safe tonight, and we can all meet tomorrow and figure out what to do. Do we have to call the police or something? Ask Chief Sangerman for help covering this up?"

"I think we just get rid of the body," Caleb says softly. "I don't think Mrs. Potter's death will lead back to us. The fewer people involved, the better."

My father nods and gets out of the car, cueing Caleb and me to follow. That's when I notice the silver Mercedes parked in the driveway, just slightly down the hill. My father sees it at the same time and frowns.

"Who's that?" I ask.

"No idea," he says. He glances at Caleb. "Stay close to Eveny."

Caleb nods, and as I fall into step behind my father, my heart thudding, I can feel Caleb behind me, his breath on my neck, his heat radiating through me. We approach the front door, but before my father can insert his key in the lock, the door swings open, revealing an old man standing there, his eyes sunken and hollowed.

He focuses first on me, then on Caleb, and finally on my father. He smiles slightly and in a low, raspy voice says, "I hope you don't mind, but Boniface let me in. Hello, son. It's good to see you."

My dad's expression is unreadable. "Hello, Father," he says.

12

We all stand motionless on the doorstep, staring at each other, until my father finally nudges me. I shake my head in disbelief as we all walk inside. I can't stop staring at the bald, weary-looking man in the foyer. He looks like an older, far more worn-out version of my father.

"Now, what kind of welcome is that, son?" the man—my grandfather—asks. He turns to me with a smile. "Eveny, it's lovely to see you again, my dear."

I have no memory of this man, but he feels strangely familiar. "Again?" I repeat, studying him. He looks weak, gaunt, and I recall what my father said about his cancer.

"We met once before, when you were just a baby." He chuckles, but the sound turns into a cough. "Forgive me," he says, once he recovers. "My health, it hasn't been wonderful, needless to say. But yes, Eveny, I was here just after you were born. I had to see my grandchild, the heir who would carry on my family's future."

I glance at my father, who is staring at my grandfather as if he's trying to figure out a particularly complicated puzzle. My grandfather's emphasis on my status as his heir makes me uneasy; it's a reminder of just how much rests on my shoulders.

"And who might you be?" my grandfather asks, turning to Caleb. "Wait, don't answer. Let me guess. You're Eveny's protector. Charles Shaw's son? I'd nearly forgotten about him, the one who was responsible for protecting Sandrine. I met him when I was here just after Eveny's birth."

I can feel Caleb stiffen. "Yes, sir. I'm Caleb."

"Ah. Of course. Well, Caleb, you don't need to stand so close to my granddaughter. I don't bite, I promise." My grandfather smiles as Caleb clears his throat and takes a small step back.

"Father," my dad says, seemingly finding his voice at last, "you still haven't said why you're here. Or in fact, *how* you're here, inside the town's walls."

My grandfather chuckles again. "Well, I hate to be the one to tell you, but your protective gate seems to have shorted out. I'd recommend fixing them as your first order of business. I could have walked right in on my own, but I'm a gentleman, so I went through the proper channels."

"Channels?" my father asks, his forehead creasing.

"Bill Saxon. Young Bram's uncle," my grandfather replies,

glancing at me. There's something about his expression that makes me feel like he can see beneath my skin, can read my mind. "Of course you remember they live in Carrefour now. So," he adds, clapping his hands together, "what do you say we do something about this mess you've gotten yourselves into?"

Boniface prepares the guest bedroom for my grandfather, and my father disappears for a while, mumbling an excuse about needing to call Simon, so I'm left with my grandfather and Caleb.

"Perhaps you could go help Boniface for a little while so that I can catch up with my granddaughter," my grandfather says, turning to Caleb.

Caleb glances at me, and I try to tell him with my eyes that I'd rather he stay, but he either doesn't understand or he's feeling just as awkward as I am, because he shrugs and says, "Sure." He strides out of the room without looking back.

"Pleasant young man," my grandfather says.

I nod, unsure how to reply.

"He certainly seems fond of you," he goes on, raising an eyebrow meaningfully.

I shrug. "So," I say quickly, changing the subject, "what brings you here?"

"Ah, a young woman who cuts right to the chase. I like that. Well, Eveny, you see, I've come because you need me, and I need you, and when families are in need, they should stick together. Don't you think?"

"But why come back now?" My grandfather's absence in my life doesn't sting as much as my father's does, but it's still disconcerting that he's shown up suddenly after so many years, talking about how family is important.

He frowns. "Things are coming to a head, aren't they? Today's events are a perfect example."

"You mean . . . ?"

"Scarlett St. Pierre," he says. "The attack. It's only the beginning, Eveny."

"How did you know about that already?" I ask. Then I realize I know the answer to my own question. "Bram's uncle told you?"

He nods. "I had just arrived in town and was meeting with him before coming to see you and your father when I got the news. I think you'll agree that there's no time to waste."

"What do you mean?" I ask, leaning forward. But my father interrupts us by walking back into the room.

"You okay, Eveny?" he asks.

"She's just fine, Matthias," my grandfather answers, his voice flat. I can practically feel the awkward tension in the air between them.

My dad stares at me and then turns his gaze back to his father. "I'm afraid we don't have much in the way of dinner, but Caleb and Boniface are putting some cold cuts out for sandwiches. Shall we head into the kitchen?"

"Whatever you say, son," my grandfather says. I follow the two of them into the other room, where Caleb and Boniface are spreading out deli meats and cheeses on a plate.

"Mind slicing a tomato and onion, Eveny?" Boniface asks, winking at me.

I nod, grateful for the distraction. I grab a knife and stand beside Caleb, but it's only when I begin to cut the onion that I realize my hands are shaking. Caleb notices too, and he takes a small step closer.

"You okay?" he whispers.

I nod. "Just completely weirded out."

We all prepare sandwiches and settle around the dining room table. Boniface comes in with a pitcher of iced tea and pulls up a chair, which is unusual, because he typically declines dinner invitations. I can tell by the way he's looking at my grandfather, though, that he's not sure whether he can trust him or not.

"So?" my dad says after we're all settled. "Shall we talk about what you're doing here, Father?"

"As you know, son, I'm very ill," my grandfather begins. He's interrupted by another coughing fit, and when he straightens back up, he's looking right at me. "Lung cancer," he adds. "Not a particularly pleasant cancer to be dying from."

"I thought you were receiving chemotherapy," I say.

"I've been receiving treatments in Miami for the last couple of months, but it appears my time is finally up. The chemo, well, my body just can't take it anymore. And the cancer has metastasized and spread. So I've come here, to spend my final days with the people I love most in this world: my son and my granddaughter."

"I'm so sorry," I say. As uncertain as I feel about his sudden arrival, it makes me sad that he knows his days are numbered.

"Don't worry about me, Eveny," my grandfather says, looking into my eyes. "I'm at peace with my fate. We all have a destiny, and it's not always the one we hope for. My only goal now is to make the most of the rest of my time on earth."

He looks at my father, and the two of them hold each other's gaze. My dad blinks first. "How are you feeling, Father?" he asks.

"Weak," my grandfather admits. "But being here, seeing you, fills me with strength. In any case, enough about me. Shall we discuss the attack on the St. Pierre woman?"

"Something has to change," my father says right away. "If Main de Lumière is here . . ." He shakes his head. "With the gate open and their operatives hiding in plain sight, I'm afraid things are more dangerous than ever."

My grandfather looks at me. "Will you consider going to Caouanne Island until the storm has passed, Eveny?"

I shake my head. "No. There's no way to keep the people of Carrefour protected if I leave."

"But perhaps it's not your job to protect them," he says. "The things that are happening now are things your sister queens and their mothers have brought on themselves by years of misusing their powers. They wouldn't be in Main de Lumière's crosshairs if they had practiced more responsibly."

"But they've also been weakened for years because my mom's gone," I point out. "If she'd been here to cast charms with them, the protections around the town never would have crumbled. And that's not their fault."

"It's certainly not *your* fault," my grandfather says.

"But it's my responsibility. I'm my mother's daughter, and this is her legacy. This town was her home, and the people under attack are her sisters. *My* sisters. I have to stay."

"I suppose that's very noble of you," my grandfather says.

The doorbell chimes, interrupting us. I exchange looks with my father as Boniface stands to go see who's here. "Go with him, Caleb, just in case," my father says.

A moment later, they return, accompanied by Bram. Our eyes meet, and a sizzle of heat runs through me. I look quickly away.

My father asks if he's hungry, and he says no, then turns to shake my grandfather's hand. He seems to bow to him slightly, which reminds me just how important my grandfather is among andaba practitioners. None of us have eaten more than a couple of bites, and as I look down at my sandwich now, my stomach lurches. I push my plate away.

"I hope you don't mind that I've invited Bram Saxon to join us," my grandfather says, glancing at me and then at Caleb, who seems tense and on edge. "I thought it would be helpful to put our heads together about this Main de Lumière problem. And I have some news I'd like to share."

He looks around at all of us before continuing. "While

I was in Miami, I had some dealings with muerdaya practitioners from Haiti. They're not on Main de Lumière's radar to the same extent we are, which has allowed them to gain more insight into the organization. In a ceremony last week, a group of priests managed to coax some information out of the Main de Lumière general assigned to their region." He pauses. "Then they killed him."

I'm surprised by how much this bothers me. There's simply too much bloodshed, no matter which side it's on. I feel a surge of guilt, like I should be doing something to stop all of this. But it's a chain of events that was set in motion long before I got here, and I know I have yet to understand even a fraction of it.

"So what did he say?" my father asks.

My grandfather pauses dramatically. "There's infighting within the Main de Lumière ranks," he says. "A split between those who believe the organization has gone too far and those who believe that the only way to cleanse the world is by spilling the blood of all who have magical ties."

I swallow hard. "I thought they *all* believed in killing us."

"They do, to an extent," my grandfather says. "Main de Lumière was founded on the idea that magic—in any form—is the work of the devil and that they're doing something virtuous by eliminating us. But finally, there's a faction within the organization that believes murdering innocents is wrong. The problem is that there's a disagreement about what makes a person innocent. Are we guilty the moment we draw upon our powers for the first time? Or are we only guilty if we use our abilities to do harm?

"That's exactly why the split within Main de Lumière focuses largely on Eveny," he adds, turning to me. A chill runs through me as he goes on. "For those who believe that magical blood alone isn't reason enough for punishment, you've become almost a symbol of a movement. But this has only infuriated the others, who harp on the idea of your great potential for power—and thus your great potential to do harm."

"But I'm not planning on doing harm!"

"Still," my grandfather continues, "you remain a symbol to both sides, which makes you more important and interesting to Main de Lumière than ever before. When you were younger, they feared that your power would one day be a threat to them. Now you're a threat regardless of your power, because you're capable of dividing them and turning them against each other."

My head is suddenly throbbing. I close my eyes.

"What are we supposed to do with that information?" my father asks.

My grandfather leans back in his chair. "Be aware. Defend ourselves. Darkness is coming, but it may not come from the places we expect. Who knows? There may even be people within Main de Lumière who wish to help us."

"You think we should work *with* Main de Lumière?" Caleb says. "You can't be serious!"

"Oh, I'm very serious, young man. And you should be at least considering the possibility too, if you truly want to save Eveny's life."

"Of course I do." Caleb looks at me, pauses for a second, and then looks back at my grandfather. "It seems like what they're afraid of is that she has andaba powers too. That's just making things worse."

"But isn't it her zandara side that's been getting her into so much trouble?" Bram counters. "What if andaba isn't a complication? What if it's something that could help?"

"That's insane. How could it help?" Caleb says. "It's making Eveny a target."

"It's not andaba that's making her a target," Bram says. "It's the fact that she has two kinds of magical blood."

"Including andaba," Caleb says.

"*And* zandara," Bram replies.

The two of them glare at each other.

My grandfather holds up a hand. "You both have different reasons for protecting her. But looking at Eveny's face now, I don't imagine your war of words is making much of a difference."

They both turn to me. I'm tired of being asked to pick sides, to turn my back on a part of my own history.

I take a deep breath. "I just want all of us to survive. I don't see why I have to choose one tradition over the other. Wasn't I born to practice both? Isn't that who I am?"

I don't wait for an answer. I get up from the table and head for the back door, leaving a divided room full of people staring after me.

13

Caleb follows me outside, as I knew he would, but he stays in the shadows as I walk through the garden. "I know you're out here to protect me," I say after a moment. "But honestly, all the lurking gets a little creepy after a while."

There's a rustling behind me, and Caleb steps out, looking guilty. "I didn't want to bother you. You okay?"

"No," I say. "As a matter of fact, I'm not."

"Everyone just wants what's best for you, you know."

"Do they?" I ask. "Or does everyone want what's best for their own magical tradition? I'm tired of feeling like a pawn in a game I don't understand."

I sit down on the stone bench in my mother's rose garden and gesture for him to join me.

"I'll stand," he says awkwardly.

"I'm not going to throw myself at you, if that's what you're worried about," I say. "I'm capable of controlling myself."

"Yeah, well, I'm not sure I am," he says, looking away.

I can feel his defenses up, the chill in the air, and as I look up at him, I suddenly feel angry. You can't practically rip someone's clothes off one night and then turn around and ice them out. I know there are forces at work that are bigger than us, and I know Caleb thinks he's doing the right thing. But I happen to believe that following your heart is the only right way, regardless of the rules. And I can only bang my head against the wall so many times before I start to get a pounding headache.

"So then leave me alone, Caleb, okay?" I say. "If you can't even bring yourself to sit with me, then just go."

"I'm supposed to stay and protect you."

"You're not the only one who can do it."

"You're talking about Bram," he says.

"He's capable of protecting me too. Remember? He's a king." I know from the look on Caleb's face that my words are hurting him. I continue anyway. "And he actually seems to want to be around me. So if I'm such a burden to you, go. I don't need you."

"Eveny—" he says, but he doesn't continue. Instead, he hesitates for a second, then turns quickly and walks away.

I blink back tears and close my eyes, breathing in the scent of my mother's Rose of Life flowers as Caleb's footsteps fade. "Mom," I say loudly, "if you can hear me, I need your guidance more than ever."

I don't know how long I sit there before I drift off to sleep. In my mind, I can see my mother coming toward me, a vivid memory from my childhood. I'm standing in the garden, and she walks out of the house with a glass of lemonade for herself and a little plastic cup for me. She's smiling at me, and in her long, white dress, with her red hair billowing in the breeze, she looks a bit like she's floating. "Eveny," she says, the sound clear and sweet.

I'm so startled to hear her voice that my eyes snap open and I lose my balance. I reach out to stop myself from falling, and when I do, I accidentally scrape the back of my hand against one of my mom's Rose of Life bushes. A thorn jabs into me, and I wince. I look down to see that I'm bleeding.

"Ow," I mumble, rubbing my hand once I regain my balance. A drop of blood falls onto one of the rose blooms, and instantly, a translucent white cloud begins swirling in front of me. It's so faint that I can barely make it out in the darkness, but I can feel it more than I can see it. "What the . . . ?"

"Eveny?"

I whirl around to see Bram walking toward me from the direction of the house, looking concerned. "Who were you talking to?" he asks.

I look back to the rosebush in front of me, but the white cloud isn't there, leaving me unsure whether I really saw it at all. I shake my head, perplexed. "No one," I say. Then, when I realize he looks skeptical, I hang my head and say, "My mom. Not that she can talk back."

He sighs and comes to sit beside me on the bench. "Losing her must have been so hard on you."

I nod. "I just wish I could ask her for advice, you know?" I hesitate. "I feel like I'm being pulled in a million different directions. Everyone in my life seems to want something from me right now."

"I don't want anything from you," Bram says softly. "Nothing you don't want to give, anyhow."

"But that's not really true, is it? You want me to embrace andaba, and it seems like my dad does too. I think Peregrine and Chloe want me to turn my back on it and only practice zandara. But no one really cares what I want, do they?"

"What *do* you want, Eveny?" His voice is low, and there's a sudden intimacy to it.

"I don't know," I say.

"Sure you do." His stormy eyes bore into me, but instead of making me uneasy, his gaze makes me feel safe, protected, understood. Exactly the opposite of how Caleb has been making me feel lately.

"Fine. I want to make the right choices." I pause. "I want to find a way to keep everyone safe. I want to do what my mom would have done if she were here. And I want to make a better future for everyone. We can't just keep living in fear."

"You sure have a lot on your shoulders, don't you?" he says after a moment. He puts a hand on my leg, just above my knee and squeezes gently. "You don't have to carry all of this alone. I mean, I know you're confused right now and you're not sure who to trust. But you can trust me."

I sigh, my heart racing from his touch. "I want to believe that's true. But I don't know you yet, Bram."

"Are you sure?" He holds my gaze. "Think about it, Eveny. I mean, really think about it. Isn't there a part of you that knows me too?"

I'm about to tell him that I don't know what he means, but then, suddenly, I realize that in fact I do. There's something about him that tugs at the corners of my memory, just like my visit to Caouanne Island seemed to trigger something embedded in my genetic code. "Did we ever meet before Saturday?" I ask.

He smiles. "No."

"So why do you feel familiar to me? Because you're my brother king?"

"So you *do* feel it."

"Feel what?" I ask, although I know exactly what he means. He's talking about the way being with each other is inexplicably comfortable, the way every glance and touch between us feels natural.

But he doesn't reply. Instead, he stands and offers me his hand. I take it without even thinking about it, and before I can consider pulling away, he helps me up. I'm expecting him to say something romantic, because it suddenly seems like that kind of a moment. But instead, he asks, "Eveny, do you want to learn a little more about andaba?"

I nod. "You'll teach me?"

"Sure." He takes my other hand and leans forward so that his forehead is touching mine. I can feel his warm breath against my cheek as he says, "I know your father explained about reaching out to the spirits, but did he show you how to channel power from the living too?"

"No," I whisper. Is Bram using magic on me now? Is that why I feel so warm and syrupy inside?

"It's why we're so powerful together," he says. "In and-aba, you can be even stronger when you rely on channeling another king's thoughts and feelings."

"I don't understand," I say, but I realize I don't want to move; there's something about the heat of his skin against mine that's making me feel peaceful.

"Close your eyes," he says softly, "and focus only on what's flowing through me to you. Imagine my blood coursing through your veins. Imagine my heart beating in time with yours. Imagine our minds opening to each other so that all of our thoughts and hopes and dreams flow back and forth."

My own heart is thudding now, but I close my eyes and try to do as he says. At first, I feel self-conscious and strange, but after a moment, I can feel my head heating up, starting from where we're touching and spreading outward, slowly and gently. I can sense his heartbeat, the cadence of his breath, and without meaning to, I can feel my own body's rhythms slowing to match his. The sense of strangeness that filled me a moment ago is dissipating, and as soon as I realize we're breathing in unison, something strange happens. My whole body begins to tingle, and as I crack my eyes open, I can hear his voice, like a humming in the back of my brain, although his lips aren't moving.

"What?" I ask softly.

Listen, his voice says in my mind, and I'm so startled that I almost pull away. But although it should seem strange, there's also something very natural about all of this, so my instinct overrides my fear and I stand still. After a moment, I hear the faraway whisper again: *You have no idea how deeply I care for you.*

My breath catches in my throat, and this seems to break the link between us. Bram pulls away, and when I open my eyes, he's smiling. "Did you feel that?" he asks.

I nod slowly. "Did you . . . say something?"

"You heard words?" He looks surprised but pleased. "You're better at this than I thought you'd be, Eveny. You heard what was going through my mind."

"I . . . I heard your thoughts?" I ask. Then something occurs to me. "Could you hear what I was thinking?"

"We can only hear our brother kings—and in your case, our sister queen—but that person must consciously open his or her own mind to us."

"So you meant for me to hear what you were thinking?" I ask, feeling a blush creep up my cheeks.

He takes a step closer, but this time, he doesn't lean his head toward mine. Instead, he takes both of my hands in his. "Yes," he says softly.

"Oh." My cheeks are on fire now, and I don't know what to say.

He lets go of my right hand and reaches up to touch my cheek gently. "You feel it too. The connection between us."

"I—I think so," I whisper.

"Good." He only has to lean forward a couple of inches to kiss me because we're standing so close, but when he does, it doesn't feel like a surprise at all. Nor does it feel like we're doing something wrong, although perhaps it should. As his tongue gently parts my lips, I don't taste regret the way I do when Caleb kisses me. Instead, there's only the sweet taste of desire and the warmth of belonging. And so I kiss back, and as he bites gently on my lower lip, a shiver goes through me.

When he finally pulls away, I feel dizzy.

"Wow," he says, looking into my eyes.

"Wow," I echo. "That was . . ."

"It was what?" he asks gently when I don't continue.

I hesitate. "Unexpected."

"Was it?" He looks amused. "Or did it feel like that was exactly what was supposed to happen."

"I don't know," I admit. The guilt is finally trickling in, though. "Look, I should tell you that I sort of have something going on with Caleb."

He nods. "But he's pushing you away."

"How do you know that?" I wrap my arms around myself, suddenly feeling violated.

"I couldn't hear the words in your mind," he says. "But

sometimes you can get whispers of what's in someone else's heart. I could read that in yours."

"And you kissed me anyhow?"

He reached out to touch my cheek. "I thought it was important for you to know that you would never have to worry about that with me. I would never push you away."

"But you don't even know me yet," I say, suddenly wary. "And this isn't going to make me choose andaba. Is that what this was about?"

He looks surprised. "No. Not at all. I'm not trying to make you do anything, Eveny." He holds my gaze for a long moment and adds, "After all the noise fades away, the only thing you'll be able to hear is your own heart."

We head back toward the house in silence, and although Caleb is nowhere to be seen—which I'm grateful for—my grandfather is standing at the back door with a knowing look. And suddenly, I have the feeling that he saw everything.

The next morning, I head downstairs after a troubled night's sleep to find Peregrine and Chloe standing in the front hall-way with my father. "Your friends are here," he says.

"Thanks," I say as he heads back upstairs. I turn to Pere-grine, who has Audowido wrapped around her shoulders like a shawl. "What are you guys doing here?"

"Would you stop referring to us as *guys*, Eveny?" Peregrine says. "We are ladies."

"It's just an expression."

"Yes, a thoroughly improper one," she says. "In any case, we're on our way to school, and we dropped by to tell you when to join us for the ceremony we're doing tonight. We'll be meeting at midnight in the crossroads of the cemetery. You might want to be a few minutes early."

I glance at Chloe, who's looking intently at the floor. "What kind of a ceremony are we doing, exactly?"

Peregrine rolls her eyes and sighs. "As you may recall, Eveny, Chloe's mother was attacked yesterday? We need to draw some significant power in order to address the gaps in our protection. Unless you'd prefer to be a sitting duck?" She makes a face and adds, "Besides, you'd be helping Caleb."

"Caleb?" Guilt surges through me as I think about Bram's kiss last night.

Peregrine examines her nails. "In addition to helping secure the gate, we'll be charming a potion for our three protectors, to help safeguard them against harm."

Chloe finally looks up. "This really *is* important. It will make sure the guys stay as safe as possible."

"I thought the Mardi Gras ceremony was supposed to do that," I say suspiciously, glancing back and forth between them. "Isn't that why we had to rush to New Orleans the night Drew tried to kill me? You acted like it was the most important ceremony of the year."

"Try to keep up, Eveny," Peregrine says. "That ceremony was to bank power. This is the first time we're calling in some of the power we've reserved. Understand?"

"Fine," I say. I blink and glance at Chloe, who's nodding. "How's your mom doing?"

She sighs. "Better. Physically, she's okay. But I think she's just really on edge."

"That's why we need to do the ceremony," Peregrine says. "Close the gate, help our protectors, get back to normal." She looks so sure of herself.

"But what if it doesn't work?" I ask. "What if normal isn't going to exist for us again? What if we can't fix what's broken?" I hate to sound so pessimistic, but it feels like things are unraveling. There's no guarantee that a few charms or ceremonies will change that. I want to make sure we're considering all the alternatives. "Are we sure this is the right thing to do?"

Peregrine's expression hardens. "What, would you prefer to sit around and let your andaba brothers control things? Is your father telling you to turn your back on us?"

I clench my fists in frustration. "No! No one's telling me anything, and I'm not turning my back on you—or on them!"

She snorts. "You sure about that? Because you seem awfully interested in andaba lately."

I feel like I want to scream. Nothing I do or say seems right. I grab her arms and force her to look at me. "Peregrine. You are my sister. Chloe is my sister. I care deeply about this town, and I'm not going anywhere. You can choose to believe me, or you can keep being a bitch, but honestly, that's just going to make you look like an idiot when it turns out I'm telling the truth."

She studies me. "Did you just call me a bitch?"

I'm too tired to smooth it over. "You heard me. Deal with it."

To my surprise, a genuine smile crosses her face. "Good. That's the fighting spirit I was looking for. I believe you."

I stare after her, baffled, as she turns to go.

14

My father and Caleb join me for breakfast, and when I tell them I'm going to take the day off from school, neither of them argues.

"I'll stay home too, then," Caleb says, glancing at me. I turn away from him.

"Go to school, Caleb," my father says. "I know you want to look out for Eveny, but she'll be perfectly fine here with her grandfather and me."

Caleb looks uncertain, but he nods and then heads upstairs to get his books. I follow him with my eyes, feeling sad. He's so close yet so obviously out of reach. A moment later, he comes back down the stairs, waves halfheartedly at us, and disappears out the front door, leaving my father and me alone.

"Since you're staying home today, would you be interested in learning a bit more about andaba?" my father asks after a long silence. He looks nervous but hopeful, and I realize this is his version of extending an olive branch.

"Bram already taught me a little." My lips tingle at the recollection.

"I see." He pauses. "Would you like to know more?"

I look directly at him. "I'd like to learn how to protect myself and the people I love. Can you teach me that?"

"I can try." He stands and beckons for me to follow him. "First of all, you need to know that andaba and zandara are very different, although they both rely strongly on calling on the spirits for help," he says as he leads me out through the back door into the garden. "In many ways, they're opposites."

"Opposites?"

"The biggest difference is that zandara deals in life—flowers, herbs, trees. Andaba deals in death. Graveyard dirt, for example, is used for protection and increased power."

I shiver in the damp morning air. "Well, that's creepy."

He smiles slightly and begins walking deeper into the garden. "I suppose zandara would seem creepy to someone unfamiliar with it too. The truth is, whenever you're trying to reach over to the other side, we have to use elements that would make the average person uneasy." He nudges me. "But you're not an average person, are you?"

"Apparently not."

"Muerte dust is another thing we use that you don't have in zandara," my father continues. "I know you saw us use it in the ceremony we performed on Caouanne Island. All sorts of magical sects have their own proprietary recipe for it, as do we. In andaba, it's a mixture of grave dirt, ashes, ground turtle shells, gold dust, and pulverized dirt dauber nests. They're little bugs."

"Ew."

My father smiles. "I know this must be weird for you. I can stop, if you want me to."

"No. I need to hear this."

"Very well. Muerte dust is made by one individual in each generation of andaba kings. It's one of the most sacred things in andaba, because its combination of elements is made to work with the charms we already have in place." My father digs in his pocket and pulls out a small leather cuff with a tiny glass ball attached.

"I've filled this globe with muerte dust," he says, handing it to me. "If you keep it with you at all times, you'll be more connected to your andaba powers—sort of like your Stone of Carrefour better connects you to your zandara powers. I'd suggest wearing it around your wrist, like I do." He rolls up his sleeve to show me an identical tiny globe on his own arm. I'm surprised I've never noticed it before, but I realize as he pulls his sleeve halfway back down that he typically keeps his arms covered.

I take the cuff from him hesitantly. "What do I do with it?"

"Say someone tries to inflict pain on you, you can inflict identical pain on them with muerte dust and a charm. You just have to know who your enemy is; the charm must be directed toward a specific person to be effective. And it can only be used when you're under direct attack." He holds up his own wrist, smiles slightly, and says, "Hit me."

I blink at him in confusion. "What?"

"Hit me," he repeats. "Just lightly, on the shoulder. I want to show you how this works."

"You want me to hit you?" I say. He nods, and I shrug. I reach forward to punch him lightly on the left arm, but before I can make contact, he touches the glass ball on his cuff and says quickly, *"Con mi sangre, regreso a su intención."*

Instantly, I feel a dull pain in my own left arm, and I recoil, more startled than hurt. "Ouch! What did you just do?"

He smiles. "I turned your intention around on you. The words mean literally, *With my blood, I return your intention.* The muerte dust itself is powerful enough to reverse something minor, like you just saw, but when you touch your blood to the globe of dust and say the words, you can ward off much more powerful advances. You want to try it on me?"

"What do I do?"

"I'm going to come at you, but you won't know where I'm planning to hit you. Just touch your cuff, say the words, and focus on returning the aggression to me."

I nod, and he smiles at me, then lunges forward. Quickly, I hold up my wrist, place my finger on my cuff, and murmur, *"Con mi sangre, regreso a su intención."*

Instantly, my father recoils, grasping his forearm. "Very impressive," he says. "I was going to pinch you, and instead, I felt the pinch. You're a natural at this. But it's something you'll get better at the more you practice. So I'd suggest rehearsing the words in your mind all the time until they come naturally. Sometimes, you have just a split second to react before someone is able to hurt you. And if your thoughts are clouded at all, it gets in the way of your magic."

I hold up my wrist and stare at the cuff. Already, I feel a little stronger, a little safer. "What else?" I ask. "What else can you tell me about andaba?"

"Well, you know that in zandara, you draw energy from love," my father replies. "The more love you feel, the stronger your charms are."

"Right."

"In andaba, it's different. We draw energy from anger. It's not a bad thing," he adds quickly. "It's just a different source of emotion. Anger and love aren't exactly opposites, but they're on different ends of the spectrum. Your mother and I always found that fascinating."

I consider this, the idea that embracing the anger that sometimes courses through me could actually make me more powerful.

"You're good at this, you know," my father says after a while. "All of it. I've seen you in action in zandara and now in andaba, but more than that, I've seen you beginning to believe in yourself a little more. That's wise; you *should* have faith in yourself. Sometimes, when we're in the most danger, our gut feelings are all we can rely on. And your instincts are solid,

Eveny. You have a good head on your shoulders." He pauses. "Your aunt raised you well."

I nod, accepting the compliment as the peace offering I know it is. "Thanks."

"I'm proud of you," he adds softly. "I know I wasn't always here, but I've always been proud to be your dad."

I dodge two calls from Bram that afternoon and one from Liv. Bram's message tells me he missed me at school and adds that he hopes my absence didn't have anything to do with last night.

"Because last night, well, it meant a lot," he says. "I hope you agree. Call me if you need anything."

I can feel myself blushing and I hurry to erase the message. I don't call back because I don't know what to say. The truth is, it meant something to me too. But how can it, when I still have feelings for Caleb? Yes, I'm attracted to Bram; that much is obvious. But Caleb isn't pushing me away because he wants to. He's doing it because he thinks it's the right thing—because he thinks it's what magical forces beyond our control dictate. What if I can persuade him—and everyone else—that this isn't the case? I owe it to him to at least try, even if I keep getting hurt in the process.

I'm the first one to arrive at the cemetery that night, just before midnight. I hear twigs snapping nearby, and I whirl around to see Caleb approaching from the direction of my house.

"Hey," he says, shoving his hands in the pockets of his jeans as he approaches. I can't help but notice how perfectly his black polo shirt stretches over his muscular chest. "You're here already."

"Uh-huh," I say, my throat suddenly dry.

"I would have walked here with you. I *should* have walked here with you."

I tear my eyes away and pretend that I don't care, because it's easier that way. "I didn't need you to."

Before he can reply, Peregrine and Chloe arrive in the clearing, trailed by Pascal, Margaux, and Arelia. Chloe's in a velvet romper and platform wedges, while Peregrine's wearing a sparkly silver minidress and bejeweled Christian Louboutin platform heels that should be sinking into the graveyard dirt but aren't. She has a designer bag slung over her shoulder, and I can see Audowido peeking out from inside, his tongue darting in and out.

"Hi, you two!" Peregrine chirps as she glides over to Caleb and me. "Don't you look cozy."

"Yo," comes a deep voice from behind us. I squint into the darkness and a moment later see Oscar and Patrick. "Are we late?"

"No, you're not late," Peregrine says, looking Patrick up and down. "But you *do* smell like cigarette smoke. You realize that if you give yourself lung cancer and die, you won't be able to look after me, right?"

"Yes, ma'am," Patrick says, giving her a dark look.

"Hi, Oscar," Chloe says much more politely to her protector.

"Howdy," he says, then spits.

"Charming," Peregrine says. "Now shall we get started?"

Shooting an uneasy glance at me, Caleb moves into the center of the crossroads along with Oscar and Patrick.

"Where are your mothers?" I whisper to Chloe. "And Patrick's and Oscar's dads? Shouldn't they be here too?"

"They're doing a protection ceremony with their own sosyete," she says. "Don't worry." She raises her voice and turns to Margaux, Arelia, and Pascal. "Just hang out over there for a few minutes. This first ceremony is just the queens and their protectors. We'll need you for the second charm, though."

"Whatever," Margaux says with a sigh.

I glance back at them and see Pascal staring directly at my butt. I clear my throat, and he raises his eyes slowly to meet mine, then waggles his brows suggestively. I make a vomiting motion, and he laughs.

I watch as Peregrine sets her bag down in the clearing and lifts Audowido gently out. He slithers toward the three protectors and curls himself in the center of their little circle.

Next, Peregrine pulls out three zandara dolls and hands one to me and one to Chloe. I look down and realize that the one I'm holding looks like Caleb: brown fabric skin, short-cropped black yarn for hair, eyes sewn from brilliant blue thread. It's wearing a school uniform—khaki pants, a pale purple oxford—like the one Caleb wears every day. I squeeze it a little tighter and for a second I wish I was the kind of girl who felt like it was okay to cast love charms using zandara dolls.

I swallow hard and look up to see Caleb watching me.

"Light the fire, would you, Chloe?" Peregrine says as she digs in her bag, and Chloe nods and moves toward the guys.

Five minutes later, Chloe has used a lighter to set a pile of twigs aflame, and Peregrine has pulled three long poles with hooked ends, a bottle of water, and a small, black cauldron out of her bag. She hands the poles to the three guys, and I watch as they expertly thread their hooks through the cauldron's handle and take a step back, so that the cauldron is suspended in the middle of their circle. Calmly, Peregrine pours the bottle of water into the cauldron and moves away. "To the fire, boys," she says.

Caleb, Oscar, and Patrick move together over to the small fire Chloe has built, positioning the cauldron directly over it. It only takes a minute for steam to begin to rise.

"Shall we, ladies?" Peregrine asks brightly. She places Audowido on the ground, where he immediately curls into a coil. He watches as she pulls a sachet from her bag. With the other hand holding her zandara doll of Patrick, she goes to stand behind her protector. She nods at Chloe and me to do the same. As Chloe lines up behind Oscar and I line up behind Caleb, Peregrine begins to chant, and Chloe and I automatically join in.

"Come to us now, Eloi Oke, and open the gate," we say in

unison. "Come to us now, Eloi Oke, and open the gate. Come to us now, Eloi Oke, and open the gate."

There's a whoosh through the trees and a familiar change in air pressure. Peregrine roots around in her bag briefly before pulling out a small handful of pink flowers and stepping up to the cauldron, which is now bubbling and hissing. She throws the flowers in and says, "Antennaria blooms for invincibility."

Next, she withdraws a handful of tiny white flowers and pale green leaves, murmuring, "Rattlesnake weed for protection and luck." She also throws in lemon balm to ward off curses and blackberry to enable the three protectors to harm their enemies if necessary. Then she gestures for me and Chloe to hold our dolls up in the moonlight. All three of us do so as the fire dies out. The guys continue to hold the cauldron as it stops steaming, while Peregrine, Chloe, and I begin to dance in the moonlight.

"Spirits, we ask you to grant our protectors strength," Peregrine says in a low voice, holding her Patrick doll up to the sky.

"Spirits, we ask you to grant our protectors intuition and foresight," Chloe says, holding her Oscar doll up.

They both look at me expectantly. "Just wish for something to help the guys," Chloe whispers.

I clear my throat and hold my Caleb doll up. "Spirits," I say, "please watch over our protectors and keep them safe. This fight isn't theirs, and they are risking their lives for us."

"Let's chant together, ladies," Peregrine says. "For each ray of light, there's a stroke of dark," she begins. My heart thuds a little faster; it's the beginning of the verse that's etched on a plaque in my front hallway, the verse I first heard my sister queens chanting the night I learned that zandara existed.

"For each possibility, one has gone," all three of us chant together. "For each action, a reaction. Ever in balance, the world spins on."

"Now, the potion," Peregrine says. "Boys?"

The guys set the cauldron gently down in the dirt and begin taking off their shirts. Patrick and Oscar whip theirs off immediately and toss them aside, but Caleb glances at me before pulling his black polo slowly over his head. He sets it carefully on the ground as I stare at him, my breath caught in my throat. Seeing him nearly naked—the bulge of his biceps, the ripples of his abs, and the flat, V-shaped plane of obliques—still makes it hard for me to breathe.

Caleb turns away and bends at the waist, so that his muscular back is nearly parallel with the ground. The other guys do the same, and I manage to tear my eyes away from Caleb long enough to look questioningly at Chloe.

"We douse them with a bit of the potion," she says. "That's what delivers the power of the spirits to them."

Peregrine reaches for the cauldron first and carries it over to where Patrick is standing, his back flat and pale in the moonlight. She holds it over him and looks skyward.

"Won't she burn him?" I whisper.

Chloe shakes her head. "It cools quickly. They'll be fine."

I watch as Peregrine says, "To Patrick, power," before pouring a small amount of the liquid inside the cauldron onto his back. He flinches as it hits his skin, but I'm relieved to see he doesn't seem to be in pain.

It's Chloe's turn next. She takes the cauldron from Peregrine and does the same with Oscar, saying, "To Oscar, power." Then she passes the cauldron to me and says, "Just pour a little bit out. They all have to drink from it too."

I nod and approach Caleb. His skin glistens in the moonlight. "To Caleb, power," I say before pouring a small amount of liquid onto his back. The droplets bead and run slowly toward his waist. After a pause, he straightens up and turns. Our eyes meet for a second.

"Eveny?" Peregrine says. "Give Caleb the cauldron."

I blink and hand it to him. I feel something electric pass between us as our hands touch and our gazes lock. But then he looks away, takes a sip of the potion, and passes it to Oscar.

Peregrine uses the last of the potion to dunk the feet of all three zandara dolls, and then hastily, Chloe and I bury them in the dirt.

"*Mesi, zanset,*" we all say together. "*Mesi, zanset. Mesi, zanset.*"

The air seems to get lighter and Caleb, Oscar, and Patrick pull their shirts on and step back toward the trees.

"Now it's time for the rest of you to join us!" Peregrine singsongs.

Margaux, Arelia, and Pascal step forward into the circle, along with Caleb, who's the only protector who's also a practicing member of our sosyete. I wind up with Pascal on my left and Chloe on my right. My eyes meet Caleb's across the circle as Peregrine puts Audowido down in the center of the clearing.

"Okay, ladies and gentlemen," Peregrine begins, clapping her hands together like she's the head cheerleader at a school pep rally. "As some of you may have guessed, attempting to repair the protection of the gate is a very big deal, and I don't believe there's any way to do it tonight without performing a *Renmen Koulèv*."

"The possession ceremony?" I ask. I've only been involved in one of these, but they're downright disturbing. The last time Peregrine and Pascal allowed themselves to be possessed, the spirits inside of them practically had sex in the middle of our circle. "You didn't mention we'd be doing that tonight."

Peregrine smiles. "Then I must also have neglected to mention that tonight, we'll need you to be the one who opens herself up."

Beside me, Chloe squeezes my hand, and it takes me a second to register what Peregrine means.

"Me?" I say. "You want me to be possessed?"

"Everyone keeps saying how powerful you are because of both your andaba and zandara sides," she says. "What better way to repair the gate than to allow a powerful spirit to inhabit someone so unique?"

"I don't like it," Caleb says, stepping forward and glancing at me.

"Well, it's not up to you, is it, Caleb?" Peregrine says. She turns to me. "It's up to Eveny. Will you do it?"

I know it could be risky; something can always go wrong when you let a spirit in. But Peregrine is right. I could be stronger than anyone else here, thanks to my dual heritage. And a true queen puts the people she's responsible for above herself.

So I take a deep breath and try not to imagine what might happen next. Possessions are all kinds of creepy, but having our lives in peril is worse. "I'm in," I say.

15

As I step into the center of the circle, my legs turn to jelly. I've only been possessed once, and I didn't like it at all. Having someone else inhabit your body is terrifying, and after the possession ends, you're left feeling completely drained. Besides, when you open yourself up during a ceremony like this, you never know who will wind up taking your body over and what their motives will be.

"We'll keep you safe," Chloe says, apparently reading my mind. "As long as we're in the ceremony with you, the spirits can use your body, but they can't hurt you."

"Okay." I glance at Caleb, who looks nervous too. I turn back to Chloe. "Are *Renmen Koulèv* ceremonies always as . . . sexual as the last one was?"

She looks uneasy. "Not always, but usually. It'll be over quickly, though, and then they'll help us."

My stomach swims as I turn to Peregrine. "How do I start?"

She withdraws a large triangle from her tote bag and hands it to Pascal. "I'll handle the chanting. You just open yourself up to possession. Keep your mind as blank as possible, and when it's time, you can invite the spirits to take you over. Remember what to say? *Move lespri, pran kò mwen. Move lespri pran tèt mwen.*"

I nod and repeat the words softly. Pascal strikes the triangle and everyone around me joins hands.

"Come to us now, Eloi Oke, and open the gate," Peregrine chants. "Come to us now, Eloi Oke, and open the gate. Come to us now, Eloi Oke, and open the gate."

The breeze suddenly stills. Peregrine lets go of Margaux, who's on her right side, and reaches into her pocket. She pulls out a small cluster of herbs and sets fire to them with a lighter. "Ashes to ashes," she chants as they burn in her hand. She drops them on the dirt and nods at me.

I take a deep breath. *"Move lespri, pran kò mwen,"* I chant, trying to clear my mind. *"Move lespri pran tèt mwen."* Around me, the others in the circle seem to be slipping into trances one by one. They sway, hum, and move their feet as I repeat the words again, sending the song to the nether. *"Move lespri, pran kò mwen. Move lespri pran tèt mwen."*

Audowido makes his way toward me and begins to move up my leg. At first, I'm totally creeped out, but then I remind myself that this is part of the ceremony, and the sooner I get used to it and allow it to happen, the sooner it will all be over. So I focus on my breathing. Suddenly, there's a dull but insistent pressure at the back of my skull—a spirit trying to get in.

My first instinct is to push it away, but I force myself to accept the intrusion. It's what we're here for. My Stone of Carrefour begins to burn against my chest, and just as it's beginning to hurt, the pain dissipates and a warm, fuzzy feeling spreads through my whole body. It takes me a second to realize that I can no longer feel my limbs.

A voice sounds in my head. *Hello*, it says, soft and feminine, and although I know it means that the spirit is now within me, I don't feel as freaked out as I thought I would. This spirit feels gentle and nonaggressive, not what I would have expected after what happened last time. Instead of shoving her way into my brain, it's like she's taking polite steps forward.

I try to respond, but my tongue is frozen, and as the warm syrupy feeling spreads to my head, I know the spirit has taken control entirely.

I hope you don't mind, she says, *but my boyfriend and I, we've been waiting for an opportunity like this. We'll help you. But first we want to be together once more.*

She doesn't wait for an answer; instead, she looks around the circle, her eyes resting on Pascal and then on Caleb. "He's the one," I hear myself say, but my voice isn't my own; it's the spirit speaking through me. "I want him."

I want to ask the spirit in my head what she means, but I

can't form the words. I realize in a moment, though, what's happening. She has selected Caleb as the body for her boyfriend to inhabit. I watch as Caleb's eyes roll back in his head and he steps into the center of the circle with me. He twitches a little, and then his body goes still. A second later, all of his limbs seem to turn rubbery, and he slides and lurches toward me with what seems like great effort. It's as if whoever is controlling him hasn't quite gotten the hang of possessing someone yet.

"Is that you, Megan?" Caleb asks, but it's not his voice. His accent sounds like it's from Boston.

"Yes, it's me, Brett," I hear myself reply. "Come here, baby."

My heart thuds faster as Caleb approaches and puts a hand on my face, trailing it down slowly to my collarbone. I'm vaguely aware of the sensation of his touch, but it's like I'm feeling it through several layers of clothes. It makes me realize that the spirit inside of me—Megan—has taken control of all of my senses too. She's feeling Caleb's hands on her.

"It's been so long," she says through my mouth, as Caleb, his eyes wide and unfamiliar, leans toward me and kisses me lightly on the lips. I can barely feel it, but I hear myself moan with pleasure. "Oh, Brett," I hear myself say.

The others in the circle take up the chant. *"Move lespri, pran kò mwen. Move lespri pran tèt mwen."* It's background music to a slow dance of seduction as Caleb circles me and then pulls me close, pressing his body against mine. Even through my blurred senses, I can feel that he's excited, and I know Megan feels it too, because she presses my body closer to Caleb's and says, "I want you, baby."

And then, Caleb's lips are on my lips, and his tongue is in my mouth, and it's one of the strangest things I've ever felt, because the emotions attached to this encounter aren't mine, and I'm only conscious of a fraction of the physical sensations. Although I'm seeing the scene through my own eyes, it's also like I'm floating above it, watching two people I don't know make out.

Fear tickles at the back of my mind as the kisses turn more passionate. My concern grows as Caleb begins peeling off my shirt and then my bra. He tosses them aside, and then his hands are on my bare skin, but the part of me that should feel violated and exposed is buried too deep. Megan's enjoying this too much, and her happiness is tangible as she uses every one of my pain and pleasure receptors to feel her boyfriend's touch.

I should be humiliated that I'm standing in the middle of the cemetery topless, but that emotion too is buried somewhere too deep inside of me to reach. Instead, I focus on allowing Megan to use me, and for the next few minutes, she and her boyfriend kiss passionately and grope each other, but they don't go any further.

Suddenly, I can hear Megan's voice in the back of my head again, whispering to me. *Don't worry, Eveny,* she says. *I can feel your fear, but I just want to kiss him for a while. That's the most romantic part, don't you think?*

I can feel her sadness, and it fills me with the immediate and overpowering urge to cry. I wonder how and why Megan and her boyfriend ended up in the nether, but I have the feeling she has said all she wants to say, and now she just wants these precious moments with the boy she loves.

Finally, I can feel Megan's spirit withdraw from my body a bit, allowing more of my senses to return, so I'm aware of it when she takes a step back from Caleb. *I'm fading*, she whispers in my head. *Tell me what you need before I go.*

So I summon all my strength and reply in my mind, *The gate to our town is open, and we need to close it, to restore its power. We're all in danger.*

There's silence for a moment, and I can feel her pondering. *I will get it done. I'll hold it closed as long as I can*, she says, and I believe her. There's a long pause and she adds, *The people who are after you, they claim to be soldiers of the light?*

Startled, I manage to reply in my head, *Yes. Main de Lumière.*

I can sense them out there, she says. *But there's a divide within their group. Some could be your allies. You must look for the good in them but prepare for the bad. No one is what they seem.*

I swallow hard. Already, I can feel her energy seeping out of me, and I know the possession is almost over. She's gotten what she wanted, and she's promised to help us with the gate. But there's one more thing I want to know.

In the spirit world, I ask in my head, *can you see the other side? Do you know who my mother is? Can you see her?*

Megan pauses before saying, *No, but I can feel her. She's moved on, but she's nearer than I would think she'd be.* There's another pause, and I can feel her fading. *Eveny?* she whispers faintly.

Yes?

I can't promise that the danger isn't already here.

And then she's gone, and suddenly, I'm conscious of my own body, the weight of my own limbs again, and I sink to the ground. I see Caleb sitting down, rubbing his head beside me, and Audowido coiled between us, looking back and forth. Around us, the others are still chanting and swaying, their concentration unbroken.

Caleb looks up at me. "Is that you, Eveny?" he asks, and he sounds as weak as I feel. "You're back?"

I nod. "Your spirit is gone too?"

"Yeah. That was . . . heavy."

"Was that your first time being possessed?"

He nods. "I hope I didn't do anything that hurt you. It was really hard to feel what the spirit inside me was actually doing. It was like my eyes were closed, and I couldn't feel my body."

"You were fine," I say. "We just kissed."

I see his eyes travel down my body, and I realize suddenly that I'm missing my shirt and bra. "Oh God," I croak. I grope around me on the dark earth, but it's Caleb who finds them first and hands them to me, averting his eyes. I pull them on quickly and let him help me up.

"You sure you're okay?" he asks.

"I promise, nothing happened." I want to tell him about Megan, what she said about Main de Lumière, but already, I can feel the darkness and exhaustion pouring in. All at once, I can barely keep my eyes open. "How do we snap the others out of it?" I ask.

"I think you just finish with *Mesi, zanset*," Caleb says. "Want to say it together?"

He grabs my hands, and we chant the phrase three times, closing the ceremony. The air pressure changes; the others open their eyes; and the charm is broken.

Peregrine's eyes find mine in the darkness, and she too looks drained and disheveled. "Did it work? Did the spirits say they would help?"

I can only manage a simple, "Yes," before my legs go out from under me.

Caleb scoops me up effortlessly, although he must be exhausted from the possession too. "I'll carry you home, if that's okay."

"Thanks," I murmur.

I'm dimly aware of Peregrine checking to make sure the fire is fully snuffed out. Audowido crawls back into Peregrine's bag, which she hoists over her shoulder. In silence, our whole group begins trudging back toward the three mansions at the cemetery's edge. As we walk, Audowido hisses gently. A few times, I could swear I hear twigs snap nearby. Each time, I turn and stare into the darkness, but nothing moves, and I'm forced to admit to myself that in my exhaustion, I must be imagining things.

Still, as our houses come into view, I have the strange feeling that someone is watching us. The hairs on my arms stand on end until long after we've made it inside my house and locked the door behind us.

I sleep soundly that night and wake up before my alarm goes off the next morning, still groggy and disoriented from the possession ceremony. My grandfather is the only one in the kitchen when I walk in.

"Looks like you had a rough night," he says, pausing midway through pouring himself some coffee. He gestures to his mug. "Can I get you a cup?"

"No thanks." I cross to the fridge and get a glass of orange juice. My head is clearing a little as I wake up, and I feel a sense of relief knowing that Megan has promised to help seal the gate. I know it's not a solution that will last forever, but every little bit helps, and this should give us at least a few days of protection. Spirits in the nether have the ability to control some mortal affairs, and I believe Megan when she says she'll do what she can to keep danger out of Carrefour.

"How did it go last night?" my grandfather asks as he settles down at the table and takes a sip from his mug.

I nod. "I think the ceremony worked." I pause. "But I'm not sure how long the protection of the gate will hold this time, since Main de Lumière has seemingly already found a way to disable it."

"A very valid concern." My grandfather begins to cough

violently, so I stand and pat him on the back a few times, feeling sad for him. He sounds awful.

"You okay?" I ask when the coughing finally subsides.

He sighs. "Oh, my dear, it's been a long road. My time is growing short."

"Don't talk like that," I say. "Maybe we could find you another doctor, maybe do a different type of treatment . . ."

He smiles. "Eveny, it's okay. Chemotherapy was very hard on me. Maybe it's not meant for someone with magic in his blood; maybe that made the treatments more difficult. I don't know. But I do know that if it was meant to work, it would have already. I've accepted what's happening to me. My one wish is to know that the future of andaba is secure before I leave this earth."

I feel a surge of sadness. "I promise I'll do all I can to make sure andaba is okay," I tell him. "I'm not going to walk away from my responsibilities to the people on Caouanne Island."

"A nice sentiment, dear, but your allegiance is divided, isn't it?"

I begin to protest, but he holds up a hand, and I stop.

"I didn't mean it as a criticism," he says. "I understand the pull you feel from both sides. Your situation is unprecedented. Of course your loyalties are split."

"I'm doing the best I can." I look away, out the kitchen window toward the garden. I imagine my mother must have felt torn too, and suddenly, Megan's words from last night come back to me. *She's moved on, but she's nearer than I would think she'd be.* If only I could reach across the divide and ask my mom how she balanced her love for my dad with her love for her sister queens.

"What are you thinking about?" my grandfather asks.

"Just my mother," I say.

"She was a fascinating woman, Eveny. I see much of her in you."

"You do?"

My grandfather looks out the window for a long time before responding. "Yes. But perhaps it was her naiveté that led to her death, my dear. I hope you have the wisdom to prepare for whatever lies ahead, because I have the feeling the greatest battle of your life is on the horizon."

16

That day at school, I can't seem to concentrate. My head is swirling with thoughts of Main de Lumière and my grandfather's strange warning this morning. Plus, Megan's words are haunting me: *I can't promise that the danger isn't already here.*

What if she's right? What if it's foolish of us to assume that closing the gate will make us safe? What if we need to do more?

Peregrine and Chloe catch up with me after fourth period and ask me if I want to join them at Cristof's Salon for a little makeover.

"Now?" I ask them.

Peregrine shrugs. "Who cares about the rest of the school day? We'll cast a charm so that our teachers think we're here."

"No, I meant *now*. In the midst of everything, pampering's your priority?"

Chloe looks uneasy. "Look, I know what you're saying, Eveny. But the ceremony last night worked. Our mothers went out to the gate early this morning, and they verified that the protection has been restored. We're safe."

I stare at her. "Are you crazy? What about Mrs. Potter? What if there are others, like my father's sosyete told us? They could attack at any time!"

Peregrine makes a face. "Our protectors are well aware, Eveny. No one's getting past them now. And our mothers are working on a charm to identify people who are betraying us before they strike. It's all under control." She pauses. "Now, are you going to come with us or not? No offense, but you look like roadkill."

I give her a look. "Thanks for the compliment, but I'm going to decline. You two enjoy."

They totter off on their sky-high heels and I sigh. It's hard to imagine that they're supposed to be responsible for protecting this town too. But at least the news from their mothers makes me feel a bit better.

I head into the caf and glance up toward the Hickories, but Caleb isn't up there yet; it's just Pascal. Since I have no particular desire to get hit on for the next hour, I decide to sit with Liv, Max, and Justin instead. I'm glad that Liv trusts me again, and I could use an easy lunch hour of watching Max and Justin flirt; the way they are with each other reminds me that it's still possible to be normal. Maybe one day, when we've figured out how to defeat Main de Lumière, I can have a normal relationship too.

I run into Bram as I get in the caf line. "I thought you ate a catered lunch up there," he says, nodding toward the Hickories with a smile.

Every nerve in my body is suddenly on edge. Standing so close to him makes me think of the way I could hear inside his head, the way it felt so perfect when he kissed me. "The girls aren't here this afternoon," I manage to say. "They went to the salon."

"The *salon*? Now?"

"I know." I feel annoyed and embarrassed to be associated with them, but at the same time, I find myself holding back on saying anything further.

"Just as well." A small smile plays across Bram's lips. "I don't think Peregrine would let me sit up there if she knew how I feel about you."

I can feel myself blushing. "How you feel about me?"

"You heard what was inside my mind, Eveny. But I'll say it out loud this time: I think you're extraordinary. You're beautiful, you're smart, and you have the biggest heart of anyone I've ever met. The way you care about people, well, I can only hope that one day I'm lucky enough to have you care about me."

I can feel my cheeks turning warm. No one has ever said anything like that to me before, not even Caleb in the whispered moments when our defenses were down. The truth is, I can't ignore the pull I feel to Bram. But I'm not ready to leave Caleb behind. Not when he's so willing to lay his life down for me. So I clear my throat and say brusquely, "Thanks. Anyway, um, I'm going to eat with Liv, Max, and Justin today."

He looks unshaken by my lack of reaction. "Mind if I join you?"

"Um . . ."

His smile widens. "I'll take that as a yes unless you say otherwise."

An awkward silence descends over us as the line inches forward. Five minutes later, we've both ordered giant muffuletta sandwiches—a regional specialty of cold cuts piled high and topped with marinated olives—and we're headed toward Liv's table in the middle of the caf.

"What are you doing here?" she asks, looking up at me in surprise and then blinking at Bram.

"Is it okay if we eat with you?" I ask, ignoring her question.

"Of course." Her eyes dart to the Hickories. "I guess Chloe and Peregrine and their minions have left for the day? We're plan B?"

I open my mouth to reply, but she nudges me and says, "Kidding. It's fine. But who's this?"

I'm surprised to realize that she and the guys haven't met Bram yet. "This is Bram. He's new in town."

"He's cute!" Liv whispers once I've slid onto the cafeteria bench beside her. I can feel my cheeks heating up as Bram settles in on my other side.

"I guess," I whisper back, which makes Liv raise an eyebrow knowingly.

Bram strikes up a conversation with Max and Justin about freshwater fishing versus saltwater fishing as we all dig into our lunches.

"You're still thinking about Caleb, aren't you?" Liv asks as she takes a bite of the peanut butter and marshmallow sandwich she's brought from home.

"Hard not to," I say before I can stop myself. "Considering he lives in my house."

"Wait, what?" Liv's eyes practically pop out of her head. "I'm sorry, but I swear you just said Caleb Shaw is living in your house."

I hesitate and try to come up with a lie that sounds plausible. "His mom's an old family friend. He needed a place to go, and my dad gave him a spare room. No big deal."

Liv stares at me and then shakes her head. "You have the most bizarre life of anyone I know."

"You have no idea."

"Okay," she says after a pause. "Well, is he being any less weird with you?"

"He's being even weirder, actually."

"Then for the thousandth time, Eveny, you've got to move on!"

We both glance over at Bram, who's animatedly explaining something to the guys about casting a fishing line. When I look back at Liv, she's grinning at me.

"Eveny, maybe Bram being here is some kind of a sign, you know?" She pauses and I force a smile. "Ask him out," she says. "Why not?"

I sigh and glance sidelong at Bram. "Look, I can't," I whisper, turning back to her. "I know this doesn't make any sense to you, but Bram just isn't . . ." I pause, trying to think how I can explain it. "Bram isn't the direction I want my life to go in right now."

"Not this again, Eveny. Fate and all that crap? Just live a little. I mean, look what happened with Drew. He *died*, Eveny. He died right when I was finally getting to know him."

I look away. "I'm so sorry."

"It's not like it was your fault," she says, which makes me feel even worse. "But what I'm saying is, you never know what's going to happen. Life is short. And I think it's too valuable to waste on a guy who doesn't like you back."

I take a deep breath. "Look, you don't know *how* Caleb feels."

She doesn't quite meet my eye. "I saw him with someone else, Eveny."

She blurts the words out so quickly that I'm sure I've misheard her. "Wait, what?"

"I saw Caleb with someone," she says again. "Another girl. I'm sorry, but you should know."

I can feel color rising to my cheeks. "I'm sure it was just a friend."

"Do you hold hands with your friends?"

I blink at her a few times. "Caleb was holding hands with a girl?" My first instinct is to believe there's some mistake, but he'd warned me, hadn't he? I just didn't expect it to happen so quickly. "When?"

"Yesterday."

I feel sick. "Who was it?"

"I'd never seen her before; maybe she goes to Carrefour Secondary. But they looked pretty close, if you know what I mean."

"Now you're just trying to hurt me," I say.

"No. I just want you to take this seriously. You're hanging on to some guy who gave you a tiny bit of attention forever ago and made you feel special. But he's moved on, Eveny. You should too." She looks over at Bram and gets a mischievous look on her face. "Hey, Bram?" she says, ignoring the death stare I'm giving her. "Eveny and I have a quick question for you."

"What's up?" he asks, smiling at me, then focusing on Liv.

"Just a hypothetical here," she says. "But imagine you were Eveny, and imagine that the person you liked was dating someone else."

"Okay," he says, looking at me.

"Wouldn't you move on too?" Liv says. "To, for example, someone who actually had the potential to be interested in you?"

"Of course," he replies instantly. "A person would be nuts not to."

He smiles at me. I can feel myself blushing furiously.

"Well, there you have it," Liv says. "It's unanimous." Looking amused, she turns to say something to Max.

"What was that all about?" Bram asks, leaning in.

"Don't worry about it," I say. But as his arm brushes mine, I can feel my body temperature rising again.

I can't stop thinking about Caleb holding hands with some other girl, so I do my best to ignore him in fifth period, and I make a big point of talking to Bram and choosing him as a study partner when we're asked to pair off. I can feel Caleb looking at me, but I don't give in to the temptation to turn around.

On the way out of class, he catches up with me in the hall. "Did I do something to piss you off?" he asks.

"Nope! I'm fine."

He touches my arm lightly. "Is this about the ceremony? Because if I did something—"

"No," I cut him off. "It's not about that. I'm fine." I hurry away before he can say anything else.

After school, I've just started walking home when Caleb pulls up beside me. "Need a ride?" he asks.

"Nope," I say without turning.

"Eveny . . ." His voice trails off. "Would you just get in?"

I stop walking and consider my options for a second. I'd love to maintain some pride, but the afternoon is hot and humid, and Caleb's air-conditioned Jeep is tempting. I sigh and open the passenger-side door.

"What's wrong?" Caleb asks after I've buckled my seat belt.

"Just drive."

He studies me for a moment and puts the car back in gear. We ride in silence for a few minutes before I blurt out, "So you were out with some girl? Holding hands?" I hate how jealous I sound.

He looks startled. "Where did you hear that?"

"It doesn't matter. Is it true?"

He doesn't say anything for a minute. "I went out to dinner last night. Before the ceremony."

"With who?"

"You don't know her. She goes to Carrefour Secondary."

I flinch. "So it was like a date?"

He hesitates. "Yeah."

I'm unprepared for how much the admission hurts, and I'm not sure how to speak past the lump in my throat. Finally I manage, "I can't believe you're dating other people already. After what happened the other night in my room . . ."

He sighs. "Eveny, I don't want to hurt you. But it's time we both move on. I—I'm trying to do that. I don't have a choice. It's the only way for me to get over you."

The words sink in. "Who says you have to get over me?"

He laughs bitterly. "You know the answer to that," he says. "And you know it's the right thing."

I squeeze my eyes closed for a second and press my temples. I can't believe we're having this conversation again. "Caleb, I thought we'd been over this."

"Besides, your dad told me about Bram," he says after a moment.

My heart stops. "What about Bram?"

"About you kissing him. Apparently your grandfather saw you."

I open my mouth to defend myself, but it's not like I can deny it. I feel humiliated, and I'm suddenly furious with my father. "It didn't mean anything," I whisper, although I'm not sure that's true.

"Look, I'm not mad," Caleb says. "If you hadn't done that, well, I'd probably still be sitting here agonizing over what to do about you. So in a way, I owe you. You made me realize that this is really over, okay? Your dad's right. You and I, we're bad for each other. So go out with Bram. He's a nice guy, and life with him will be a whole hell of a lot less complicated than life with me."

"No," I say. "I don't want a life with him."

"Well," Caleb replies as he pulls into my driveway, "I can't control what you do with Bram. But it's time for me to move on. I know that now. And I think deep down you do too."

He cuts the ignition and gets out of the car without another word. By the time I get ahold of myself and make it inside, he's long gone.

My grandfather finds me a little while later in the parlor, my head in my hands.

"Anything you want to talk about?" he asks, sitting down beside me and putting his hand on my back. I can feel him trembling, and I'm reminded of how sick he is.

"Don't worry about it," I say, feeling guilty because after all, my problems pale in comparison to his. I feel foolish worrying about boys when he's facing a slow death. "It's not a big deal."

We sit in silence for a while, then he takes his hand off my back and reaches for a smooth, oval-shaped crystal that hangs from a chain against his chest, beneath his shirt. He pulls it out and holds it up to catch the light. "Have you seen one of these before, Eveny?"

I stare at it. "No. What is it?"

He smiles slightly. "It's my Mind's Eye. It acts like a crystal ball in a way, but it shows only the past, not the future. And it can only project events that the bearer has witnessed or taken part in. It brings them back with complete clarity. Here, take a look."

I look at him in confusion, then I peer in. He closes his eyes, and to my surprise, an image begins to play across the crystal, as clear as a television show on a high-definition TV. My breath catches in my throat as I realize what I'm seeing: it's my mother, years ago, walking across our rose garden toward my father. She's in a flowing white gown with a veil covering her long, red hair, and he's in a gray suit, with a rose in his lapel. I realize with a start that it's their wedding day.

"You went to my parents' wedding?" I ask in confusion. "I thought you were against their marriage."

"Is that what your father told you?" He sighs. "I've made a lot of mistakes over the years, Eveny. But it's important that you know I never disliked your mother personally. I just disapproved of the decisions your parents made. I used to believe that tradition should come before all else, and that your parents were making a mistake. But how could I miss the wedding of my only son?"

I watch, transfixed, as my parents exchange vows, promising their futures to each other while Aunt Bea, Peregrine's mother, Chloe's mother, and a handful of others look on. As the ceremony ends and they kiss, I realize I'm crying, but I wipe the tears away quickly and watch as the wedding guests turn and follow my parents. My grandfather seems to have paused in the garden for a few minutes to gaze around, and when he finally enters the house and approaches my parents, they're deep in conversation with each other, holding hands and looking into each other's eyes.

You have to promise me, my mother is saying to my father as my grandfather joins them, *that if we have a child together, you'll do everything you can to protect her, even if it means putting the future of both andaba and zandara at risk. You and I both know that there's more to the world than magic. There's family, and there's love. I need to know that for you, those things will always come first, as they will for me.*

I promise, Sandrine, my father says, leaning in to kiss her gently. *On the grave of my mother, I swear it.* They both turn and smile at my grandfather, and for a second, my heart skips. It looks like they're smiling right at me through the glass. And then, suddenly, the image is gone.

I gasp as my grandfather pulls the Mind's Eye away and slips it back under his shirt. I want to reach for it, beg to be shown more, but he's already moving on.

"You see, Eveny, your parents went against tradition. They chose love. It wasn't what they were supposed to do or what those in power would have liked them to do, but ultimately, they charted their own course."

I blink back tears. "So what are you saying?"

"That the doors that seem closed to you today may not always be closed. That you have to fight for what you believe in."

"But how?" I ask. "Everyone keeps insisting that everything is already laid out for me."

"And maybe it would be if you were only a Queen of Carrefour. But you're not. You're a Queen of Caouanne Island too, and maybe that changes everything. Have you ever stopped to consider that the feelings you're having for Caleb have something to do with that?"

"How do you know what I feel for Caleb?"

He smiles slightly. "Eveny, it's plain just from looking at you, from seeing the two of you together."

I can feel myself blushing. "Okay, but you're saying that maybe my andaba side is somehow influencing my feelings?"

"No. I'm saying that perhaps the two sides of you are canceling all of the rules out. I'm saying that you need to learn to listen to your own heart. I'm saying that the only thing that's true is how *you* feel."

I look at him. "I would have thought you'd be trying to persuade me to forget Caleb and go out with Bram. You know, secure the future of andaba."

I'm surprised when he chuckles. "Eveny, I'm an old man. And one thing I've learned over the years—a lesson my own son taught me—is that in life, sometimes all you can do is sit back and let nature take its course." He pauses and studies me.

"Do you feel something for Bram too?"

I hesitate and consider dodging the question, because, after all, it's a little weird talking to my grandfather about my love life. But oddly, he seems to be the only person who understands. And I'm realizing he's a different man than my father described. Maybe that means he's changed. He seems to believe, as no one else around me does, that I have the right to make my own choices. And that's what makes me speak the truth now.

"Yes," I whisper. "But it's strange, because I've felt all . . . fluttery around him since the first time I saw him. Almost like . . ." I pause. "Almost like I already had feelings for him before we'd even met. That sounds crazy, right?"

I expect my grandfather to look amused, but instead, he appears to be considering my words seriously. "You know," he says after a moment, "sometimes the way we respond to people the first time we meet them is a sign of what lies deep within our hearts, in the places we can't quite reach. Remember, Eveny, you're not like other people. You have magic in your blood, and that means that your intuition—your ability to read others—is that much stronger. Maybe deep down you're reacting to who Bram really is and feeling a connection with him because of that."

I nod slowly. "It's how I felt when I first saw Caleb too. Like something I couldn't explain was drawing me to him."

"Are you sure it was the same thing? The same way you felt for Bram?"

I consider this. "Yes. But what does that mean? How could I feel that way for two guys?"

My grandfather frowns. "I don't know, Eveny." He begins to cough, and then he stands. "In any case, my dear, I need to get some rest."

"Oh." I'm disappointed. "Okay."

He smiles. "It will all work out, my dear," he says. "Just follow your heart. Eventually, it will tell you what to do."

17

I skip dinner that evening, because I don't want to face Caleb. Besides, I don't have much of an appetite. My insides feel like Jell-O, and I have the uneasy feeling that something terrible is about to happen. All has been quiet in Carrefour today, but I realize I don't believe that the evil lurking in the shadows has really disappeared.

I wander outside just after nightfall and find Boniface carefully trimming my mother's roses in the darkness.

"What are you doing out here so late?" I ask.

"Missing your mother," he says. "On nights like tonight, I find myself thinking of all the things that could have been."

"Nights like tonight?"

"Nights where the world feels unsettled," he says. "Don't you feel it?"

My heart thuds a little harder. "I thought it was my imagination."

He looks off into the distance. "No. I think you just have very good instincts, my dear." He turns back to me and pulls a tiny sachet, not more than an inch square, from his pocket. It's pale purple and laced with gold ribbon. "I've been waiting for the right time to give this to you," he says, handing it to me. "Your mother made me promise that if there were ever a threat to your life and safety, I would make you one of these from the flowers and herbs she loved most. It has Rose of Life petals to help keep her close to you, sage to sharpen your wisdom and clarity, and fig leaves for luck and protection. She was very specific about the ingredients."

I lift the sachet to my nose. It smells strongly of my mother's favorite flower, the hybrid she created with my dad. "Thank you," I say.

"Keep it close to your Stone of Carrefour, and when the time is right, I believe you'll find the answers you're meant to find." He reaches over and ties it firmly onto my long necklace, just beside my stone.

"But . . . how?"

"By trusting yourself," he says. He kisses me gently on the cheek, and as he walks away, my Stone of Carrefour heats up and buzzes against my chest, as if it's directly reacting to the sachet that now hangs beside it.

I sit by myself in the garden for a long time after he goes. There are so many questions swirling in my head about what to do. Peregrine and Chloe seem to believe the threat to the town is gone right now, but I'm becoming more and more confident that they're being naive. And the more I think about it, the more convinced I am that I need to talk to my sister queens about the possibility of reaching out to Main de Lumière. *Some could be your allies*, Megan had said during the possession ceremony. I believe she was telling the truth, and if there's a chance she's right, I need to look into it.

I find myself thinking of the brief andaba training my father gave me in the garden. *"Con mi sangre, regreso a su intención,"* I say aloud, holding up my andaba cuff. I wish that the words could somehow send all of my confusion back to the people who are making me feel like this.

There's an increasing pressure on me to choose one magical tradition over the other, or at least to show allegiance to one town over the other. But what if I don't choose? Both zandara and andaba are centered around a need for sisterhood or brotherhood; we're always stronger when we cast with others. But what if I already have a higher level of power within me because of my strange blend of both forms of magic?

What if andaba and zandara coexist within me, making me different from everyone else who has come before me? What if I'm only weakening myself by trying to figure out where to fit? Perhaps it's not about fitting in but rather about charting my own course. I suspect I won't be able to do anything truly powerful on my own—you need three zandara queens or three andaba rulers to enact powerful magic. And all logic dictates that andaba and zandara shouldn't be able to mix; my ancestors on both sides specifically set up their magical traditions that way to protect themselves and their descendants.

But what if my very existence overrides those rules?

Suddenly, I'm convinced that if I can somehow summon Captain Cabrillo using my zandara herbs instead of the blood and muerte dust used for andaba, there might be some truth to my theory. I probably won't be able to get Cabrillo to actually do anything for me without the help of the other kings—or at least until I get better at harnessing my magic—but I'm desperate to know whether my zandara and andaba can work together.

I stand up and close my eyes, trying to remember exactly what happened in the ceremony on Caouanne Island. I think I can remember the words to the andaba charm my father chanted, but the key will be figuring out whether I can use zandara flowers and herbs to call Captain Cabrillo.

My mind spins through the various herbs I've learned about over the last few months. Finally, I settle on hollyhock, a plant closely linked with summoning helpful spirits. I know there's some growing on the side of the house, so I quickly go and grab a handful of its pink and purple flowers before returning to the garden.

I take a deep breath, pray this will work, and begin. *"Guardabarrera, ¿está usted ahí?"* I say aloud, knowing that my Spanish accent is probably terrible. *"Dejarnos entrar, señor. Dejarnos entrar,"* I chant a moment later, repeating the words of my father's andaba brothers.

I don't remember much else, but this seems to be enough. Once I've repeated *"Dejarnos entrar, señor. Dejarnos entrar,"* twice more, the air suddenly feels thin.

"Captain Cabrillo?" I venture into the silence. "Are you there?"

There's no reply, but I realize that the night air is now devoid of even the chirping of crickets or the far-off croaking of frogs in the swamps. I've managed to do *something*. I take a deep breath and continue.

"I know this isn't traditional," I say, "calling on you like this by myself. But if you can hear me, well, please, I'm begging for your help."

Still, nothing happens, and my heart sinks. I stand there for a moment, feeling dejected, until I realize that if I'm invoking zandara herbs, perhaps I need to do so using zandara traditions, even if I'm ultimately calling on Cabrillo. So I try again, chanting the words to summon our gatekeeper. "Come to us now, Eloi Oke, and open the gate. Come to us now, Eloi Oke, and open the gate. Come to us now, Eloi Oke, and open the gate," I say, and in an instant, the air grows thicker and heavier. There's a low rumbling, like thunder, all around me, and I wonder if it's the two spiritual worlds pressing up against each other.

I turn my attention to my Stone of Carrefour and try to clear my mind. "Hollyhock, I draw your power," I say, focusing on the flowers in my hand as I feel my stone heat up. "Please, zandara spirits, help me to communicate with Captain Cabrillo, who assists my andaba brothers in the nether."

For a second, there's no response. But then, the rumbling stops, and a faint wisp of fog begins to materialize in front of me. Within a few seconds, I can just barely make out the face of a man.

"Captain Cabrillo?" I ask, although the image is much less clear than it was when he materialized from the smoke of a fire on Caouanne Island.

"I am here," a deep voice hisses, and I recognize the accent. My heart swells with relief.

"It's . . . it's Eveny Cheval," I say.

There's silence, and for a moment, I'm sure he won't reply. But then he says, "You summoned me alone?"

I can't tell if he's angry or just surprised. "I—I wasn't sure I could do it. But yes."

"Remarkable." The cloud swirls and shakes a little, and I can see that he's laughing. "I wouldn't have thought it possible. Perhaps you really are the miracle they fear you are."

"Who? Main de Lumière?"

He pauses. "Yes. Among others."

"Who else?"

"You will see one of my sailors through?"

I'm confused briefly, but then I remember that in the ceremony we performed on Caouanne Island, my father promised one of Cabrillo's men safe passage to the other side—heaven, I assume—in exchange for assistance. "I don't know how."

"Speak with your father," Captain Cabrillo says. "I cannot help you for free."

I nod. I should have expected that. "I'm sorry. I only wanted to see if I could summon you. I forgot that I'd have to pay you." I feel like an idiot. "It's different in zandara."

"In zandara, you have other forms of payment," Captain Cabrillo says. "Possession ceremonies, I believe. I don't ask that of you. But my help comes at a price."

"Of course. Look," I say quickly, "while you're here, can you just answer one question for me?"

The cloud swirls silently, and I'm afraid Cabrillo won't answer. But then, finally, he responds. "It depends what the question is."

"Are we still in danger? Can you tell me that?"

He considers the question. "I only answer you, Eveny, because I see how great your power is and how useful you can be to me in the future. So the answer to your question is this: the enemy may be focused on you, but I believe it is your sister queens who are in danger now. They are seen as expendable, a means to an end."

"They're in danger? Now? From whom?"

"That is all I will say until you have something for me in return."

My heart is thudding. "But you say they're a means to an end? What end?"

He chuckles. "You, Eveny. You're the end goal."

"Me?"

"Don't summon me again until you can pay the price. *Adiós*."

And with that, Cabrillo and his cloud of white smoke are gone, whisking upward until they disappear. The air pressure returns to normal, and I stand there in the darkness, breathing hard.

"I can't believe I just did that." But before I can feel any pride over having summoned Cabrillo alone, using zandara instead of andaba, I'm overwhelmed with concern for Chloe and Peregrine. I have to warn them.

I consider briefly stopping in the house to let Caleb know where I'm going, but an image of him with another girl fills my head. I shake it away and hurry out back, through the cemetery. Cabrillo said I wasn't in jeopardy at the moment. I have to believe that's true—for now at least.

18

"You're in danger," I blurt out when Peregrine opens her front door twenty minutes later. Audowido is around her shoulders, and she's wearing a skimpy pink robe and a facial mask that looks like it's made of red clay. I have no doubt that it's one of the magically charmed beautifying masks her mother uses.

"Hello to you too," she says, stepping aside and gesturing for me to come in. "What is it this time?"

"I summoned Captain Cabrillo," I say quickly as she shuts the door behind me. "He said that my sister queens are in danger. Peregrine, I think this means the gate ceremony didn't work. Or maybe the threat is from people who are already here, like Mrs. Potter. Either way, we have to—"

She cuts me off. "Wait, wait, wait. Go back. You said you summoned Cabrillo? That andaba spirit?"

I nod.

"By yourself?"

"That's not the point."

"The hell it's not! You're coming over here telling me you're doing powerful andaba on your own, and I'm not supposed to react to that?" she asks. "Mom!" she calls, her voice shrill.

I can hear her mother click-clacking down the hall. A moment later, she appears in the doorway to the parlor, Chloe's mother behind her. They're both wearing heels and long, flowing gowns.

"Hello, Eveny," Peregrine's mother says, looking me up and down.

"Hi, Ms. Marceau. Ms. St. Pierre." I gaze at them nervously.

"Mom, Eveny is practicing andaba," Peregrine says.

"Is this true, Eveny?" Peregrine's mother asks.

I glance at Peregrine, but she's focused on her cell phone. I know she's texting Chloe. I'm beginning to feel ganged up on. But then I remember I haven't really done anything wrong.

"Look," I say, drawing myself up to my full height. "Yes, I used andaba. But I used zandara too. I'm not choosing one over the other."

Peregrine's mother snorts. "Could have fooled me."

"Wait," Chloe's mother says. "Just give her a chance to explain." She turns to me. "Eveny, go on."

I nod at her gratefully. "Zandara and andaba coexist in me, okay? I can't do anything to change that, and I don't want to. I think they're like . . . yin and yang. Or something. Two halves of the same whole, but they make me who I am. This is *me*."

The mothers stare at me. "Eveny, that's nonsense," Peregrine's mother finally says. "Yin and yang? This isn't ancient Chinese philosophy. This is real life. What if the spirits who help us think you're defecting? I'm sorry, but the longer you spend flirting with the idea of embracing andaba, the more damage you could be doing to us."

"But that's not true," I say. "I'm not doing any damage. I'm just existing. I'm being myself."

"Well, your mother would be very disappointed in you," Peregrine's mother says.

I can feel tears stinging my eyes. "No, I don't think she would be. I think she'd be proud that I'm finding my own way."

After a moment, Chloe's mother speaks up. "You need to be who you are, honey. We may not understand. But we've never been in your shoes." I'm surprised to hear her say this.

"Scarlett—" Peregrine's mother begins in a warning tone.

"No, Annabelle," Chloe's mother cuts in. "Eveny's mother was always different from us, and so is Eveny. Maybe that's a good thing. Maybe it's the differences that will save us in the end." She nods at me once and holds my gaze for a long time, then she grabs Peregrine's mother's arm and begins pulling her toward the front door. "Come on, Annabelle. I think the girls have had just about enough input from us. Let's head over to my house and let them talk this out amongst themselves."

Peregrine's mother follows Chloe's mother, muttering to herself. Just before they disappear, Chloe's mother shoots me a small smile, then she closes the door behind her.

When I turn around, Peregrine is glaring at me.

"Chloe's on her way over," she says. "And then we're going to talk about this."

"Good! We need to figure out a way to protect ourselves."

"I mean we're going to talk about whether you can use andaba," she says. "We need to set some rules here, Eveny."

"No. We don't. That's my decision. What we need to talk about is the fact that you're in danger."

"According to your ridiculous andaba spirit," she says, rolling her eyes. But an uneasy expression flickers across her face, and I know I've gotten to her.

"Peregrine, you know as well as I do that when we receive a warning like this, it's important we listen." I take a deep breath. "We need to do something."

She stares at me for a long moment, then nods. "Fine."

As she turns and begins walking toward her living room, I hide a smile. I know I've won this round.

Chloe arrives ten minutes later, looking concerned.

"Did your mother tell you about what Eveny said?" Peregrine asks after ushering her into the house.

She shakes her head. "She wasn't home yet when I left, and I didn't see her on my drive over." She turns to me. "Eveny, what happened?"

I carefully recap exactly what Cabrillo told me.

"He called us *expendable*?" Peregrine asks when I'm finished. "You can't tell me that's not extremely insulting."

"I don't think he meant it as an insult," I say. "I think he was explaining how Main de Lumière views us."

"Apparently they don't view *you* that way." She glances at Chloe. "What do you think we should do?"

"I think the three of us should figure out a way to protect ourselves," Chloe says.

"But we *are* protected," Peregrine says. "Don't you remember doing the ceremony to restore the gate?"

"If the gate was breached once," Chloe says, "it could be breached again. Maybe Main de Lumière has found a way to manipulate our charms."

"Impossible," Peregrine says, but she looks worried.

I finally muster the courage to say what I'm thinking. "I think we should try to meet with them," I say. Both girls instantly stop talking and turn to me with wide eyes.

"Meet with Main de Lumière?" Peregrine says.

I nod. "Megan, the spirit who possessed me, said Main de Lumière has some sort of internal division. It's what my grandfather said too. If that's true, maybe there's a way to ally with one of the sides."

"Did you smoke something before you came over here?" Peregrine asks, her expression incredulous. "Because you're really not making any sense."

"Actually," Chloe says, "I see her point. If there's a divide in the organization, maybe we can somehow benefit from it. But I don't know. It seems really dangerous. Main de Lumière is our sworn enemy. What if the spirit was wrong? Or what if she was lying to you?"

"I don't think she was," I say.

"We could be walking right into a trap," Chloe says.

"But maybe that's a chance we have to take." I pause. "Everything we've been doing so far is reactive. They attack; we respond. But what if we're proactive instead? What if we stop them before they can come after us again?"

"And you think you can do that?" Peregrine asks.

"I think *we* can do that," I say. "If we work together."

Chloe and Peregrine exchange looks.

"Now you want us working with you?" Peregrine says. "Because just a minute ago, you were all about doing weird andaba ceremonies on your own."

"Peregrine, I've always wanted to work with you two," I say. "And I always will. But you have to trust me. You were wary of me when I got here, and I understand that. And you've been worried ever since you learned about my andaba side. I get that too. But we're sisters. We're supposed to be friends. I think if you keep pushing me away, it's just going to put us in more danger."

She looks surprised, and I can almost see the war going on in her head as she considers how to respond. She blinks rapidly a few times and narrows her eyes, then her expression softens. "Fine," she says at last, so quietly that I think I heard her wrong.

"What?"

"Fine," she says a bit more loudly. "Maybe you're right. Okay?" She glances uncertainly at Chloe. "So? What now?"

For the next few hours, we talk, and for the first time, the conversation with my sister queens doesn't feel like an uphill battle. Chloe listens intently to everything I have to say, and Peregrine manages to keep her snarky comments to a minimum.

We're still in the midst of a conversation a few minutes after midnight when we're interrupted by the sound of men shouting outside.

"Was that Patrick?" Peregrine asks, her eyes wide as she looks at Chloe and me.

"I think it was his dad," Chloe says, looking worried.

Another voice cries out, and this time, the words are crystal clear. "Annabelle! Annabelle! Oh no! No! My God!"

Peregrine's on her feet and headed for the door before I can stop her. "Mom?" she cries.

I jump up. "Peregrine! Come back! We don't know what's going on out there!"

But then I hear her anguished scream from the front door, followed a second later by Chloe crying out. I take a deep breath and hurry after them. If there's danger lurking outside the door, I have to face it with my sister queens.

Still, I'm unprepared for the sight that greets me.

Peregrine has collapsed on the front lawn. Chloe is running down the driveway screaming. Oscar, Patrick, and their fathers are hunched together, all of them choking on their sobs.

And hanging from one of the branches of the massive oak tree that stands in front of Peregrine's house are the lifeless, bloodied bodies of Annabelle Marceau and Scarlett St. Pierre, their white, gauzy gowns fluttering around them in the silent breeze.

19

A heaviness settles over Carrefour as my father and Caleb arrive and we spend the next few hours trying to figure out what happened. By dawn, we still only have snippets of the story, and the parts we haven't pieced together are the ones that horrify us most.

Patrick's and Oscar's fathers had set out to accompany the mothers to Chloe's house, hanging back in the shadows, as is their protocol. Ms. Marceau and Ms. St. Pierre decided to cut through the cemetery rather than drive, and just after they'd made it across the crossroads, at least two assailants—maybe more—leapt out from behind a cluster of tombstones and took Patrick's and Oscar's fathers by surprise. Using some sort of drug—chloroform, Patrick's father, Benjamin, guesses—the assailants knocked the two men out in virtual silence.

"The last thing I saw," Oscar's father, Anton, says, "was

Scarlett and Annabelle walking on ahead, with no clue that we'd been overpowered."

When the two men regained consciousness, they realized they were bound and gagged in the cemetery and the mothers were gone. They quickly freed themselves and called their sons for help, but by the time they got back to Peregrine's house, it was too late. The two women were already hanging lifeless from nooses. But they didn't die that way; they were both stabbed through the heart—Main de Lumière's hallmark. They were strung up after the fact, apparently as a macabre warning to all of us.

Benjamin and Anton are beside themselves, and at first I think it's because of the horrible curse on them; the deaths of the mothers mean the protectors are doomed too. But soon I realize it's something more; the two men are actually grieving.

"I've—I've been looking out for her my whole life," Anton says, sobbing loudly. "She was practically my family. And now I've failed her."

Benjamin is just as emotional about Peregrine's mom. "I've let this happen," he says, "and now a daughter is without her mother."

Peregrine and Chloe are inconsolable. I sit with them as the hours tick by, and while Chloe hasn't been able to stop crying, Peregrine is sitting silently, completely unresponsive. My father, Caleb, Patrick, and I keep trying to talk to her, but it's as if she doesn't hear us at all.

"She's in shock," my father says. "I can't blame her."

The mothers' sosyete members trickle in before sunrise, and together, we all decide to let the police launch an investigation.

"We can't cover something like this up," says Maxine Pace, the café owner downtown who has been a member of the mothers' sosyete for years.

"But an investigation would put us in the limelight," Cristof, the town stylist, says. "We'll risk exposing zandara to the town. Annabelle and Scarlett never would have wanted that."

"I'm pretty sure they wouldn't have wanted to end up dead either," my father says, which earns him glares from the other sosyete members. "My point is, we're playing a new game with new rules here. We have to think on our feet. There's no way to conceal the very public murder of two of the town's most well-known citizens. If we try to, it's only going to make us look like we have something to hide."

"Besides," I say, feeling uneasy as all eyes turn to me, "maybe the police can help us."

"Only the police chief is a member of the sosyete, Eveny," Sharona, Cristof's assistant, says. "Not the officers."

"But we have no idea who killed Peregrine's and Chloe's moms. And if the gate's protection has been restored, and I think it has, the only answer is that the killer is someone who lives in Carrefour. Or killers, if you take into account the fact that it took at least two men to overpower the protectors."

"What are you saying, Eveny?" Cristof asks.

"That whoever is attacking us is probably hiding in plain

sight. If the police are looking for the killers, maybe they'll do a better job of finding them than we will."

Everyone stares at me. "You know, Eveny has a point," Cristof says. "The police don't have to know about our magic to follow the trail of a murderer."

I nod and continue. "So I say we're as honest with them as possible. I say we tell them everything, except about zandara, of course. Maybe they'll be the best chance we have."

"My, my, my, Eveny," Cristof says, "you're really turning into a queen, aren't you?"

I open my mouth to reply, but he holds up a hand.

"I mean it as a compliment, young lady," he says. "And with Annabelle and Scarlett gone . . ." He pauses and wipes away a tear. "Well, let's just say that this town is going to need your leadership. I hope you're up for the challenge."

I glance over at my sister queens. Chloe is hunched over, still gasping through her tears, while Peregrine is staring out the window in silence. They'll need me too. "I'm up for the challenge," I say.

My father pats me on the back. "Okay. I'll call the police. The rest of you, go home for now. We'll reconvene later to talk next steps."

The sosyete members stand and exchange uneasy looks. "How do we know we'll be safe until then?" Maxine asks. But the question isn't directed at my father; it's directed at me, and I realize that already, they're looking to me for answers.

"We don't," I say, looking them all in the eye, one by one.

"That's why we have to be extra careful. Stay together, if you can. Don't cut across the cemetery or anywhere else deserted. Stay in public. Don't give Main de Lumière a chance to come after you."

"This is just the beginning, isn't it?" Cristof says as he hugs me good-bye.

"That's what I'm afraid of," I reply.

Police Chief Sangerman arrives just past dawn with four other officers and the town doctor. Carrefour is small enough that we don't have detectives—the senior officers and the chief himself are supposed to be in charge of investigations—and our town's one general practitioner, Dr. Caldwell, also serves as a medical examiner on the rare occasion that one is needed.

"You just found them like this early this morning?" Chief Sangerman asks, staring at the bodies, which are still strung up. I swallow hard and avert my eyes. It's a horrible thing to look at. "I'll need to talk to their daughters."

"Of course," my dad says. "But I don't think they're in any shape right now."

Chief Sangerman frowns. "Very well," he says after a moment. "But I'll need their statements as soon as possible. Do we have any idea who did this?"

My father stares him down and waits until the officers are involved in a discussion. "Your guess is as good as mine," he says, raising an eyebrow meaningfully.

Chief Sangerman swallows hard. "Main de Lumière?" he

asks, his voice lowered to a near whisper.

"Looks like it."

"Benjamin Payne and Anton Galea were with them?" Chief Sangerman asks.

"Yes," my father says quietly, again glancing at the officers, who have walked over to the base of the tree and appear to be discussing the best way to get the mothers down. "They were drugged."

The chief looks startled. "Benjamin and Anton? The two most experienced protectors in Carrefour?"

"I know," my father says, glancing at me. "It worries me too."

The chief glances at me and sighs. "Such a shame. And their lives will be cut short now. Hardly seems fair."

My father's jaw flexes. "Not at all."

"Well," the chief says a moment later. "Let me get started with the two men. Maybe they saw something, and I'd rather talk to them before my officers do." He glances at me. "I'll need to talk to Eveny too."

"She had nothing to do with this," my father says immediately. I'm grateful for his attempt at shielding me, but at the same time, I know I need to cooperate.

The chief's eyes harden. "Mr. Desjardins, I know you're new here, so I'll cut you a break this time. But in this town, when it comes to the law, I decide who has to do with what. And if I think Eveny may know something, well, then, I need to talk to her to find out."

"It's no problem," I say before my father can reply. "I'm happy to talk to you, Chief. But for now, I need to make sure my friends are okay."

I stay with Peregrine and Chloe all day, but after Chloe finally cries herself out, an exhausted silence fills the void, and I realize it was more comforting to see her tears. Now, she just seems numb like Peregrine. I can't convince them to leave the house—or even to talk to me—so I call my dad and tell him not to expect me home tonight.

I'm surprised when he shows up around six thirty with a foil-covered dish. "Boniface made his crawfish casserole," he says, holding it out to me like a peace offering. "I hear it's pretty spectacular. There's enough in here for all three of you girls, and for Caleb."

"Caleb?" I ask, startled. I've been so focused on Peregrine and Chloe that I haven't given him much thought.

My father nods. "He's been walking the perimeter of the house all day, along with Patrick and Oscar. They're all on high alert."

"Of course," I say. "How are Patrick and Oscar doing? Considering their dads are . . . you know." I can't even bring myself to say aloud that their fathers are now cursed to die.

"They're holding up all right," my father says.

I nod, my heart heavy. "Well, I'll thank Boniface later, but I'm not hungry. I don't think the girls are either. Caleb, Oscar, and Patrick can have our share."

"You have to eat, Eveny," my father says, and I'm caught off guard by the depth of concern in his eyes. "You have to keep up your strength."

"I'll be okay," I say. "Seriously, give the casserole to the guys. They've been on their feet all day."

He returns a moment later and follows me into the parlor, glancing at Chloe and Peregrine. They're slumped against each other on the couch in the corner, both of them staring at the wall.

"How are they doing?" he asks.

"They haven't said a word all day," I say. "I don't know what to do."

He looks at the two of them, then sighs and beckons for me to follow him out to the hall. "I'm sorry for your friends," he says once we're out of their earshot. "I really am. I know how devastated they must be. But it's time for us to go."

"What?"

"It's time," he says. "You can't stay here any longer. I was patient while you restored the gate, and I was willing to see how things would go. But Carrefour's a lost cause right now, Eveny. You have to admit that. The fact that two of the town's most powerful queens could be murdered right outside their own homes . . . Well, I can't in good conscience let you stay here any longer."

I stare at him. "You can't *let* me stay here?"

"Let's not do this again," he says. "I know it's hard for you to adjust to having me back. But I'm still your father, and I have the right to make decisions about the things that will keep you safe."

"No," I say. "You don't. You have the right to *suggest* things that you *think* will keep me safe. You have the right to give me advice and try to explain your point of view. But we're not like other fathers and daughters, Dad. We never have been. I've been making my own decisions for years, and that's not about to change."

"Do you really think this is the time to be arguing just to assert your independence, Eveny?"

"How could you think that's what I'm doing?" I say. "I'm trying to make the right choices for everyone. I'm trying to protect all of the people I love. I'm trying to save this town."

"But what about yourself? What about trying to save yourself?"

I shake my head. "What do you want me to do, disappear and leave Peregrine and Chloe all alone to defend Carrefour?"

"We could bring them with us. Keep them safe on Caouanne Island."

"But what about everyone else? If we leave, what's to say that Main de Lumière won't destroy Carrefour and the people in it while they try to find us? Dad, these are my people—everyone in Carrefour. Are we going to bring the entire town to Caouanne Island?"

"You know that's impossible."

"And that's why I have to stay. Now that Ms. Marceau and Ms. St. Pierre are gone, the three of us are all this town has," I say, gesturing to my sister queens. "If we leave, innocent people die. And I can't live with that."

"Most of them have nothing to do with the Secret of Carrefour," my father says.

"Do you think that'll stop Main de Lumière?" I ask. "They killed Glory Jones, didn't they? There was no real point in killing her, but they did it anyhow. You think they won't do that again?"

"Look, long ago, I promised your mother that I would do everything I could to protect you."

"I know," I say. I watched him make the promise in my grandfather's Mind's Eye, but I don't have time to explain that now. "And you're doing exactly as she asked, Dad," I say. "You're trying to protect me. You're keeping that promise. But the choice is in my hands, and I choose to stand up and do what's right. This is my town. It's the town Mom loved. It's where I was born, and it's where I'm meant to be. It's also the home of my sister queens, who may not be perfect, but they're my family as much as you are. I know there's goodness inside both of them, and I know that when the time comes, they'll stand with me."

"I'm ready to stand with you now," Chloe says from the doorway.

My father and I turn to look at her in surprise. I hadn't realized she had followed us into the hall, but now, her red-rimmed eyes are a little brighter, her expression a little more resolute.

"Hey, you," I say softly.

She smiles slightly, and her eyes fill with tears again. "We can't let them die in vain," she says. "Their lives can't be a waste. We have to fight."

"I'm in too," Peregrine says, coming up behind Chloe in the doorway. Her face is still stony, but her eyes are flickering. "It's what our moms would have wanted. And it's what I want too. You can't leave, Eveny."

"I know," I say. "I'm not going anywhere."

20

My father leaves an hour later after finally realizing that he's not going to change our minds.

"You can go back to Caouanne Island with him if you want," Peregrine says after we close the door behind him. "I wouldn't hold it against you, and I don't think Chloe would either."

"You have the right to choose," Chloe says.

I reach out and squeeze their hands. "I choose you. Now, why don't you two head upstairs and try to lie down for a bit? You need to get some sleep."

They agree, and I lead them up to Peregrine's bedroom. After they've both fallen into bed, huddled against each other, I close the door behind them and head back downstairs alone.

The tears that I've been holding back all day finally fall.

Not only have my friends lost their mothers, but two of the last remaining links to my own mother are gone now too. For all their faults, Ms. Marceau and Ms. St. Pierre were still my mother's sisters, like Peregrine and Chloe are mine. They were the two most constant things in her life, except for perhaps Aunt Bea, and now they're gone. It's the end of an era. The sound of the doorbell disrupts my train of thought. Instantly, I'm on edge, but I remind myself that Caleb, Oscar, and Patrick are guarding us from the outside.

My heart hammering, I hurry to the front hall and peer through the peephole. I'm relieved to see Caleb standing there, but I'm surprised when he moves aside and I see the person next to him: Aunt Bea.

"You okay?" Caleb asks as soon as I open the door.

"Yeah. You?"

He nods. "I just—I feel terrible for Peregrine and Chloe. Are they doing okay?"

"They'll get there." I pause. "How are Oscar and Patrick holding up?"

Caleb looks away. "It's hard to know that your father's days are numbered."

"I'm sorry," I say, and I hope he knows that I'm apologizing not just for Patrick and Oscar, but for the way he lost his own father too.

Behind him, Aunt Bea clears her throat and steps forward. "Can I come in?" she asks.

I nod and step aside. I'm surprised when she crosses the

threshold and gives me a quick hug. "I'm glad you're okay," she says.

I manage a nod. "Thank you."

I look back at Caleb, who's standing on the doorstep. "Want me to stay?" he asks.

"You're welcome to come in if you want," I say. "But I'm all right."

"I'll head back out to help the other guys patrol, then," he says. "Call me if you need me."

I nod and watch him as he returns to the perimeter of Peregrine's property. Then I shut the door and turn back to Aunt Bea.

"How are the girls doing?" she asks.

"Not great," I tell her.

"It's terrible to lose someone you love," she says. And then, all at once, she's sobbing—big, body-wracking sobs.

"Aunt Bea?" I say, stepping closer and putting a steadying hand on her back. "What's wrong?" After all, she wasn't that close to Peregrine's and Chloe's mothers. In fact, I'm pretty sure she disliked them.

"It's just that it's happening again," she finally manages to say through her tears. "I lost your mother, and now you're going to be taken from me too."

"Aunt Bea, that's not going to happen."

When she looks up, her eyes are blazing. "You think you have a choice, Eveny? You think your mother had a choice? She didn't think she was going to die either. But if I fail you the way I failed her . . ." Her voice trails off. Finally, she adds in a whisper, "How will I live with myself?"

"You didn't fail her," I say. "And you're not failing me. Besides, the situations are different. Main de Lumière didn't kill my mom."

"So they claim," Aunt Bea says. "But we don't know for sure, do we? There's so much we don't know. No one in this damned town is what they appear."

"I am," I say. I wait for her to look up at me. "I'm the same person you've always known. I'm the person you raised. And I'm the person who's going to make everything right."

"Oh, Eveny. Your mother thought she could change things too." It takes her a moment to look up and meet my eye. "All of this, Eveny, it's wrong. It's been wrong from the beginning, from the birth of zandara. Don't you understand that?"

"What do you want me to do?" I ask.

"Walk away," she whispers. "Walk away before you die. I'm begging you."

"I can't, Aunt Bea."

"Of course you can! You're choosing not to."

My heart hurts as I look at her. "Maybe. But it's the right choice. Can you say the same thing about walking away from me?"

"I didn't walk away from you! I just couldn't be there with your father anymore."

"You still walked away," I say firmly. "You had your reasons, and that's okay. But you abandoned me when I needed you. Do you know how much that hurts?"

"I couldn't stay," she says, her eyes filling with tears again.

"But you have to understand that I feel differently. I *have* to stay. It's my responsibility. My life."

She stares at me in silence. "Then I guess you're a better person than I am," she says after a long pause. She turns to leave without another word.

I follow her outside, hoping to stop her, but she's already hurrying down the front walkway. "Aunt Bea!" I call, but she doesn't turn. She gets into her Volvo without another word and drives away.

I sit down on the top step of the front porch and put my head in my hands for a long time before looking up again. Outside, in the darkness, I can see shapes moving around the outskirts of the property, and I know it's our three protectors doing their job. But will any of us ever feel safe again? Will any of us *be* safe? I fear that the events happening now—and the way we're all reacting to them—will be the things that shape the rest of our lives. Still, I don't know what to do to change that, to make the future secure for all of us.

I'm not sure how long I spend sitting there, gazing out at the yard and then up at the speckled sky above, but I'm startled some time later by a huge gray hawk sweeping across the front yard, its wingspan so wide that for a moment, it obscures the pinprick stars. It circles twice before landing mere inches away from me. I'm so shocked that I don't move; I just stare.

It stares right back, and that's when I notice that it's carrying something. I blink and lean closer. It's a scroll of some sort. I reach for it tentatively, and as my fingers close around it, the hawk releases its grip and lifts off again, its expansive wings slicing through the humid air.

I stare after it in confusion, then I look down at the tube of parchment I'm holding. I unroll it slowly, and I can feel my eyes widen as I read the note.

> Dear Ms. Eveny Cheval,
>
> Please accept my condolences for the loss of two of your queens. As you may know, Main de Lumière has split into two separate factions: one that wishes you dead, and one that's interested in working with you to build a better future. I'm a leader of the latter, and of course the former group was responsible for the events that occurred in Carrefour earlier today.
>
> I hope that you, like me, are tired of all this bloodshed and war. If you're open to discussing how to end this feud, I would ask that you meet me, alone, in the St. Louis Cemetery No. 1 in New Orleans at the stroke of midnight tomorrow, at the tomb of Marie Laveau. I would like to discuss a solution.

I very much hope that you will consider my proposal. But you must tell no one, for it is impossible to know who we can trust. I believe you know that as well as I do.

Sincerely,

Jean-Luc Gerdeaux

I stare in disbelief at the note, a thousand thoughts running through my head. If the note really *is* from a leader of Main de Lumière, how do I know it's not a trap? What guarantee is there that he's not trying to get me alone so he can kill me? If I let that happen, my father and aunt would be devastated, and I'd be cursing Caleb to death, not to mention destroying the future of zandara and andaba.

But couldn't ignoring the note come with the same perils? What if Jean-Luc Gerdeaux is exactly who he says he is, and this is my one chance to put an end to this century-old feud? What if I can change our future? What if this is exactly what I'm meant to do?

I go home the next morning after Peregrine and Chloe have woken up. There's a funeral to plan, and as somber as that is, it seems to be giving the two of them a purpose. They're past the initial shock of their mothers' deaths, and now they just seem morose and subdued. There's little more I can do than provide moral support, so I promise I'll be back at dinnertime.

"Go home and get some sleep," Peregrine says with a small

smile. "I know you were up all night."

"How do you know that?" I say, startled.

"Because it's what I would have done if the roles were reversed," she says. "And maybe we're not so different after all."

My father is out when I get home, but he's left a note saying that he's meeting with the police chief and that he has his cell phone if I need him. Boniface comes in to give me a hug and make sure I'm all right, but he must sense that I'm exhausted and not in the mood for company, because he leaves right away.

I lie down on the living room sofa and try not to be conscious of the fact that every five minutes or so, I see Caleb pace through the garden as he does his rounds on my property. He must be bone tired, and I consider inviting him in, but I'm too exhausted myself to deal with him right now. Besides, I have the feeling he'll say no.

My mind is spinning as I try to decide what to do about the invitation from Main de Lumière, but fatigue finally gets the best of me, and I doze off sometime before noon. I wake up to the sound of the ringing doorbell, and I scramble off the couch and check my watch. Just past one in the afternoon. I only slept for slightly more than an hour, and I feel woozy and disoriented. *Get it together, Eveny*, I tell myself as I make my way toward the front door.

Out the peephole, I see Caleb, and beside him, an annoyed-looked Bram. My stomach twists, and I pull open the door.

"Eveny," they both say at the same time before pausing to glare at each other.

"I came over to see how you're doing." Bram is the first one to speak again. "But Caleb stopped me in the yard like I was some kind of intruder."

"Just doing my job," Caleb says.

"Yes, well, obviously I'm harmless," Bram says.

Caleb shrugs and looks away. "Are you?"

"Can I come in?" Bram asks, ignoring him.

"Yeah, of course," I say, moving quickly aside.

"You okay?" Caleb says, his eyes following Bram as he enters the house.

"I'm fine," I say. "Thanks, Caleb."

We stare at each other for a moment before I close the door.

"He's very protective," Bram says when I finally turn around.

"That's kind of his job."

"Yeah, well, I think we both know that's not all it is," Bram says. He puts a hand on my shoulder and changes the subject. "So how are you? I wanted to come check on you when you were over with Chloe and Peregrine, but your dad thought I should give you some time. You doing okay?"

"As well as can be expected, I guess. Thanks for asking."

"Of course. How are the girls holding up?"

"I don't think they've fully processed everything. Witnessing something like that . . . well, it's horrible." I pause and think of the memory I have of my own mother's death. "You never get over it."

"I'm sorry." He puts a hand on my cheek, and when his skin makes contact with mine, I suddenly feel like every nerve ending in my body is on high alert. As he trails his thumb down toward the corner of my lips, I feel a shiver of pleasure ripple through me, and I take a step back, my heart racing. Surely in the midst of everything—the mothers' murder and the danger swirling around us—I can't be having a physical reaction to Bram's touch.

But he just smiles. "Don't fight the way you're feeling, Eveny," he says.

He steps closer and pauses, perhaps waiting to see if I'll move away again. But I'm frozen in place, torn between logic—which says I have more important things to worry about—and emotion—which is telling me to stay right here. Emotion wins out, so I don't move when he leans forward. As soon as his lips touch mine, it feels like an electrical spark has been ignited within me, throwing everything off balance. The world begins to spin.

He reaches up to gently cup my face with his hands, and I hear myself sigh, my knees suddenly weak. Kissing Caleb always made my heart race and my body temperature rise, but it never felt like this.

When Bram finally pulls away and takes a step back, I'm hit with a wave of dizziness.

"Why did you do that?" I whisper.

He smiles. "Because you need someone to lean on. And I'm here, Eveny. I'm here to protect you and stand with you and do anything else you need."

"But . . . ," I say, letting my voice trail off. My brain still feels fuzzy. "But what about Caleb? I can't do this. Not while he's out there risking his life for me."

"Don't you understand that I would lay down my life for you too?" Bram says.

"But . . . why? I don't understand."

He holds my gaze. "I know you feel it too." There's a strange charge in the air, but I can't explain it. Before I met Bram, I was so sure that I could never feel this way for anyone but Caleb. And now, in a matter of days, it's like my heart has been invaded. I nod slowly.

He reaches out and touches my face again, looking deep into my eyes. "You'll choose me in the end."

"You don't know that."

"But I do, Eveny. I've always known. You're my intended."

I blink at him a few times before pushing his hand away from my face and taking a few steps back. "Wait, I'm your what?"

He looks startled by my reaction. "My intended. Our sosyete paired us together when we were just babies."

Suddenly, my stomach is churning. When I asked my father whether someone had been chosen for me in the bizarre andaba tradition, he had dodged the question, and I'd assumed the answer was no. Now I realize I was wrong. "What exactly do you mean?" I say.

He looks surprised. "You were the next girl born after me to a royal family, and even though you have powers too, the sosyete decided to pair us when you were about six months old." He laughs uneasily. "I think we're supposed to be some big power couple or something."

"No," I whisper. The realization that someone has magically tinkered with something so personal makes me feel violated. An instant later, I find myself wondering if my parents knew this charm had been cast. How could they have been okay with such a thing?

"How exactly does this pairing thing work?" I finally ask.

"From the time we turn seventeen, it makes us fall more and more deeply in love with each other every day," Bram says. I gasp, and he reaches for me, but I dodge him. He hesitates and adds, "Please don't worry. The sosyete is very careful. There's never been a bad match."

"So you're saying I have no choice about falling in love with you? Marrying you?" I say, incredulous. He takes a step forward, but I back away. I don't want him touching me now. I don't want to feel my heart thudding and my skin sizzling. I don't want to feel myself wanting his lips on mine. It's not real.

"Trust me," Bram says, "it's how the charm works. You'll feel it more as you get older."

"No," I say. "I don't want to."

He looks like I've slapped him across the face. "Eveny, I promise you'll feel differently when—"

I cut him off. "I don't want to feel differently, Bram. I want to fall in love—whether it's with you or with someone else—because my heart tells me to. I want to fall in love because a guy is good and kind and smart and funny. I want to fall in love with someone who gets me and someone who wants all of me, the good and the bad, the natural and the supernatural, the complicated and the simple. I don't want to fall in love with someone who only loves me because of magic."

"Eveny, how can you think that?" he says. "I love all of those things about you. And I know I'll love you more and more as I get to know you better."

"Because you've been forced to! By something *you* didn't ask for and *I* didn't ask for. Don't you see? This isn't real!"

"It *is* real," he says. "If you'll let me explain—"

I cut him off again. "I'm sorry. You seem really nice, Bram. But knowing that I'm supposed to love you kind of ruins it."

Bram takes a step back and smiles at me sadly. "I thought that too, Eveny. But just wait until you get a little older. Magic takes over. You'll feel the link between us too. You'll feel what I feel. And when you do," he adds, "I'll be here. Waiting."

He leaves without another word, and I stare after him, confused and shaken, long after the front door has closed behind him. It's only when he's gone that I realize I already miss him.

21

"Why didn't you tell me?" I say as soon as my father walks in the door a half hour later. I've spent the time since Bram left sitting in the kitchen, trying to figure out how I'm supposed to stop feeling something I've been magically forced to feel.

He looks startled. "Tell you what?"

"About Bram!"

"What about him?"

"How I'm apparently supposed to *marry* him? Didn't you think I deserved to know that?"

"Oh." My father looks guilty. "I'm sorry."

"You're *sorry*?" All of my frustration is pouring out now, sharpening my words. "You're sorry that you didn't respect me enough to tell me something so important? Or you're sorry that when I specifically asked you about it, you basically lied to my face?"

"I didn't lie to you," he says. "I just didn't answer completely. Besides, it didn't seem as important as some of the other things we're dealing with now."

"It didn't seem *important*? How can the outcome of my life not be important to you? How can the feelings I have not be important to you?"

"I don't mean it like that," he says quickly. "I just mean that we're under attack. Your life is in danger. I have to focus on saving you."

"Why? So that I can marry a boy you chose for me a lifetime ago? So that I can go on to follow some path you laid out for me when I was just a baby? So that I have absolutely no control over my own destiny?"

"Eveny, you're overreacting," my father says. "I'm not pushing you toward Bram, nor am I trying to take away your control. I *do* believe you have the right to choose, just like your mom and I did."

"But you and Mom agreed to let your sosyete cast this charm to bind me to Bram? How could you?"

He shakes his head. "Believe me, I voiced my concern, and I refused to take part in the ceremony, but they did it anyhow. They only needed three kings to cast, and I was outvoted. Your mom was furious when she found out what they had done, and she made me promise that I'd support you in whatever you chose in the end."

"Now you're saying I have a *choice* in the matter?" I ask, unable to keep the bitterness out of my tone.

"You *do*," my father replies. "Just like I did when I chose your mom. It's difficult to turn your back on the things you've been magically predisposed to feel, but it's not impossible. Regardless, I think you and I can both agree that Caleb isn't the right decision for you. And I don't see why you shouldn't give Bram a chance, when you get right down to it. He's a good guy, Eveny. And at the end of the day, I only want what's best for you."

"Yeah, well, funny how what's best for me looks an awful lot like what's best for you and your sosyete."

I storm up the stairs and slam the door to my bedroom, ignoring him as he calls after me. For the first time all day, I'm beginning to feel like meeting with Main de Lumière is my only option, regardless of the risks. After all, I can't even trust the people who are closest to me.

Caleb calls a few times, but I don't answer, and finally he texts me to ask if I'm all right.

Don't worry, I write back.

I'm still outside if you need me, he replies instantly. *Whatever it is, it's going to be okay.*

A new wave of guilt washes over me. How could I have given in to whatever I was feeling for Bram when Caleb is out there risking his life for me around the clock? What kind of a person does that?

I sit at my window for a few minutes and stare out at my mother's Rose of Life blooms, lit by the evening sun, and beyond them, the cemetery, which now lies in shadows. I think of my mother and wonder what she would have done if she were in my shoes. I can't help but feel disappointed in myself for having feelings for Bram, even after realizing I'm fated to. My parents, it seems, were stronger than that; they let their own passion for each other guide them rather than buying into their magical destiny. I wrap my arms around myself as I watch Caleb cross the garden on his nightly rounds. He looks up at my window, meets my gaze, and gives me a small wave. I feel tears in my eyes as I turn away.

There's a knock on my door and I call out, "I don't want to talk about it, Dad."

"It's your grandfather, Eveny."

"Oh." I hesitate. I'm not sure how he can help me now, but based on our conversation the other day, I'm hopeful he'll be sympathetic to my plight, at the very least. "Come in."

As he opens the door and settles himself onto the edge of my bed, I'm struck by how drained he looks. "Your father told me what happened," he says. "With Bram."

I look away. "Let me guess. You're here to tell me you agree with him? That I should just marry Bram and move back to Caouanne Island and forget all about Carrefour?"

"No," my grandfather says. "I'm here to tell you that I think you have the right to choose, just like your parents did."

"You do?"

"Tradition means a lot, but sometimes we have to rely on ourselves to make the best choices." He pauses. "Here. I have something I'd like to show you, if you'll come sit beside me.

I think that your mother would have agreed with me about relying on yourself too."

He chants something under his breath and pulls his Mind's Eye out from under his shirt as I move next to him. The crystal flickers to life, and it takes me a minute to realize that the scene appearing in the glass is taking place on Caouanne Island. A second later, a young version of my mother walks into the frame, and my breath catches in my throat. She looks so real, so alive in the tiny image. It makes my heart ache.

"This was the first time I met your mother," my grandfather says. "Your father brought her home to Caouanne Island to show her where he'd grown up. She must have been twenty-one or twenty-two."

I watch, transfixed, as my mother throws her head back and laughs. She looks hopeful, like anything is possible. "She seems happy," I say.

"She was."

We continue watching the scene, from my grandfather's point of view, as he meets my mother for the first time. They hug, and she chatters nervously about how happy she is to be on Caouanne Island.

The image flashes forward to what I assume is later that same day, because my mother is wearing the same flowing emerald green dress. My grandfather approaches from behind, and as he gets closer, I see that she's sitting on the back deck with my father, his arm slung around her. *Are you two almost ready for dinner?* I hear my grandfather ask, and

my parents turn to smile at him. I gasp as I see how young my
father looks too.

I watch as my father kisses my mother tenderly on the
cheek and heads into the house, leaving her alone with my
grandfather. He moves closer to her, and her whole face seems
to light up as she smiles at him. *Mr. Desjardins, thank you so
much for inviting me here*, she says.

But of course, my dear, my grandfather replies. *I know how
deeply my son loves you. And please, no need for formalities.
Call me Gregore.*

My mother blushes and smiles, and when she looks up
again, her eyes are filled with tears. *I know there are some concerns on Caouanne Island that I'm going to take Matthias away.
But I promise, that isn't my intention. We plan to be together,
but one day, we both hope that our magical faiths can be united.*

United? My grandfather's tone sounds surprised.

Oh yes, Gregore, my mother says, grasping his hands. In
the Mind's Eye, it looks like she's staring right at me. I'm startled to see the depth of resolve in her eyes. *Matthias and I
want to fix the things that are wrong with andaba and zandara,
the way they've been misused, and return both magical faiths
to their former glory, so that we can change the world for good.*

Sandrine, you're dreaming big, my grandfather replies. He
pauses and adds, *Then again, the world never changes unless
someone has the courage to lead. How can I help?*

My mother beams at him. *You're already helping, just by
accepting the love between Matthias and me. Thank you for*

opening your mind and your heart to me. I promise, I won't let you down.

The image flickers and vanishes, and my grandfather lowers the Mind's Eye and looks at me. I'm struck by how kind he was to my mom, which isn't at all what I expected after what my father told me.

"My mother wanted to unite zandara and andaba?" I ask after a moment.

He nods. "She never got the chance. But you do, Eveny. You have the opportunity to make that kind of change."

I wipe away a few tears and feel a new sense of hope.

"The stakes are so much bigger here," my grandfather goes on. "So much more important than which boy you'll wind up choosing."

"I know," I say, embarrassed.

"Eveny," my grandfather says after a pause, "do you know that anyone wearing the Mind's Eye can harness its power?"

"You mean I could see one of my own memories?" I say, surprised.

He nods. "The Mind's Eye is already charmed. You just have to focus on a specific moment in time." He hands me the crystal. "Do you want to try it?"

I take it hesitantly. "I don't know what to look at."

He pauses again before asking, "Do you remember the night your mother died?"

My breath catches in my throat, and I nod.

"Could you show it to me in the Mind's Eye?"

"But why?" I ask. I can't imagine anything more painful to witness again.

"Because her murder was never solved, Eveny," my grandfather says. "And things are happening in Carrefour again, terrible things. What if what's happening now is tied to what happened to her? What if your memories hold the key to saving us?"

I hang my head. He has a point. "You're right. I'll give it a shot."

"You're doing the right thing." He chants softly as I close my eyes and force my mind back to that terrible night fourteen years ago. When I open my eyes again, the scene flickering on the surface of the Mind's Eye is painfully familiar. The closed door of the parlor in our front hallway. A scream, light pouring out from beneath the door as someone flips a switch, Peregrine's mother crying out *Sandrine!* in a strangled voice. Peregrine's and Chloe's mothers bursting from the parlor and running right past me, both of them stained by my mother's blood.

And then, the image begins moving into the parlor, as I knew it would. I was three years old, and the room looks huge around me as I make my way inside. I can hear my mother gasping for air, a terrible, rasping sound that I now know comes from the jagged wound to her neck. *Mommy!* I hear myself cry.

And then the image bounds across the room as I dash to my mother's side. She's in a filmy white gown that's already soaked crimson, and her arms are twisted at a strange angle. Blood pumps from her slashed neck in an even, slowing rhythm.

No, Mommy, no! I whisper in the image, and I begin to cry now as I watch my tiny toddler arms wrap around my mother, trying to fix her, trying in vain to stop the life from seeping out of her.

Eveny, my mother says, so low that I can barely hear her. *I live on in you.* Then her eyes close and her body goes limp.

Mommy? Mommy, wake up!

Sobbing, I hand the Mind's Eye to my grandfather and turn away, trying to get ahold of myself.

"I'm sorry," my grandfather says, rubbing my back. "I'm very sorry I asked you to do that."

"No, you were right. If it could help us now, I had to try," I tell him. "Did you see anything important?"

He shakes his head. "You obviously didn't see the killer."

"No," I admit. I think about what I saw for a moment and add softly, "She said she lives on in me. What do you think she meant?" Hearing her voice again, her dying whisper, has undone me.

He hesitates. "I think she wanted you to know that you're magical too. She wanted you to be here, in this moment, knowing the extent of your abilities and of your responsibilities. What a wonderful gift."

"You're right." I feel a surge of power. My mother would have wanted me to fight, to stand up for all the things I care about and believe in.

And just like that, I know for sure that I need to go to New Orleans tonight. I need to meet with the Main de Lumière faction if it means I have a chance to save this town. It's what my mother would have done. *I live on in you*, she said. I have to do a better job of becoming the kind of queen she believed I could be. "Thank you," I say, turning to my grandfather with a small smile. "Thank you for reminding me who I am."

For a moment, I consider telling him about my plans. After all, he seems to be supporting my right to choose my own fate. But then the words from the scroll come back to me, and I worry that if I involve my grandfather, the man from Main de Lumière will know, and our meeting will be off. I can't take that chance.

He stares at me before nodding and standing up. "I'm proud of you, Eveny."

He kisses me on the cheek and walks slowly out of the room.

I drop by Peregrine's place just past six to check on my sister queens.

"We've chosen coffins," Peregrine says after leading me inside, her eyes empty and sad. "The nicest ones we could find."

"Good." I give her a hug. "Your moms would be grateful." It seems like the wrong thing to say, but she hugs me back.

She ushers me into the living room, where Chloe looks up at me blankly. "Hi, Eveny," she says, her voice flat.

"Hey. How are you holding up?"

She shrugs. "I don't know. I don't know how to feel. I don't know what to do. I've never been so helpless."

Peregrine nods. "How do we avenge our mothers if we don't even know how to find their killers?"

"I know the feeling," I say. "It's been fourteen years, and I still have no idea who killed my mom."

"We have to avenge her death too," Peregrine says. "We'll all work together from now on. Finding the people who took our mothers will be the most important thing we've ever done."

We're all silent for a moment, and I look away, guilt surging through me as I think about how I'm about to go off on my own to meet with the group that could very well be behind their mothers' murders.

"What is it?" Peregrine asks.

"What's what?"

She narrows her eyes. "I feel like you're hiding something."

"Nope," I say, shaking my head. "I'm just upset."

She looks at me suspiciously before sighing. "Sorry. My emotions are so jumbled right now that I don't know what to think anymore."

I make them some spaghetti for dinner, and we eat in silence, each lost in our own thoughts. My phone rings a few times, and Bram's name shows up on my caller ID, but I don't answer, and after his third call, I finally silence it.

"Looks like someone really wants to talk to you," Peregrine says, glancing at my phone.

"It can wait," I tell her, and she gives me a small smile.

Just before ten, I tell the girls that my dad needs me home, and they both thank me for coming over. "That's what sisters do," I say, hugging them both extra tight. After all, I don't know what will happen tonight.

"You sure nothing's up?" Peregrine asks.

I force a smile. "Positive. Get some rest, okay?"

I head toward the back wall, intending to cut across the edge of the cemetery to my property. As I expected, Caleb catches up with me before I leave Peregrine's yard. "Where are you going?" he asks.

"Home."

"Why didn't you wait for me?" He sounds frustrated. "You know I'm supposed to stay with you."

"I knew you'd catch up," I say without looking at him.

"What did Bram want today?" he asks after we've walked for a few minutes.

"What do you care?"

He's silent for a minute. "You know I care. Would you stop all this self-defensive bullshit, Eveny? Just be honest with me."

"There's nothing to tell you, Caleb," I say, looking straight ahead. "It was just a conversation between friends."

We part ways without another word at my back door, and I slip into my house. The living room is empty and silent, and I venture a guess that my grandfather is asleep upstairs and my father is out meeting with the mothers' sosyete, trying to figure out a way to find the mothers' killers. I glance out front and see only my grandfather's silver Mercedes in the driveway.

I wait until I see Caleb head toward the back of the yard, then I grab my grandfather's keys from the hook in the front hall and hurry outside. I climb into his car and turn the key in the ignition, offering a little prayer of thanks when it starts up quietly. I've only driven a handful of times, but as I pull the car out of the driveway and begin making my way around Cemetery Road, I call on Eloi Oke and ask the spirits to help me get safely to New Orleans tonight.

"*Mesi, zanset,*" I whisper three times aloud as I reach the gate some fifteen minutes later, after cutting across the Périphérie. I've just gotten out of the car to unlock the gate—a necessity when coming or going—when I see a pair of headlights slicing through the darkness behind me.

"Crap." My hand shakes as I turn the key and the gate begins to creak open. I hurry back to the car. If the person behind me intends me harm, leaving Carrefour is the stupidest thing I could do right now, because I'm much more protected within the town walls. But on the other hand, if I wait around and it's just another Carrefourian headed out of town, I'd be wasting valuable time—time when my father or Caleb could realize I'm missing. I have to go.

The gate opens completely, and I quickly push down on the gas pedal, but the headlights are suddenly upon me. I see a dark vehicle pass my car and screech to a halt in front of my bumper, blocking the road. Panicked, I put the Mercedes in reverse, and that's when I realize that I recognize the other car. It's Caleb's Jeep, and Caleb is leaping out of the driver's seat and striding toward my car, looking furious.

I shift the Mercedes into park and hesitantly roll the window down.

"What the hell?" Caleb says, leaning in my window. His eyes are flashing.

"Oh, hey," I say. Guilt for trying to evade him surges through me. I know he's mad.

"Where do you think you're going?"

"Out?"

He glares at me before reaching over me, turning off my engine, and pulling the key out of the ignition. "Get out of the car," he says.

Feeling like a child being scolded, I do as I'm told, because after all, there's not much I can do without the keys. As soon as I'm out, he gets into the driver's seat, shifts the car into reverse, and parks it by the side of the road. He climbs out and crosses back over to me. "Get in," he says, gesturing to his Jeep's passenger seat.

I nod, already putting together an argument about why he should let me go to New Orleans as I scramble into his car. "I can explain," I say after he's gotten in and started the engine.

"I sure hope so," he says without looking at me. "Buckle up." He puts the car in drive and accelerates through the gate just as it begins to swing closed.

"Wait," I say, turning around and looking behind us. He's already gaining speed as we make our way down the bumpy country road that cuts through Fantome Swamp. "Where are we going?"

"You tell me," he says.

I stare at him. "I thought you were coming to take me home. You're going with me?"

He gives me a small smile. "You didn't think I'd let you take on Main de Lumière by yourself, did you? Now, are you going to give me directions, or am I going to have to guess?"

22

I explain the note from Jean-Luc Gerdeaux on the way, and Caleb, in turn, tells me how he knew I was up to something. "You wouldn't meet my eye," he says, glancing at me. "Besides, Peregrine called and asked me to check on you. She said you were being weird."

"Look, I'm sorry I didn't tell you, but Gerdeaux insisted I come alone."

"And you just took orders from a Main de Lumière guy?" Caleb shakes his head. "Seriously, Eveny?"

"But what if he's for real? What if you being here with me ruins everything?"

"And what if he tries to kill you?" Caleb shoots back immediately.

That silences me for a moment. "I can take care of myself."

"I'm sure Annabelle Marceau and Scarlett St. Pierre felt that way too," Caleb says.

"It's not the same thing."

"The hell it's not." Caleb says. "Actually, your false sense of security is even dumber, because you're outside the gate. I don't have the same ability to protect you out here."

"I know." I gaze out the window at the endless cypress trees that line the road. They droop under the weight of hanging Spanish moss, and I think about how they, like me, are carrying more than they should be able to bear. "You can't come with me, though," I add after a minute. "Not to the meeting. You have to hang back. I can't risk Gerdeaux getting spooked and leaving."

I'm sure Caleb's going to protest, so I'm surprised when he says softly, "All right. But you need to take every precaution to stay safe."

I hold up my andaba-charmed cuff and then pull out my Stone of Carrefour, which is pressed against the sachet of Rose of Life petals Boniface gave me. "My armor," I say with a small smile.

Caleb gives me a look. "If you think that's going to protect you against Main de Lumière, you're even crazier than I thought."

Being back in New Orleans with Caleb sends a shiver of sadness up my spine. As we exit I-10 at Orleans Avenue and merge onto Basin Street toward the cemetery, I look out the window at the faded blacktop and squat palm trees that line the road. We're near the French Quarter, but not in it, so I don't have to be reminded directly of the insane Mardi Gras Possession ceremony that nearly claimed my life there. We pass the St. Louis Cemetery No. 1 on the right, and in the darkness, its chipped and faded brick wall, surrounding a small town of tombs, reminds me a bit of the wall that encircles Carrefour.

We're silent as Caleb continues down Basin, makes a right on Canal, and then another sharp right onto Treme Street. He pulls into a parking space on the side of the road, flicks off his headlights, and shuts off the Jeep's engine. "What now?" he asks.

I look at my watch: 11:35. "Now we wait."

A few minutes tick by before Caleb turns to me in the silent darkness. "About Bram," he says. "If you have feelings for him . . ."

"I don't," I say.

Caleb raises an eyebrow.

"I mean, I do." I pause. "But not like you think. It's complicated."

Hurt flickers across his face. "Oh."

"It's not the same as how I feel about you, okay? What I feel for Bram—and what he feels for me—is because of an andaba charm that was cast on us when we were just babies."

"An andaba charm? What are you talking about?"

"It's a long story. But the feelings aren't real."

"Yeah, but what if your feelings get stronger?" Caleb asks. "What if you can't fight them?"

Something occurs to me then. "You're jealous," I say softly. "You are, aren't you?"

He opens and closes his mouth. After a moment he says, "Damned right I'm jealous, Eveny. From the second I first saw you, I felt something for you. And it's real. It's not because of some stupid magical crap. In fact, it's *despite* magic. And I've been trying so hard to turn all of that off, because it's the right thing to do. I know I told you to move on, but I was just trying to do the right thing. But what if the right thing is being together?"

"Haven't I been saying that all along?" I ask.

"It's not that simple, Eveny," he says. "How do I accept that if I let myself love you, the protector link between us gets weaker? What kind of a trade-off is that? The more feelings I have for you, the less safe you are. That's what I'm wrestling with, and meanwhile, Mr. Southern Prince Charming waltzes in and sweeps you off your feet because of some stupid charm? How is that fair in any world?"

"It's not."

"So that's it?" he says. "Sorry, Caleb, game over, Bram Saxon wins because he has magic on his side and you're just some protector?"

"Not at all. My dad had someone he was supposed to marry too, and he went against everything to be with my mom instead. So it's possible. Maybe the more you love someone else, the easier it is to counteract the charm."

"How do you know?"

"I don't. But in my parents' case, my mom wasn't afraid to love my dad back. She knew she was risking being ostracized from her sosyete, and she did it anyhow, because it was the right thing. She listened to her heart. Maybe it's time you listen to yours, Caleb, or there's no point in talking about any of this."

"Eveny—" he begins, but I look at my watch and interrupt him.

"It's time. I have to go."

He blinks a few times. "You sure you want to do this?"

"I'm sure."

He hesitates, then leans across the seat and kisses me lightly on the lips, lingering for a second. My heart flutters with hope. "Be safe. I'll be waiting right here."

I can feel his eyes on me as I hurry up Treme and turn right at the corner. As I turn onto Basin to head toward the cemetery, my pulse starts racing. I looked the place up online before coming, so I know the gate is closed and locked at night, and I'll have to climb over the wall on Conti Street.

I find a few bricks missing, and I use the gaps as footholds to boost myself up. It takes me a minute, and I almost lose my grip, but climbing over the wall in my own backyard on a regular basis has made me better at this than I should be, so I eventually manage to heave myself over the top. I land in the darkened cemetery with a thud and try to get my bearings. The tomb of famed 1800s voodoo queen Marie Laveau, which is where I'm supposed to meet Gerdeaux, should be just up ahead to the right, so I make my way there silently, doing my best not to freak out. I'm used to the Carrefour Cemetery, which is spread out and fairly well-lit by the moon at night. This one, however, is so packed with vaults and crypts that it's hard to move.

I find Marie Laveau's tomb easily and check my watch. It's 11:58. The seconds crawl by as I wait.

At precisely midnight, a church bell tolls ominously somewhere in the distance, and I hear a rustling sound just a few feet away from me to the right. I gasp and turn, blinking into the darkness as a man in a dark suit emerges from the shadows.

"You're early," he says, his words tinged with a French accent that, under other circumstances, might actually be charming. He's absurdly tall—at least six foot seven—with white-blond hair, ice blue eyes, and skin so pale and smooth that it seems to glow, catching the light of the moon and reflecting it. As he smiles coldly at me, his too-white teeth seem to glisten too.

I can feel myself shaking, and I will myself to stop. "You're right on time," I say, surprising myself with how even my voice sounds.

"I'm pleased that you chose to come."

"If I can help save my town, I have no choice."

I can almost feel his eyes raking over me, probing me, trying to figure out if I'm hiding something. "You brought someone with you," he says finally, his cold smile morphing into a sneer. "Against my wishes. Didn't you?"

I hesitate and consider lying, but there's something about this man that makes me think he'll see right through me. "My protector. Caleb. He wouldn't let me leave town without him. But he's not here. He's several blocks away, waiting for me in the car. I came alone, as you requested. It's the best I could do."

He studies me. "You're honest. I didn't expect that," he says. "Fine. Let's not waste time, Ms. Cheval. As I said in the letter, I'm one of the leaders of Main de Lumière. I know you met one of our generals, Aloysius Vauclain, not that long ago, but let me assure you, he did not speak for our group. I am at the top of our hierarchy. When you speak with me, you speak with Main de Lumière."

"How nice," I say, barely keeping the acid out of my voice. "The group that's been trying to murder me."

"You have no reason to believe me, but I assure you, Ms. Cheval, I am not interested in eliminating you. Nor was I responsible for the regrettable murders that just took place in Carrefour."

"What about the guy who attacked me in my garden last week?"

"I'm afraid that was my fault, to an extent. He was tasked with delivering you to us peacefully, without causing you harm. I was hoping we could talk before things got out of hand." He clears his throat. "Clearly, he failed in his mission. I apologize."

I shake my head. "And Drew Grady?"

"He went off the rails, Ms. Cheval. When he tried to kill

you, he wasn't working under my orders. He had taken on a mission of his own. I suppose we owe your friend Caleb a debt of gratitude for ending him before he became even more of an embarrassment to our organization."

I suddenly feel sad for Drew, who got caught up in something far bigger than himself. "So I'm supposed to feel better now?" I ask. "You have soldiers out there trained to hate me, and apparently they have the tendency to go rogue, but I'm not supposed to worry, because you don't really mean to hurt me?"

He doesn't answer right away. Instead, he begins to pace. I'm struck by how silent he is, almost as if his feet aren't touching the ground. "As I mentioned in my letter," he says finally, "Main de Lumière has split into two factions, and that's at the heart of our problem here. But in order to understand this, you must understand how Main de Lumière works."

He begins pacing more quickly as he goes on. "You see, we formed not long after zandara and andaba developed, and my ancestors must have been of the same mindset as yours, for they set up our organization as a triumvirate based on paternal succession."

"But you're not magical," I say, shaking my head in confusion. "Are you?"

He makes a cold clucking sound. "Obviously not. We deplore magic and all those who practice it. Surely you know this already."

"Right."

"Now, while your order of succession is tied to the transference of powers from generation to generation, ours is simpler.

A leader's firstborn son is always next in line to a governing position, and a leader is thus obligated to continue producing children until he has a son."

"Sounds normal," I say. "Not a screwed-up system at all."

He ignores me. "For more than a century and a quarter, this system has worked fine. Each leader has always had a successor, and each successor has taken over when his father reached the age of sixty-five, which is our official retirement age. It has all gone smoothly."

"How lovely for you."

He glares at me. "I could do without the sarcasm, Ms. Cheval." He clears his throat. "In any case, it has long been Main de Lumière's policy to kill magic practitioners first and ask questions later. In other words, we were operating on the principle that the practice of dark magic is inherently wrong, and thus, if a person is born with magic in his or her blood, it is our right—our *duty*—to eliminate that person.

"But," he goes on, "in the last generation, Main de Lumière began to split. My father and one of the other leaders started to believe that the murder of magic practitioners was not, in fact, justified unless that person had used his or her magic in a way that was evil and destructive. The third of our three leaders—a distant cousin of my father's—strongly disagreed."

"Looks like leader number three got his way," I say, "since you're still running all over the world killing people like me."

"Actually, there's been a lot of infighting over just that issue. My father and Gilles—the other leader who agreed with him—condemned many of the killings over the years. But

Yves—the leader who took the hard-line view that all magic practitioners deserved death—continued to order executions.

"And then," he goes on, "for the first time in our history, we were presented with a serious problem. I was my father's firstborn. A man named Vincent was Gilles's firstborn. But Yves's wife gave birth to *twin* sons, Bruno and Gustave. Both had a legitimate claim of succession, although Gustave is, how can I put it nicely, a bit of an imbecile. And when their father turned sixty-five, both of them claimed his vacated seat of power."

"So you're saying you have four leaders now instead of three?" I ask.

He nods gravely. "Which might not seem like a big deal to you. But three was always a number that worked, because we could keep each other in balance. Four, on the other hand, can be split down the middle. And that's exactly what has occurred.

"Bruno and Gustave have separated into their own splinter group, which we've come to refer to as *Les Jumeaux Noir*—the dark twins, for they were both born with dark hair and coal-black eyes, very unusual for Main de Lumière, as you know. They've taken many of Main de Lumière's chief generals and high-ranking soldiers with them. Vincent and I have kept the majority of Main de Lumière's followers, but more and more are leaving by the day, not because they necessarily believe in Bruno and Gustave's hatred of all magic-doers, but because Bruno and Gustave are offering rich financial incentives. They've been blackmailing magic-doers into creating great wealth for them and then killing them anyhow. They have amassed a fortune this way, and money speaks, Ms. Cheval. Money speaks loudly."

"Wait, so they're using magic for their own personal gain?" I ask. "And they don't see that as hypocritical?"

"They see themselves as well within their right," he says. "They believe they're using magic against itself, and that it's therefore justified. But yes, of course they are hypocrites of the highest order. And the more power they amass, the more fearless and deadly they become. If they manage to lure a third leader to their side, Vincent and I—and the moderation for which we stand—will be dead."

"I don't understand," I say. "A third leader to their side?"

"Yes," he says. He stares off into the distance for a long time before turning back to me. "Main de Lumière was always meant to be run by three. That's what our followers are comfortable with. If Les Jumeaux Noir succeed in adding a third, the vast majority of our remaining followers will likely join with them. And they'll kill the followers who don't switch to their side."

"But how will they get a third leader?" I ask. "Didn't you just say you need to be a firstborn son of a Main de Lumière leader to get power?"

"Usually, yes," he says. "But if they can find someone with magic in their blood who's willing to become their third, it will trump everything we have to offer."

Now I'm completely lost. "But they'd never work with someone magical, would they? They hate magic!"

"Not as much as they love power. Don't you see, Ms. Cheval? Power is at the heart of everything. Bruno and Gustave are savvy. They'll offer a king or queen the chance to save his or her own sosyete. And in turn, they'll be able to leverage that sect's magic to eliminate every other sect in the world, one by one."

My mind is spinning. "So you're saying Les Jumeaux Noir are seeking a magical ally? And if they find someone to join them . . ." My voice trails off as I realize the enormity of the situation.

"Exactly. You and all of your magical friends will be wiped out with the greatest of ease."

He lets the words settle, and I can feel myself beginning to shake again. "What can I do to help you stop them?"

"I'm so glad you ask, Ms. Cheval. You see, this is a new world, and we want you to be a part of it, to help us guide Main de Lumière in a new direction. I don't want our organization to be about punishing those who haven't yet sinned. I want it to be about morals—about keeping those with magic in their blood from doing harm. You can help us do that."

I blink at him. "Wait, you want me to join *you*? You want me to become *your* third?"

"How better to help us minimize bloodshed?"

"But you kill!" I exclaim. "You destroy. You murder innocent people!"

"But it doesn't have to be that way, Ms. Cheval. If you work with us, we can change things from the inside. We'll listen to you. We'll respect your opinion. Our followers may finally begin to understand that magic isn't inherently evil; it's the misuse of magic that we should oppose. Furthermore, joining us will guarantee that we'll leave Carrefour and Caouanne Island alone—forever."

I consider this. I have the gut feeling he's being honest with me, but what guarantee is there that his fellow leader—Vincent—and their followers will agree with his plan? What if he's overruled at some point in the future, and my very involvement with him makes my two homelands *more* of a target? And even if that never happens, can I really work in good conscience with a group that's done so much harm in the past, even if they're vowing they've changed? "What happens if I don't join you?" I ask.

He smiles, but the expression doesn't reach his eyes. "It's important you realize you're not the only fish in the sea, Ms. Cheval," he says. "You're just our favorite fish, because we see great potential in your power, and so far, you've only used your abilities for good. But if you don't become our ally, we'll have no reason to fight for your right to survive anymore."

I swallow hard. It's not exactly a threat, but the message is clear. If I'm not with Main de Lumière, I'm against them. "I need some time to think about this."

"Of course. You're a very wise queen. But please consider our position carefully, Ms. Cheval. I'm a reformer like you are. I see a better future for all of us, one where magic isn't used for harm, where we don't feel we have the right to kill kings and queens just because of what's in their blood."

He takes a step closer and takes both of my hands. His touch is icy, and my whole body suddenly feels cold. "If you choose us," he says, "everything can be different. I'll expect your answer in forty-eight hours. Meet me here, in the cemetery. If you don't show, I'll take that as a no."

I nod, but before I can say anything else, he's backing away. In seconds, the shadows swallow him, and he's gone.

23

I fill Caleb in during our drive back to Carrefour, and then we call everyone in our sosyete, as well as Aunt Bea. Caleb insists I call home too, and although my dad is furious that I snuck out of town without telling him, he agrees to coordinate a meeting at our house.

When we pull into my driveway, there are already several other cars there, including Aunt Bea's and Bram's. All of a sudden, I remember that I basically stole my grandfather's Mercedes and left it by the gate.

"Crap," I say as we get out of the car.

"What is it?" Caleb asks.

"My grandfather's car."

He cracks a small smile. "Yes, brilliant move. I'll get it in the morning, okay?"

I nod, and we hurry inside. My grandfather greets us at

the front door with a stony look on his face. "I'm so sorry about your car," I blurt out immediately.

He looks perplexed. "You took *my* car to New Orleans?"

"Not exactly. But I was going to. I promise, I'll have it back by the morning."

"That's the least of my concerns right now, Eveny," he says, turning and striding away before I can say any more. I swallow hard and turn to Caleb, who just shrugs.

We follow my grandfather into the parlor, where I'm surprised to see everyone already gathered. Peregrine and Chloe are perched on the love seat, looking like zombie versions of themselves. Aunt Bea is there too, sitting beside Boniface on the sofa. Pascal, Margaux, and Arelia are on the couch on the other side of the room, looking uneasy, and on two chairs beside them sit my grandfather and Bram. As we walk through the door, Bram's eyes flick from me to Caleb, and his face falls.

"As you all know," my father says, entering the room behind us, "Eveny met with Main de Lumière a few hours ago without consulting any of us." He pauses to glare at me. "Do you want to tell us what you learned, Eveny?"

Everyone's eyes shift to me, and I clear my throat. For the next ten minutes, I explain exactly what Jean-Luc Gerdeaux told me in the New Orleans cemetery. When I'm done, there's stunned silence, and then everyone begins speaking at once.

"Wait!" my father shouts, standing and holding his hands

up until everyone quiets down. "Arguing and talking over each other isn't getting us anywhere. Let's take turns."

My grandfather stands, and the room falls silent. He turns to look at me, and at first, I'm sure he's going to take my side. But instead, he says, "We have no way of knowing that the faction Eveny met with is telling the truth. What if these supposed Les Jumeaux Noir fighters are actually the ones who are on our side?"

"But then why would Gerdeaux meet with me?" I ask, hurt that my grandfather is acting like I've made a foolish mistake. "And if he was the evil one, wouldn't he have just killed me right then and there?"

"Not if he needed something from you," my grandfather says. "Not if he hoped you'd come back here and try to persuade us to join with him. I think you're being played."

"But to what end?" Aunt Bea speaks up, and I'm surprised that she seems to be agreeing with me for once. "I mean, what would Gerdeaux's motive be? If we decide to back him, what could he possibly gain from it?"

"Giving us a false sense of security, that's what," my grandfather says. "Making us feel like we've reached a truce when in reality, we've just gotten into bed with the enemy."

"So we keep our guard up," I say. "We don't let ourselves buy into everything he's saying. But what if he's right? What if by ignoring him, we're effectively opening ourselves up to attack? He said that up until now, he's been fighting for my survival. What if this changes his mind about me? About us?"

"I think you're very naive to be taking the word of a leader of a cult that has set out to destroy you," my grandfather says, his eyes flashing. The anger in his voice surprises me.

"But wasn't it you who said we should think about working with them?" I ask.

He stares at me in disbelief. "That was before they murdered your two best friends' mothers."

"Gerdeaux said that wasn't him!" I say. "It was Les Jumeaux Noir."

My grandfather laughs. "And you believe him?" He turns to Chloe and Peregrine. "Do you want to take that risk? Do you want to work with the man who might have ordered the murder of your mothers?"

I look reluctantly at my two sister queens. They're both looking down, avoiding my eyes. It's Chloe who speaks first.

"I trust Eveny," she says, glancing at me. "But I . . . I think maybe the best move for now is to do nothing. Maybe Gerdeaux *is* being totally honest. But maybe this is another trick. I'm sorry, Eveny."

"I feel the same," Peregrine says, looking at me for a second before turning to my grandfather. "I'm not ready to dismiss Gerdeaux, but I can't agree to join forces with someone who might be connected to . . . what happened." Her words trail off into a stifled sob.

"But he said that if we didn't join him, he'd consider us to be against him," I say. "It might make things worse."

"I'm sorry," Peregrine whispers. "I just can't."

"I have to agree with Peregrine and Chloe," my father says, turning to me. "I'm sorry, but this is war, and the only way to win is to wipe out Main de Lumière for good. Working hand in hand with some of them might be a short-term solution, but not a long-term one."

"Then maybe we should just agree to ally with them in the short term," I say. "We don't have to work with them forever. Just until we're back on stable ground. What happened with the mothers weakened us."

"And we'll get strong again," Peregrine says. "But we have to do it on our own terms."

"In honor of our mothers," Chloe adds. "They never would have condoned working with Main de Lumière."

"Maybe they would have been wrong," I say softly.

Pascal speaks up from the couch. "Am I the only one here who thinks this could be the perfect way to get revenge on Main de Lumière? Eveny pretends to be working with this Gerdeaux guy, and we use his trust to destroy them from the inside?"

"No." Bram speaks up instantly, his tone sharp. "That would put Eveny in even more danger than she's already in. I can't allow it."

Pascal gives him a look, but I can feel Caleb, who's still standing beside me, tense up. "You can't *allow* it?" he says. "Since when are you in charge of what Eveny does?"

"I'm not in charge of her," Bram says, staring back evenly. "But I care about her. Deeply. I never would have put her in danger the way you did by driving her to that meeting."

"It wasn't my choice," Caleb says. "The decision was Eveny's, and I respected that."

The room erupts in argument again, and this time it's me who shouts, "Stop!" I step to the middle of the room and wait until everyone's eyes are on me. "For too long, we've done nothing," I say. "For too long, we've sat here, feeling confident in our safety, despite the fact that Main de Lumière has been picking us off. For too long, we've assumed that our magic would trump all. But that's not true, is it? Our magic isn't protecting us anymore. So we can continue to be sitting ducks, or we can take control and do something!"

"Why not a ceremony?" Peregrine says. "Why are we considering an alliance when we could be doing a protective ceremony instead?"

"Peregrine, we've performed plenty of ceremonies, and Main de Lumière continues to get past us," I say. "Something's not working."

"But we've never joined forces and done a protective ceremony with the sosyete from Caouanne Island," she says. She looks at my dad. "What if we did a ceremony together? Called on our spirits at the same time you call on yours? There are enough of you here to make it work."

My father glances at me. "I'm not even sure that working with both forms of magic at once would be possible."

"It would be, I think," I say. "I've tried. But I still don't think it's a solution." My dad looks at me in disbelief, but before he can say anything Peregrine speaks up.

"Let's put it to a vote," she says. "Who thinks we should try casting jointly before we even think about working with Main de Lumière?"

Hands go up all over the room; the only people abstaining are Aunt Bea, Caleb, and Boniface, who exchanges a concerned look with me before getting up and walking out of the room.

"Look," I say to everyone. "I've been thinking about it, and here's what I'm afraid of: The only way Main de Lumière could be getting past our magic is if they have some very powerful magic on their side already. I told you what Gerdeaux said about Les Jumeaux Noir trying to work with a king or queen. What if it's already happened, and that person is pulling the strings right now? How else would Main de Lumière be getting through the protection of our gate?"

"Maybe we didn't cast well enough," Peregrine says. "Or something was off in our charm."

"But . . . ," I begin.

"Eveny, casting together is worth a try," Peregrine says. "It's a better solution than working with someone who's an enemy. So let's do a ceremony after our mothers' funeral. If we feel like it doesn't work, then we can discuss what to do."

"I think that sounds like a wise plan, Peregrine," my father says before I have a chance to reply. "Now, why doesn't everyone go home to get some sleep? We have a long, sad day ahead of us."

Everyone stands and filters toward the door. On the way out, Chloe and Peregrine both stop to give me hugs. Bram lingers and reaches for my hand, but I pull away, and he looks wounded. Aunt Bea is the last one out, and as she goes, she leans in to whisper, "Whatever you decide to do, I'm on your side. Remember that."

She follows the others out of the house. Finally, it's just me, my father, my grandfather, and Caleb standing in the front hallway.

"I'm exhausted," my grandfather says, looking at my father and Caleb, but not at me. "Thanks for including me in this discussion, but this old man needs his rest. Good night." He walks up the stairs without another word. I watch him go, surprised by how hurt I am by his obvious lack of support.

My father turns to me. "I'm very disappointed that you went to New Orleans without saying anything to me."

"I was with her, sir," Caleb says. "She was safe."

"It was still irresponsible," my father says. "Eveny, you have to stop acting like a child."

The words cut me deep, and I stare after him as he walks to his bedroom, slamming the door behind him. When I turn back to Caleb, there are tears in my eyes. "Is he right? Was I acting like a child?"

"No," he says right away. "I think you did the right thing. That's why I stood up for you. What you did . . . it was brave, Eveny."

"Thanks." But after we walk upstairs and part ways in the hall, I feel more confused than ever.

The funeral is jam-packed; it seems that everyone in town has shown up to pay their respects. It makes sense, I suppose; Scarlett St. Pierre and Annabelle Marceau were arguably the two most well-known women in Carrefour, and even those who didn't really know them must have been saddened by their deaths.

On top of that, the town's weekly newspaper was filled with speculation about their strange double murder, and the police force has been asking questions all over town. I suspect that some of the mourners clustered around the gravesite are as interested in being a part of the action as they are in grieving.

"Don't you see why we can't trust Main de Lumière?" Peregrine says as we watch her mother's coffin slide into the family crypt. She walks away before I can reply.

The two sosyetes meet that night in the clearing in the cemetery's crossroads, the most powerful place in all of Carrefour. It's where the town's founding ceremony took place and where our Stones of Carrefour were first imbued with power, so our abilities are always strengthened when we call to the spirits from this spot.

Our entire sosyete plus the remaining members of the mothers' sosyete are here, all quiet and dressed in somber colors. We're joined in the clearing by my father, my grandfather, and Bram.

"Eveny, you are the link between us," my father says. "I think you'll have to be the one to light the fire and to summon all of the spirits. It's the best way for them to see, from the start, that we're working together. Captain Cabrillo already knows that you're proficient in both andaba and zandara. Perhaps it's time to show your spirits too that we're allied."

I nod and accept the matches my father hands me. Someone has already built a small fire pit in the middle of the clearing, filled with dry twigs and surrounded by a rough circle of stones. I ignite it quickly, then back up.

"Now what?" Chloe asks.

My father nods at me. I step back into the center of the circle and take a deep breath.

From my pocket, I pull a cluster of devil's shoestrings—a root from the honeysuckle family—and one of agrimony. The first is for keeping evildoers away, while the second is used to create protection from a curse and to get back at those who wish to harm you. I also pull out a few dozen basil leaves, which are for creating harmony within a family. I know this group isn't the most ordinary family, but technically, that's what it is, because I link everyone together.

I hand some of each of the herbs to Peregrine and Chloe, and I keep a small amount for myself. "The zandara side is all set," I tell my father. "Did you bring grave dirt and muerte dust?"

He nods and passes me two small sachets.

"You start the ceremony," he says, "and Bram, my father,

and I will take it from there since we have a bit more experience."

I nod and close my eyes. The others join hands, and I take a step closer to the fire.

"*Guardabarrera, ¿está usted ahí?*" I chant, calling on Captain Cabrillo.

My father, my grandfather, and Bram immediately chime in: "*Dejarnos entrar, señor. Dejarnos entrar.*" There's a familiar gust of wind, and the air seems to thin out around us as my dad starts to chant.

> "*Oh lonely warriors, spirits of the sea,*
> *Hear our cry, accept our plea.*
> *With grave dirt and muerte dust our passage fee;*
> *With the strength of our hearts, we call out to thee.*

I open the sachets my father gave me and throw most of the dirt and dust into the fire, then blow the rest into the flames, like my father did during the ceremony on Caouanne Island. I step back just as a cloud of sweet-smelling white smoke begins to rise in the center of our circle.

"Quickly, now, call on your zandara spirits," my father says. "Let's see if we can get them all here at the same time."

I nod and glance at Peregrine and Chloe. "Ready?"

Together, the three of us chant, "Come to us now, Eloi Oke, and open the gate. Come to us now, Eloi Oke, and open the gate. Come to us now, Eloi Oke, and open the gate."

I can feel the air pressure shift again, just as it always does when the gate to our spirit world opens, but this time, there's a low rumble, like distant thunder. The sound gets louder, and the ground beneath us starts to shake. The two spiritual sides must be resisting each other.

I think quickly. "Captain Cabrillo, if you can hear me, the other spirits you're sensing have been invited here too!" I call out. "Please, don't fight them." I say the same thing to Eloi Oke, the gatekeeper of zandara.

The rumbling grows louder for a second, there's a sudden snapping sound, and then the air goes still. I exhale in relief. From the strange thickness of the air—heavier than a typical zandara or andaba ceremony—I have the feeling that Captain Cabrillo and our zandara spirits are all still here.

"Good job," my father says.

I take a deep breath and turn to the cloud. "Captain Cabrillo, commander of the *Nuestra Mujer del Mar*," I say, "we reach out to you to ask for your protection and your intervention on our behalf."

"Evenyyyyyyyy," the voice hisses. I can see the lips of the foggy figure moving slowly. "We receive your *súplica*, your *petición*. On whose behalf do you make this plea?"

"On behalf of both my sosyetes. Carrefour and Caouanne Island. Zandara and andaba." I say the words as firmly as possible, and I hold my breath as the cloud swirls. Finally, Captain Cabrillo's face becomes visible in the smoke, and I can see that he's smiling.

"Good girl," he hisses. "Now, are you going to introduce me to your other spirits?"

"Yes, sir." I shakily turn back to Peregrine and Chloe. "Let's go."

They begin to chant and dance, stomping on the ground. After a moment, Pascal, Caleb, Margaux, and Arelia join in too.

I sway in time to their chanting, and after a moment, I call out, "Devil's shoestrings and agrimony, I invoke your power. Spirits, we wish to keep evildoers away and to protect the town from those who wish us harm. Basil, I invoke your power. Spirits, we wish to create harmony among the groups from Carrefour and Caouanne Island. We are all in this together, and we have to trust each other. Help us to strive toward a common goal, and please reach across the spiritual divide to work hand in hand with our andaba brother, Captain Cabrillo, who also resides in the spirit world."

Peregrine's and Chloe's dancing has gotten more frenzied as they give themselves over to the spirits, which helps strengthen my requests. It's the most I've ever directly asked for in the spirit world, and I know I'm on shaky ground. The protective charms should work, especially with so many sosyete members involved in this ceremony, but I'm not sure if they'll honor my request to work with Cabrillo.

So I'm surprised when I hear Cabrillo's voice from the swirling cloud of smoke. *"Hola, hermanos,"* he says. "Can you hear me?"

There's silence for a moment. The fire flickers noticeably higher and then dies down to almost nothing.

Cabrillo chuckles, vibrating his swirling cloud. "Eveny, it seems we have a problem. Your zandara spirits can hear me, but I can barely hear them, and we won't be able to include you in any conversation we have. If you wish us to speak on the mortal plane, one of the zandara spirits must possess one of you." The swirling cloud seems to incline itself toward Peregrine, Chloe, and me. There's another flicker in the fire and I hear Cabrillo chuckle again. "The blond one? Very well." He turns to me. "Eveny?"

"Yes?" I'm nervous about what he'll say.

"The spirit would like to inhabit the blonde."

"Chloe?" I glance at my friend, who looks worried.

Chloe steps forward and glances at me uneasily. Then she nods and closes her eyes. "*Esprits du passé, entre en moi,*" she chants in a shaky voice. "*Esprits du passé, entre en moi. Esprits du passé, entre en moi.*"

She continues to chant the words as Peregrine and I begin to hum, helping to raise her request up to the spirits. A moment later, her body twitches, stiffens, and then collapses. I gasp and move toward her, but she's already standing up on her own, her eyes wide and empty, her legs like rubber.

"I am here," she says in a voice that's not her own. It sounds like she has a British accent. "Pleased to make your acquaintance. I am Lady Margaret Sawyer."

"Well, this is most extraordinary," Cabrillo says. "Never

have I met another spirit who lives outside my realm."

"Nor have I," the spirit says through Chloe. "How charming."

I clear my throat and step between them. "Please. We don't have a lot of time. We need you to restore as much of the gate's protection as you can. We're hoping that working together will enhance our safety. Can you help us?"

"Yessssss," Cabrillo says.

"I will help you too," Lady Margaret says through Chloe. "For the price of another possession. But I must warn you. There is magic, powerful magic, working against you, so we can't guarantee—"

Her words are cut off by a bloodcurdling scream just off to our left. I spin around, and as I do, I can feel the air pressure returning to normal. The spirits are gone.

"What was that?" Peregrine says, stepping closer to me, her eyes wide with fear.

My heart thudding, I take a step closer to the tree line and blink into the darkness. As my eyes adjust, I see a familiar figure cowering behind one of the crypts, looking in our direction.

It's Liv, and she appears to be rooted to the spot, her expression terrified. But when our eyes meet, she unfreezes and begins backing up.

"Liv!" I call, but it's too late. She's already running away.

24

"We have to erase her memory," Peregrine says behind me as I watch Liv flee.

"No," I say instantly. "It's too dangerous." After all, this is our battle, not hers, and it's not right to put her safety at risk. When a charm is used to delete experiences from a person's mind, there's always the chance the magic could go too far and take bigger chunks of memory—or even motor function—out of the brain.

"But what if she tells other people what she saw?" Peregrine says. "It could create a panic! The town could turn against us. We don't have a choice this time."

"Yes, we do. I can go after her. I can explain." I don't wait for a reply. I take off running through the cemetery. I can hear Caleb chasing after me, calling my name, but I don't slow down. I know he has to stay with me in order to protect me, but all that matters now is getting to Liv.

I catch up to her at my own house's back wall. She's trying to climb over but can't get a grip on the bricks. When she finally turns to face me, I see tears streaked down her face.

"What the hell?" she says, slumping back against my garden wall. "I mean, Drew always said there was something satanic going on in this town, but I never thought *you* would be involved."

"Liv—" I begin, but we're interrupted by Caleb arriving beside us, panting hard.

"Don't you *ever* wait for me?" he says.

"Oh great," Liv says, shaking her head. "He's part of this too? Awesome. I suppose the two of you are going to do some kind of curse on me now?" She's trying to sound tough, but I know her well enough to realize she's scared.

"No, I—" But my words are cut off by another late arrival. This time it's Bram, red-faced and out of breath.

"You need me, Eveny?" he says, glancing at Caleb.

"No, Bram," I say with a sigh as Liv stares. "I'm fine. Go back to the others. You too, Caleb."

"But I need to stay with you," Caleb says. "You know it's not safe out here right now."

"Caleb, I think we restored the powers of the gate temporarily," I say, trying my best not to think about the warning Lady Margaret began to give us before she was cut off. "Just . . . I don't know, go back into the cemetery or something. I need some time alone with Liv."

"What, so you can do some weird spell on me?" she says. "No. Uh-uh. I don't think so."

"No, Liv," I say. "So that I can explain. Let me do that, at least, okay?"

Bram and Caleb exchange looks and head back toward the cemetery. Once they're gone, Liv finally turns to me.

"What are you doing here?" I ask her softly.

"You want to know what *I'm* doing?" Her laughter sounds ragged as she shakes her head. "Fine. I've been calling you all night. I was wondering how you were doing after the funeral, since I know your family goes way back with Peregrine's and Chloe's families. When you didn't answer, I started to get worried, so I drove over to check on you. I heard voices out back, and, well, I got nervous. There's a murderer on the loose, you know." She gives me a dark look.

"Oh." I feel even worse knowing that she stumbled upon our secret just because she was trying to be a good friend.

"So you want to explain why you were in the cemetery at one in the morning doing a satanic ritual?" she demands.

"It wasn't satanic, Liv. I swear."

"Right. Like I'm going to believe that. I suppose you're going to try to tell me now that you didn't have anything to do with Drew's death, either. What was that, Eveny, some kind of sacrifice to the devil?"

"What? No! How could you even think that? You *know* me."

"Do I? Because I sure as hell didn't know about this," she

says. "You have thirty seconds. Be honest with me for once, or I'm leaving."

"Fine." I take a deep breath. "We *were* connected to Drew's death."

I see her eyes widen, and I realize immediately that even with all of her suspicions, she didn't think this was true. "You killed him?" she whispers. She shrinks away like I might do the same thing to her.

"No!" I say. "I mean, not exactly. Drew was working for an organization called Main de Lumière. They kill people like me. People with magical powers. I never, ever meant for him to wind up dead. Caleb and I were just defending ourselves."

"Magical powers? Have you completely lost your mind?" She shakes her head like she can't believe what she's hearing. "And *Caleb* was a part of what happened to Drew too?"

"He protects me," I say softly. "It's what makes everything so complicated between us. He's not allowed to love me because he's my protector, which makes me feel like I've been living in one giant soap opera since I arrived in Carrefour."

"Eveny, you're making no sense."

I reach out to put a hand on her arm, but she jerks away like she's been burned. "Liv," I try again, "Drew was trying to kill me. It's why he followed me to New Orleans that night. He attacked me in an alley. He stabbed me. I would have died if Caleb hadn't gotten there."

Her eyes flick over me suspiciously. "Oh yeah? Then where are your stab wounds?"

"They healed," I tell her, and her eyes narrow. "Look, you have to understand this. I have . . . powers. So do Peregrine and Chloe and some of the other people you saw in that clearing. They healed me after Drew's attack. They healed Caleb too."

She's still eyeing me warily but I go on. "Think about it. There's something weird going on in this town, Liv. Glory dying a few months ago? Ms. Marceau and Ms. St. Pierre being murdered? My own mom's death is even connected."

Her expression softens, but only a little. "So you believe your mom was part of this whole magic thing? And that's why you got sucked into it?"

"I *know* she was, Liv. She was a zandara queen, and so am I. We're trying to make things right around here."

"What the hell is zandara?" Her eyes are flashing. "Don't you know how insane this sounds?"

"Does it?" I ask. "Or does it explain everything?"

"No. Because magic isn't real." But she looks uncertain.

In the distance, I can hear my father calling for me, and I know he's coming this way. "Look," I say urgently. "The others want to charm you to make you forget what you saw. But I told them you could be trusted."

"*Charm* me?"

"It means to cast magic. To erase your memory. But it's risky. I don't want to do that to you unless we have to. But I need to know that if I stand up for you and stop them from casting, you'll keep quiet about what you saw."

She stares at me for a long time. I can hear my father getting closer. Finally, she says, "I'm not going to say anything.

For now. But I can't promise I'm not going to go to the police after I've had a chance to think about this." She pauses and adds, "I won't do that without warning you, though."

"Thank you," I say, relief washing over me.

"Just don't ever talk to me again," she says as she turns to go. "Whatever's going on here, Eveny, I don't want anything to do with it. Whatever screwed-up crap you've gotten yourself into . . . well, you and the Dolls can take it and shove it. I'm done."

This time, she pulls herself up over the wall with no trouble and runs through my garden, around my house to the front drive.

Caleb and Bram emerge from the cemetery at the same time, frowning.

"What happened?" Caleb asks.

"She's not going to say anything."

"How can you be sure?" Bram says.

"Because she's a person who keeps her word." I glance at Caleb and add, "But I think I just lost one of the closest friends I had in Carrefour."

The next evening, after skipping school to give Liv a little time to think without having to see me around, I'm sitting in my room, trying to decide what to do about Main de Lumière, when I hear a knock on my door.

I turn to find my grandfather standing in the doorway. "Come in," I say.

He nods and enters, and I notice that he's moving with

even more difficulty than he seemed to be last week. The cancer is clearly advancing, and he's getting weaker.

"How are you feeling?" I ask him.

"Not so terrific," he says, smiling grimly. He winces as he sits down on the chair at my desk.

"Anything I can do?" I ask.

"Yes, actually," he says. He doubles over in a coughing fit, and after a moment, I stand to pat his back. I'm struck by how bony he feels, how thin and unsubstantial.

"What is it?" I ask when the coughing finally stops.

His breathing is labored as he stares at me. "You're considering it still, aren't you? Meeting with Gerdeaux again."

I hesitate. "Maybe."

"Despite what the sosyetes have advised?"

"Peregrine and Chloe are so shaken by their mothers' deaths that they're not thinking straight," I say. "And you and my dad already had your minds made up about the right thing to do, even before I told you Gerdeaux's story."

Something flickers in his eyes. "You truly are your mother's daughter, aren't you?"

"I hope so."

"Eveny," he says after a moment, "you understand that I'm dying, don't you?"

I nod. "I'm so sorry that I can't do more to ease your pain."

"But you can, my dear. You can be wiser in your role as a leader. You can be more cautious. All of that would bring me comfort and peace. But right now, I think you're seeking revenge against those who have harmed you, instead of thinking about the future."

I stare at him, wounded. "I *am* thinking about the future. I think Gerdeaux might be offering the only way for both magical traditions to survive."

He laughs bitterly. "Nothing is as it appears, Eveny. You must know that by now. Our enemies are among us, cloaked as friends."

"Yes, but sometimes our friends look like friends too," I say. "And what if that's what Gerdeaux is—a friend? Friendships don't have to be perfect to be real." I think of Liv and feel a sharp pang of sadness.

My grandfather turns to stare out the window. "Why don't you just come home, Eveny?"

"I *am* home."

"I mean home to Caouanne Island. I can guarantee your safety there."

"But how? Main de Lumière has vowed they'll find me wherever I go. And what's to say andaba won't be a target just as much as zandara?"

"You must trust me, dear girl," he says. "There are forces at work here that you don't understand. Let me protect you."

"But who will protect Carrefour?" I ask. "Who will protect Chloe and Peregrine and Caleb and Aunt Bea and all of the people I care about here?"

He stands and begins to pace. "Don't you know that your mother would have wanted you to stay safe?"

"She would have wanted me to act like a queen," I say softly.

"A queen like her?" he asks. His face is turning pink. "Eveny, I respected your mother, but she wasn't as powerful as you think. Nor was she particularly wise."

His words slice into me. "How can you say that?"

"Look at her Rose of Life! Do you know how long she worked on that? And in the end, she failed, Eveny. She wasn't powerful enough to accomplish the one thing she wanted to do with her life."

I flinch. "She didn't fail. She was killed before she could succeed."

"No, Eveny. She wasn't anywhere close to succeeding. I don't mean to offend you, but it's important that you realize this: the magic that's practiced here in Carrefour, it's play magic. Just look at what your sister queens have done with it. They've made their hair and their figures and their wardrobes better, but they haven't done any good for the world."

"But I'm going to change that."

"Why should that be your responsibility?" He's red in the face now; I'm worried that he's going to collapse at any moment. "Everything your sister queens and their mothers have done with zandara has been so selfish and meaningless. Isn't it clear to you by now?"

I stare at him until his face returns to its normal pale shade. Still breathing hard, he sinks down onto my desk chair again, exhausted. "Don't you see?" he asks. "My one dying wish is that you return home to Caouanne Island, to the place where you can be safe, to the place where you can achieve great things. Don't waste your life here."

"It's not a waste." I take a deep breath. "And you're wrong about my mom. She was powerful *and* wise. I'm so proud of her and what she was able to accomplish, and I'm proud of this place. It's a huge part of who I am, and I can't walk away from it. I won't. The people here, they're my family, just like you are."

"But you and I are related by blood," he says.

"And this town is *in* my blood. It's been my destiny all along to live here, to help protect the people who call Carrefour home."

He stares at me for a long time before getting to his feet. "So you're going tonight, aren't you? To meet with Gerdeaux."

I'm startled by the way he seems to see right through me. "I don't know yet."

"You'd be making the biggest mistake of your life."

I shake my head, frustrated. "Didn't you tell me that I might have the chance to unite both magical traditions? That I could chart my own path?"

"That was before I realized you might well destroy everything because you're incapable of thinking things through."

The words sting. "You think I haven't thought about this?" I don't give him a chance to answer. "I have to make a decision based on what I believe in my heart is right, not on what other people want me to do. I've spent my whole life making choices that way, and I'm done."

"Then I'm done too," he says. He walks to my doorway

and pauses. "One day soon, you'll rethink the decisions you're making now, but it'll be too late. I'm afraid you're being very shortsighted, and that people will die because of it—because of you." He walks out without another word.

It's only after he's gone that I realize I'm crying. I know my grandfather means well, and as he nears the end of his life, it only makes sense that he's worried about preserving his legacy and keeping his family safe. But why is it so difficult for him to understand that I have a responsibility to this town too?

I watch the sunset over the cemetery from my window, and then I call Caleb's cell. If I'm going to do this, I need to do it right.

"Would you come with me to New Orleans?" I ask when he picks up.

There's silence on the other end for a moment. "I'm glad you called," he says. "I'll meet you out front in an hour."

25

I'm standing beside Marie Laveau's tomb in the St. Louis Cemetery No. 1 in New Orleans at midnight, and as the distant church bell begins to toll the hour, I look around, expecting Gerdeaux to materialize from the darkness, like last time.

But the seconds tick by, and the cemetery remains still. I wait for what seems like forever before pulling my cell phone out of my pocket to check the time. It's 12:04 a.m., which isn't really late yet. Still, I can't fight the uneasy feeling brewing in the pit of my stomach.

By 12:15, I've realized he's not coming. I text Caleb— *Gerdeaux not here. Headed back to car.*

I make it back over the wall and find Caleb's Jeep idling by the curb. I climb into the passenger seat and glance at Caleb. He looks as concerned as I feel. "What happened to him?" he asks.

"I don't know."

"Maybe he changed his mind."

"I guess. But after the talk we had a couple of nights ago, that doesn't seem right. Besides, if he changed his mind, that's a bad thing too. Does that mean he's decided not to work with us anymore?"

"I don't know," Caleb says, but I can tell that he's nervous. "You want to head back to Carrefour?"

"I'm not sure what else we can do at this point," I say.

He nods and puts the car into drive, pulling a U-turn on Basin.

We've just gotten on the interstate when my cell phone rings. I glance at my phone and look up at Caleb. "It's Liv," I say.

"Liv? In the middle of the night?"

I nod and answer the phone. Immediately, I hear screaming in the background and a loud whooshing sound that I can't quite place. "Liv?"

"Eveny, can you hear me?" she yells.

"Liv? Where are you? Are you okay?"

The whooshing gets louder, and I hear a woman screaming somewhere near Liv. "Eveny, you have to get back here!" Liv cries. "There's a fire. A huge fire. I think there was an explosion or something! Downtown is burning!"

"Wait, what?"

Caleb whips his head to look at me.

"Eveny, if what you said about magic is true," Liv says, her voice breaking, "you have to do something. People are dying. Where are you?"

And that's when the call cuts out.

"What's going on?" Caleb demands.

I feel like I can't breathe. "There's a huge fire in Carrefour."

"A fire?" Caleb says as I try to call Liv back. It goes straight to voice mail.

"It has to be related to Main de Lumière. Caleb, what if the Gerdeaux thing was all a trap to lure me out of town tonight? What if this was his plan all along?" I feel sick to my stomach. My grandfather was right; I was foolish, and people were going to die because of it.

"You don't know that," Caleb says.

I wipe tears from my eyes. "How fast can you drive? We need to get home as soon as possible."

I can't reach anyone.

All of my calls are going straight to voice mail. As the Jeep bumps along at almost ninety miles per hour, Caleb and I are mostly silent, except for the occasional, "It's not your fault" from him.

My phone rings as we're approaching Carrefour's gate. It's Liv again, and I answer just as Caleb throws the Jeep into park and leaps out to insert his key.

"Please tell me everything's okay," I say.

But she's sobbing. "They have Peregrine and Chloe. Two men in dark suits, Eveny. They look identical. They've tied them up to stakes on the main square."

"Oh my God," I breathe as Caleb gets back into the car and begins to drive through the opening gate. "What about the others? My aunt Bea? My dad? Bram?"

She's crying harder now on the other end of the line. "I . . . I haven't seen Bram. Your dad and your aunt, they're okay. They're here, in the clearing. Margaux and Arelia are dead, Eveny. The men stabbed them right in front of everyone. I watched them die right there!"

"Liv, I'm so sorry," I say, and now I'm crying too, because as much as I disliked Margaux and Arelia, I never wanted this to happen. I can't imagine what other carnage awaits. "We're almost there."

The phone goes dead again, and I look at Caleb. We're almost through the Périphérie, and up ahead, I can see a huge, billowing cloud of black smoke.

"Margaux and Arelia are dead," I say, my voice shaking. "Peregrine and Chloe are being held by two identical men in suits."

"Les Jumeaux Noir," Caleb says.

I stare out the window in horror as we make our way through central Carrefour. My town has been destroyed. The houses that used to line the streets are burned to the ground. "It looks like there was a war fought here," I say as the broken world rolls by my window.

The smoke is so thick and dark as we turn onto Main Street that I can no longer see the sky overhead. Caleb screeches to a halt outside Aunt Bea's bakery, and after we get out of the car and begin running toward the flames, he grabs my hand. "I'm not letting you out of my sight," he says. "If it's the last thing I ever do, I'll protect you."

My father, Boniface, and Aunt Bea are standing on the edge of the town's main square, streaked with soot, when we arrive. In front of them is a chilling sight: the plaza is surrounded on all sides by a ring of fire, but it doesn't appear to be moving inward or outward. The only explanation is that it's being controlled by magic. That's when I know that what Gerdeaux said is true: Les Jumeaux Noir are working with a king or queen from another sosyete.

"Oh, Eveny!" Aunt Bea says, folding me into a hug so tight that I can't breathe. When she finally lets go, I find myself in my father's arms, and then in Boniface's.

"I'm so glad you're okay, Eveny," Boniface says, his eyes red. "We thought they had you."

"I'm so sorry I left," I say. "I was in New Orleans, trying to meet with Gerdeaux. I thought I was doing the right thing. I thought I was saving all of you."

"The important thing is that you're safe," Boniface says, and my father nods.

"What about Bram? Where is he?"

My father's jaw twitches. "I don't know, Eveny. He and my father are both missing." He glances at Caleb and says, "Your mother's okay. We checked on her earlier. She's been moved to a shelter in the Périphérie."

"Thank you, sir," Caleb says.

"They killed Margaux and Arelia," my father says.

"Liv told me," I say. "Do you know where she is now?"

My father looks confused. "Your friend who saw our ceremony last night? No, why?"

"Because," I say, "if we're going to face off against Main de Lumière, I'm going to need two females to cast with. I know Liv isn't in our sosyete, but I trust her, and she's the best I can do right now with Margaux and Arelia dead and Peregrine and Chloe out of commission."

"I don't understand," my father says.

"In the absence of three queens or three sosyete members," I say quickly, "one queen and two other women are the next best thing. I'll need all the power I can get."

"Who's your third?" Aunt Bea asks.

"You are, if you'll join me." I speak quickly. "I know you've turned your back on zandara, and I understand why. But there's magic in your blood—you're my mother's sister. Aunt Bea, I need you. If you ever loved this town, please help me."

Aunt Bea places a hand on my cheek. "My feelings about Carrefour have always been complicated. But my feelings for you, Eveny, have never been. I love you, and I'll do whatever you ask."

I hug her, but there's no time for an outpouring of emotion. "Caleb, can you go find Liv?" I ask.

He looks up. "No need. She's already here."

I follow his eyes to the edge of the town square, where

Liv is emerging from the other side of the billowing smoke. She's running straight toward us, wearing dirt-streaked jeans, an old gray T-shirt, and a look of determination. "You want to explain what the hell's going on here?" she asks when she reaches us.

"Are Max and Justin okay?" I ask instead of replying. "Your dad and your brother too?"

She nods. "They're all helping out at the shelter in the Périphérie. They're fine."

"Then what are you doing here?"

"I assumed this whole thing was connected to you," she says. "And the magical shit you're into."

"I thought you wanted nothing to do with me," I say.

"Just answer me this," she says. "Those creepy twins, were they involved in Drew's death?"

"They're the ones who recruited him, I think. The ones who sent him to kill me."

"Then I'm on your side, no matter what," she says. "I don't trust any of this. But I trust you. Okay?"

A wave of gratitude washes over me. "Thank you," I say. "Because I really need you right now."

"What can I do?"

"Will you go in there with me?" I ask, nodding toward the flames. "Into the square? Where Peregrine and Chloe are?"

"Will more people die if I don't?" she asks.

"I'm afraid so."

"Then the answer is yes," she says without hesitation. "But

you have to tell me what to do."

"I need you to trust me and try to visualize the survival of Carrefour," I say quickly. "Just focus on those two things—trust and the town's survival—as hard as you can, and I can channel that."

"I don't understand," Liv says. "How will what I'm thinking help you?"

It's Aunt Bea who replies. "Zandara uses the power of the collective consciousness to call the spirits. Eveny will basically be using you and me as conduits to strengthen her own ability to communicate."

"It will make you feel weakened," I add. "But it won't hurt. Look, this could be dangerous. So if this isn't something you want to do—"

"I'm in," Liv says, cutting me off. "It's my town too."

"Thank you." I grab her hand and Aunt Bea's, and together, we walk toward the flames. There's a small gap in the wall of fire near the town theater, and I have the feeling it's been left open for us and that I'm doing exactly what Les Jumeaux Noir want. I'm walking into a trap, and I know it, but I don't see any other way out for my sister queens.

My father, Boniface, and Caleb all follow us into the square, our own little ill-prepared army of six. The moment we're through the smoke and inside the ring of fire, I see my sister queens. They're both tied to tall wooden stakes, strung up like scarecrows. Their clothes are drenched in blood, and their heads are hanging limply.

"Are they dead?" I ask in a panic, turning to the others.

"No," Aunt Bea says.

"How do you know?" I say.

"Because you'd feel it if they were," she says. "They're your sister queens, and you're more connected to them than you are to anybody else in the world."

"Then I have to help them," I say, and before anyone can stop me, I break away from the group and run toward them.

Behind me, I can hear my father calling out to me, fear in his voice, but I can't stop. I reach Chloe first and shake her, trying to wake her up, but she won't move. I reach for her wrist and am relieved to feel her pulse thudding steadily. I run to Peregrine and do the same. Her pulse feels slower, weaker, but at least they're both alive, just like Aunt Bea said. "Wake up!" I cry, for as much as I hope Aunt Bea and Liv will be able to help me, nothing can compare to the power that would come from casting with my fellow queens. I know that they're our only real hope of survival. "You have to wake up!"

"What do we do?" Liv asks, running up beside me and putting a hand on my arm. I turn to find Aunt Bea a few steps away, with Caleb there too, looking toward the edge of the flames with his eyes narrowed. My father stands several paces back, staring in the direction we came.

"Eveny—" he begins, but he's cut off by a booming voice.

"Well, well, well, if it isn't the elusive Eveny Cheval." The voice is smooth with a French accent, and I'm not surprised when I turn and see two very tall men with jet-black hair and alabaster skin walking toward us across the clearing.

"Allow me to introduce myself," the one on the right says, stopping several feet from where Aunt Bea, Liv, Caleb, my father, Boniface, and I stand protectively in front of my sister queens. "I am Bruno Sauvage, one of the leaders of Main de Lumière. And this is my twin brother, Gustave. We meet at last."

I think of my mother's Rose of Life petals against my heart and try to summon some of her courage. This is it. The source of the evil I've been standing up against. "Don't you mean you're the leader of Les Jumeaux Noir?" I ask, trying to sound calm. "Because the rest of Main de Lumière really isn't with you, are they? You're out on your own, trying to ally with people more powerful than you, people who practice the magic you claim to hate."

His dark eyes flash angrily, but then he smiles, his expression suddenly deadly calm. "Let's not get embroiled in a discussion of what you think you know. You're a mere child, and you have no idea how the world works."

"Oh, I think I have a pretty good idea. You're terrified of those of us who have powers. So you try to wipe us from the face of the earth. You're cowards, all of you."

"We're no cowards," he snaps. "We stand for balance in the universe."

"Bullshit," I say, and his face darkens. "You stand for power—your own selfish, bloodthirsty need for power. It's pathetic."

He chuckles. "You're so self-righteous, Eveny. Can you really say that your sister queens are not the same? Do they not strive selfishly for power too?" He gestures toward Peregrine and Chloe, and that's when I realize Chloe is stirring a little. She looks up and meets my eye with a horrified expression. I force my gaze back to Bruno. Clearly, he's the spokesperson; his twin is standing there mute, glaring at us.

"They're not the same as you at all," I say. "You've used your power to hurt, to destroy, to *kill*. Here in Carrefour, we may have been irresponsible with our magic, but we never used it maliciously. And that's what makes us different from you."

He stares at me, his eyes cold and beady. "At the end of the day, though, there's little distinction, is there?" He nods at Caleb. "After all, who could forget what happened to Drew Grady? Are you telling me you didn't kill him?"

I glance at Caleb and see guilt written across his face. Liv surprises me by speaking up in our defense. "Whatever Eveny and Caleb did to Drew, they did in self-defense," she tells Bruno, her voice shaking. She grabs my hand, which makes me feel so relieved that my knees go weak. "That's not the same thing as killing people for personal gain," Liv adds. "And the way I see it, it's *your* fault he's dead."

Bruno just stares at her. "And who exactly are you?"

Liv glances at me and then fixes Bruno with the dirtiest look I've ever seen. "I'm Eveny's sister, you scumbag. Just like Peregrine and Chloe are. And no one messes with my family."

Bruno and his brother begin moving toward us, snarling like wild animals, their eyes crazed and angry. I grab Aunt Bea so we're all connected, then I use zandara to create a protective shield around us, just like the one I used to save Caleb from Drew's knife in New Orleans a few weeks ago.

I know I can't hold the protection for long, so I'm relieved but surprised when the twins suddenly stop their advance. Bruno visibly gathers himself and smiles coolly. "On second thought, I think I'll kill your sister queens first, so you can watch the life drain out of them. And then you can follow them to the grave."

"You can't hurt us," I say. "We have magic on our side."

Bruno laughs, and his creepy twin follows suit. "Oh, you foolish, foolish girl," he says. "Do you really think we'd come after you like this without magic on our side too?"

"But the gate has been fixed," I say. "You can't lay a hand on us here."

"Yes, I admit, you've restored your gate's protective abilities," Bruno says. "Too bad it wasn't before we killed your friends' mothers. The hanging was a creative touch, don't you think?"

"Go to hell," I say.

He ignores me. "Still, you've failed to consider something important. We may not be able to kill you using our own hands, but the charm that protects Carrefour doesn't prevent me from killing you using a natural force. Say, for example, fire."

I realize in a flash that he's right. The gate was set up to keep people who wished us harm—especially Main de Lumière—away. But the founders of the town hadn't counted on the fact that Main de Lumière would be working with someone magical who could summon a ring of fire—and use it as a weapon.

"You won't kill us with fire," I say, trying to project confidence. "You kill people who practice magic by stabbing them through the heart. If you burn us to death instead, there's a chance we can resurface as spirits in the nether. You know that as well as I do."

He waves off my comment. "That won't matter after we wipe out this town. Your sister queens won't be able to communicate from the spiritual plane if there's no triumvirate here to reach out to them. And after today, I assure you there won't be. Zandara will die forever."

"Then why lure *me* back?" I say, buying time. "You don't need to kill me too if you have them."

He chuckles. "Can't it be enough that I want you to watch them die? That I want you to always remember our power?"

I draw myself up to my full height and say, "Leave them alone. I'm the one you want, and you know very well that if you kill me, the future of zandara dies just the same." If the Sauvages go after me instead, we'll have a fighting chance of surviving. They'll be expecting me to fight back with zandara. But they don't know that I've been training in andaba too. I can harness both forms of magic at the same time.

"No, Eveny!" Caleb cries, his eyes filled with tears. He begins moving toward me, but I hold up a hand to stop him.

"Caleb, you have to trust me to do this on my own," I say.

He slows down but doesn't stop. "No, Eveny. I can't let you do that. I can't let you sacrifice yourself."

"Because you'd die too?"

He looks wounded. "No. Because I can't imagine a world without you in it. Because pushing you away was impossible; you live in my heart. Don't you know by now that I love you?"

I feel a surge of power shoot through me, and I know it's because his words are true. Zandara is based in love, and the more love I'm giving and receiving, the stronger I become. "Then trust me," I say. "If you love me, Caleb, you have to stay back."

He stares, his expression mournful and conflicted, but he stops. I turn to my father, who's also walking toward me.

"You too, Dad," I say. "Please. I know what I'm doing. You have to believe in me."

He looks unsure at first, but then Caleb puts a hand on his shoulder, and my father stops. I take a long look at them, drawing strength from the love I see in both of their faces.

Slowly, I turn back to the Sauvages. I spread my arms wide and think about all the love I've ever felt—from my mom, my dad, Aunt Bea, my grandfather, my friends, Caleb, Bram, even Peregrine and Chloe. I draw all of that love into me; I imagine it flowing from the air into my heart, the source of my power. My Stone of Carrefour burns hot against my chest, and I could swear that I feel the sachet Boniface made me, the one with my mom's Rose of Life petals, heating up too. *Mom, if you can hear me*, I think, *I need you now more than ever.*

"I'm here, Sauvage," I say aloud. "Do what you will."

Bruno and Gustave both smile coldly. "Oh, Eveny, how very little you understand," Bruno says. "We promised to save you, you see. As abhorrent as it is, we've made a deal."

"A deal? With whom?" Suddenly, my mind goes to Gerdeaux and the way he was trying to talk me into joining him. "I'll never work with Main de Lumière, you know. Ever. Not after this."

He chuckles. "That's not what I hear. My sources tell me you were meeting with my foolish pacifist cousin in New Orleans. Well, rest assured, Gerdeaux has been dealt with appropriately."

I swallow hard. "You killed him?"

"What's a little murder between friends?" he asks. His brother laughs and then fixes his empty eyes on me.

"Who, then?" I demand. "Who are you working with? Who wants to keep me alive while you destroy everyone else I care about?"

"The only person who'd have a motive to do such a crazy thing, Eveny," he says, his voice tinged with amusement. "The only person who'd benefit from both Carrefour's destruction and your survival. The only person powerful enough to make an alliance with him worth our while."

I stare at him, confused, before I suddenly understand

exactly what he means. "My grandfather?" I whisper.

I don't want to believe it, but I know with instant certainty that he's the only person in the world who would benefit from having Carrefour destroyed while I survive, for I'd presumably have no choice but to return to Caouanne Island and assume what he feels is my rightful place there. And because of his advanced age, he's surely one of the most powerful magic practitioners on earth, which must have made him all the more appealing to Les Jumeaux Noir. Still, how could he betray his own flesh and blood that way? "No, he wouldn't do that," I protest weakly. "He would never take your side over mine. Never."

Bruno Sauvage throws his head back and laughs. "Oh, but he has, Ms. Cheval. I can see by the look in your eyes that you already know that deep in your heart. And now, with his help, we'll destroy your town. But first, let's have a little fun, shall we?"

26

My grandfather's enormous betrayal shatters me, and for a moment, I can't breathe. But then I straighten up and manage to pull myself together. My grandfather must have been aligned with the Sauvages from the start, which means that everything he's said to me since appearing in Carrefour has been a lie. *I haven't really lost anything*, I try to reassure myself. *I never really had his love. He was pretending all along.*

The thought is little comfort, but it's enough to help me refocus on the situation at hand as Bruno Sauvage begins chanting in French. He's saying something like, *"Pour la vie que vous vivez, vous payez un prix. Je nettoie le monde de péché avec votre sang. Équilibre est rétabli."* I search my rudimentary French knowledge and realize he's saying we must pay the price for the lives we're living, that the world will be cleansed with our blood, and that balance will be restored.

Something in the air shifts, the way it does when I cast a charm, and I know now that my traitorous grandfather is close by, controlling the ring of fire with magic. It begins to close in, and I can already feel its heat, sharp and deadly. The smoke is making it hard to breathe, and as the flames get closer, I can already feel my skin blistering, turning red and raw. The pain is almost unbearable.

"It's about time you meet some of my followers, don't you think?" Bruno says, turning back to me, his icy eyes flashing. "We don't actually *plan* to kill you, of course, but if it happens anyhow, well then, I suppose you weren't as powerful as we thought. And you never know, if you get into trouble, perhaps your grandfather will save you."

"I don't need his help," I shoot back. I raise my voice and yell toward the flames, "You hear that, Grandfather? You're dead to me!"

"I'm growing impatient, and I don't have time for family disputes," Bruno says with exaggerated boredom. "Come, soldiers!" he calls toward the flames. "Come join us."

Three shadowy figures emerge, backlit by the flames. It takes me only a second to recognize them. Drew's mother; my physics teacher, Mr. Cronin; and Cristof's assistant, Sharona. They're the insiders working for Les Jumeaux Noir. And in an instant, I know they've been against us all along. Drew's mother isn't a shock, of course. I'm surprised to see mild-mannered Mr. Cronin, but I'm stunned most of all to realize Sharona is a Main de Lumière operative. After all, she was a member of the mothers' sosyete. Suddenly, I have the feeling she was somehow responsible for luring them to their deaths. I wonder if she was involved in my mother's murder too.

I stare them down, and as I think about the depth of their betrayal, my anger flares. Something in me sparks, and I can feel heat pouring into my fingers, something that has never happened before. When I hold my hands up to look at them, my fingertips are a furious red, but I'm not in pain. Instead, it feels like my whole body is buzzing.

I glance at my father, who's staring at the advancing trio. He too has his hands outstretched. His gaze meets mine for a second, and I mouth, *Andaba?* as I hold up my fingers.

He looks surprised, but he nods. "It means you're channeling a great deal of power. But I didn't teach you how to do that."

"I think my body knows how anyway," I say. After all, zandara is fueled by love and andaba by anger. The stronger the emotions, the stronger the magic, and for the first time in my life, I have both feelings flooding through me with equal strength. I can feel power pumping through my veins.

Drew's mother is the first to attack, coming at me with a knife, just like her son did a few weeks earlier. "This is for Drew!" she says, lunging for my chest. I hold my breath and force myself to focus my love and anger.

"Come to us now, Eloi Oke, and open the gate," I whisper,

just as the blade of her knife slices into my upper arm. Behind me, I can see Caleb and my father hurrying toward me despite my warnings, but I can't have them in danger too. I have to stay focused and work quickly.

"Caleb! Dad!" I yell. "I mean it! Stay back! You have to trust me or we're all going to die!" I focus on my Stone of Carrefour, and as I stagger forward with the pain of my wound, I manage to call on Eloi Oke two more times. I reach for my Stone of Carrefour and quickly chant, "Prunella vulgaris, coriander, and rue, I invoke your power. Spirits, help heal my wounds and protect me from harm." But that's just my zandara side, and I know I've tapped into only a fraction of my power.

As the words leave my mouth, several drops of my blood fall from the gash in my arm onto the dirt below me. I can feel the ground rumble slightly, and I know Drew's mother can feel it too, because her eyes widen, and she looks down. Something flickers in the air in front of us, then vanishes before I can tell what it is.

I gather myself. "I never meant to hurt your son!" I tell Drew's mother. "I didn't want him to die. But if you led him to this, to Main de Lumière, you might as well have killed him yourself!"

I'm trying to draw out the verbal battle with her, because the Sauvage twins are focused on what's happening between us and aren't noticing what's going on behind them. Liv has quietly made her way over to my sister queens and is untying them from the stakes. Peregrine is still out cold and slumps to the ground, but Chloe, although unsteady, is strong enough to begin walking toward me, helped along by Liv. I feel a surge of hope. If I can cast with another queen, my magic will be exponentially stronger. Still, to be as powerful as possible, I need three, and Peregrine is clearly not an option.

"The only thing I got wrong was trusting you and your dirty little mother, who had the gall to pretend to be my friend," Drew's mom says, lunging at me again with her knife. I dodge her blade, but Mr. Cronin moves toward me at the same time, his features warped with anger. I twist out of the path of his knife, but not entirely; the edge of the blade nicks my elbow, and I cry out in pain.

"You're dead, Cheval," he says, already preparing to come at me again. But I touch the wound and with my bloodied fingers reach for the muerte dust that hangs from my wrist cuff. I quickly recite the words my father taught me. *"Con mi sangre, regreso a su intención."*

I don't know if the charm will work in a situation like this, though, so I'm surprised when Mr. Cronin recoils immediately and falls to the ground, blood oozing from his chest, his eyes wide and lifeless. It takes me a second to realize that I've killed him the way he intended to kill me. "I'm so sorry," I whisper, because I truly didn't want him to die, but there's no time to feel bad, because Sharona is coming at me now.

"You uppity bitch," she says, swooping her arm forward and slicing the knife toward me.

"Please, Sharona, stop!" I cry, dodging the blade just in

time. I don't want to have to kill her too, but her face is twisted
with rage, and I wonder what lies Les Jumeaux Noir have been
telling her to fill her with so much hatred. She comes at me
again with the knife, and I touch my fingers to the muerte
dust cuff and repeat the words of the charm. She falls back,
wounded but not dead, and I realize that as a member of the
mothers' sosyete, she has probably cast some sort of protection
charm on herself, so she's out of commission for the moment,
but she's still a threat.

I fend off two more attempted jabs from Drew's mother
before I cry out, "Mrs. Grady, please think about what you're
doing! I don't want to have to kill you!"

But her eyes are flashing wildly, and her sneer makes her
face nearly unrecognizable. "I plan to kill you first." As she
lunges viciously for me again, I reach for my open wound,
touch the cuff, and with some regret, whisper the words to
stop her. She falls back, her eyes already wide and blank, blood
pouring from a gaping wound that's opened in her chest. Like
Mr. Cronin, she's dead in exactly the same way she planned to
kill me. A few feet away, Sharona is still unconscious. I sink to
my knees, gasping for breath.

Bruno Sauvage lets out a long, low whistle and claps a few
times as I turn back to him. "My, my, you're a worthier adver-
sary than I imagined you'd be," he says. "I hadn't expected
that you'd be so well-versed in andaba already. Still, everyone you love is going to die regardless. It's unavoidable, I'm
afraid. Your sister queens. Your father. Your protector. Your

aunt. Even your useless friend, who I'm sure will regret getting involved in this mess."

I glance at Liv, but she doesn't look frightened—she looks furious. Fortunately, Bruno still doesn't seem to be paying her any attention. She's making her way toward me with a half-conscious, limping Chloe.

I gather all my strength, struggle to my feet, and direct the andaba charm toward the twins. *"Con mi sangre, regreso a su intención!"* I shout, feeling the fury pour out of me. But nothing happens; Bruno and his brother are unharmed, and the fire continues to advance.

Bruno chuckles. "Valiant try, Ms. Cheval, but your magic can't stop us, even if you are some sort of andaba-zandara abomination. Your grandfather is much more powerful than you are, even with your dual blood. He's been practicing for years, and he has assured me that he knows all the tricks you might try. Only the power of three Queens of Carrefour could save you, and as I'm sure you've realized, that's not going to happen."

"Then where is he?" I demand, trying not to sound as panicked as I feel. "If my grandfather wants everyone I love dead, you'd think he'd have the guts to come out and face me. But instead, he's a spineless coward, just like you."

"I'm growing tired of your insults," Bruno says. "I see Chloe St. Pierre has recovered somewhat, and apparently, you think there's some use in having her join you." He pauses to give Liv and Chloe an almost amused look. "But no matter.

Your third queen seems quite unable to help, and I intend to make sure she stays that way. Without her, I'm afraid there's simply no way you can beat us."

"I'll never let you take this town," I tell him, my heart full of resolve. He's triggering a blend of emotions in me—love for my town and fury at him—that's perfectly suited to bring out my zandara and andaba powers.

"I'm not sure what makes you think you have a choice," he says. "Without the power of three queens—or at least three kings, but you don't have that either—you're just filling the last few minutes of your loved ones' lives with empty, meaningless babble." He sighs and shakes his head, as if I'm boring him. He turns toward the flames and yells, "Brother Desjardins, let's get this fire moving, shall we? I'm running out of patience."

The fire begins advancing more quickly, and Caleb steps closer to me. "We have to do something," he says. "They're going to burn us alive."

"No. I won't let that happen," I say, and turn to my father. "Is there anything I can do with andaba to stop this?"

He shakes his head miserably. "Not without another king. It's only me and you here."

That's when I notice that the wound on my shoulder from Drew's mother's knife has opened wider, and a steady drip of blood is falling onto the dirt. I reach out instinctively to stop the bleeding, to press my shirt into the wound, but there's something flickering in front of me, just like there was when my blood first hit the ground minutes ago. It looks like a faint shadow, as if I'm seeing the reflection of someone who's not really there. Each time a drop of my blood lands, the hazy image gets a little clearer and then vanishes again. "Do you see that too?" I ask my father.

"See what?" he asks.

"Eveny, you're bleeding," Aunt Bea says, stepping forward to touch my arm. I turn to her and see that her face is white.

"Yeah, well, that seems like the least of our problems right now," I say.

"No, that's not what I mean," she says quickly. "You have to tell me: do you have your mother's Rose of Life petals somewhere on you?"

I nod and gesture to the sachet around my neck. My father gasps, startling me. "What's going on?" I ask, first looking at him and then at Aunt Bea.

"I never believed it could work," Aunt Bea breathes, her eyes wide with awe. But there's something else in her expression too: hope. "The Rose of Life . . . My God. She succeeded after all."

"What are you talking about, Aunt Bea?" I ask. "What about the Rose of Life?"

The Sauvage twins are staring at us. The fire is advancing. We probably have another sixty seconds before it reaches Peregrine, another ninety before it closes in around all of us.

"Do you remember what your mother told you when she was dying, Eveny?" Aunt Bea asks urgently.

"'I live on in you,'" I say. "I assumed she meant her magic lived on in me."

"But what if she meant it literally?" Aunt Bea says. "If she succeeded in imbuing the rose with power, you can bring her back because you share her blood. But a drop here and there isn't enough. That's why you're only seeing her shadow. She's trying, but she can't cross the boundary between life and death with so little blood spilled."

The fire is roaring toward us, but suddenly, I'm very cold. "What are you saying?"

There's a faraway look in Aunt Bea's eye as she bends to pick up the knife that Drew's mother dropped when she fell. "She can be your third queen, Eveny. It's the only way. She lives on in me, too." I can see tears rolling down her cheeks, and I take a step forward, confused about what she's saying. She holds up a hand to stop me and adds quickly, "I've done all I can to protect you. Now it's up to you. I love you, Eveny. Never forget that. I'll see you again someday, on the other side."

It takes me a split second to realize what she's about to do. "No!" I cry, rushing to grab the knife from her, but she's already slitting her own wrists, slumping to the ground. Blood pours out of her onto the dry earth.

"Aunt Bea, no!" I scream again, throwing myself at her, grabbing her, trying to stem the gushing flow of her blood. But the cuts are too deep. I can't stop it. I hold her, sobbing, as the life seeps out of her. She's the one person who has been with me my entire life, and now, I'm holding her dead body in my arms. "No, no, no!" I scream. "Aunt Bea, how could you do this? What were you thinking?"

As her blood soaks the ground, something rises in the darkness, something smoky and swirling. I can hear Bruno shouting in the distance; I can feel the flames licking closer and Caleb's hands on me, trying to pull me away from Aunt Bea's lifeless body, but all of it feels very far away. I can only stare at the swirling cloud as a voice projects from it.

"The Rose of Life," it says, and in that instant, I understand what has happened. Aunt Bea has sacrificed herself so that my mother—her sister—can come back long enough to help save Carrefour. Like me, she shared my mother's blood. "Quickly," says the voice, which I now recognize as my mother's. "Pour your sachet on the ground where your aunt Bea fell. When the Rose of Life mixes with her blood, it will bring me back."

Trembling, I rip open the sachet and dump the contents onto the crimson earth. The moment the dried petals fall into Aunt Bea's blood, my mother's form crystallizes, a real human shape instead of a ghostly cloud. "Eveny," she says.

I stare in disbelief. "Mom," I say. "You're here."

27

At the edge of my vision, I see my father coming toward us. He's crying out for my mother, but she holds up a hand. "Stay back, Matthias," she says. He stops and stares at her, and I can see her eyes fill with tears. "I love you," she says. "But you need to let us do this. There's nothing you can do to help now."

My mother's gaze shifts toward the ground, where her sister lies motionless. "Oh, Bea," she says. "I'm so sorry it had to come to this."

"Mom?" I ask, wiping away the tears that are streaming down my cheeks. "Is it really you?"

"Yes, Eveny," she says, her eyes full of love. "And I'm so proud of you. You've become such a good, kind, strong young woman." She suddenly looks behind me, and I turn to see the Sauvage twins rushing toward us, matching expressions of shock on their faces. "We have to act now, honey," my mother says.

She takes my hand, her warmth and solidity startling me so much that I pull back for a second. "Trust me," she says, reaching for me again. We hurry over to Chloe, who's slumped against Liv.

"I knew that if I could get the Rose of Life to work, I'd need to make sure I could return in physical form," my mother says quickly. "Otherwise, I wouldn't be able to cast with you."

"But you're from our mothers' sosyete, not ours," Chloe says weakly. "And they're dead. How can you cast with us? Sosyetes can't overlap generations."

"Because I no longer inhabit a body on earth, my magic isn't constrained by the rules of the sosyete," my mother says.

I'm still reeling, but I know I have to focus now. The smoke is getting thicker, and all of us except my mother have begun to cough. My mother grabs Chloe's hand too and begins to chant, and because I know she's much more powerful and knowledgeable than I am, I let her take the lead. I focus on holding Chloe up and on letting my mother's words fill my already overflowing heart. As her sweet, familiar voice washes over me, my Stone of Carrefour burns against my chest.

"It's all about love," my mother says, glancing at me. "It always has been. Draw as much love to you as you can."

"But I've always had love in my heart," I say, confused.

"You've always loved others," she says. "But you have to

love yourself—trust yourself—too. You're a queen, Eveny. Believe in the power of your own heart."

And so I block out the fire, the flames, the fear, and instead, I think about Aunt Bea, who gave her life for me. Caleb, who has come to my defense again and again. Chloe and Peregrine, who for all their faults are my sisters. Liv, who has gotten involved in this despite the danger, simply because I asked her to. My father, who came back because I was in peril. I even think about Bram, who may very well be dead right now. But most of all, I let my heart fill with love for my mother and for the town she called home. And I let myself believe, for the first time, that I'm the great queen my mother believes I am.

My mother calls out for Eloi Oke, and then she invokes fern, heather, and pansy. "Spirits, please help to douse these flames right away, so that they do no more harm. *Mesi, zanset. Mesi, zanset. Mesi, zanset.*"

I look up expectantly, but nothing happens. The Sauvage twins are laughing now, and the flames are beginning to lick at Peregrine's bare feet. I see her stir, and as her face contorts in pain, I pull free of my mother. I can't let Peregrine die. I run toward her without thinking of the risks, and although my father is calling out, his voice heavy with panic, I don't slow down.

The moment I touch Peregrine, the air goes still and the fire suddenly shrinks a bit. I look back at my mother in confusion to see her smiling knowingly.

"Mom? What happened?" I call to her.

"The willingness to sacrifice oneself for another is the greatest act of love," she replies. "You tried to save Peregrine, even though you knew it could cost you your life."

I'm about to ask more, because I still don't understand, but that's when the floodwaters come pouring in. They arch over the flames from all sides, like a dam has been breached all around us. Within thirty seconds, the flames have been swallowed by the huge waves of water that are already receding.

"No!" Bruno says, looking around in disbelief. "How could you have done that? You can't defeat us! We have a king on our side!"

"Oh yeah? Then where is he?" I run back to my mother's side, confused but hopeful. Before the twins can react, I touch the blood from my wound, move my hand to my cuff, and murmur the andaba charm my father taught me, praying it'll work now that their defenses are down: *"Con mi sangre, regreso a su intención."*

The Sauvages burst into flames, even in the midst of the soaked earth. The fire licks at them hungrily, sparking as it climbs higher and higher.

"No!" Bruno cries while his brother screams in anguish. "Desjardins, save us!"

But there's no reply; my grandfather has obviously fled.

"Perhaps you shouldn't have trusted a traitor!" I call over the raging flames.

Bruno Sauvage is still crying "You can't win!" as his voice fades into the hissing inferno.

"We just did," I say. I watch until he and his brother stop moving, until the flames subside, until they're just two blackened heaps of smoldering ash on the wet earth.

It's over.

"I don't understand what changed," I say, turning to my mother. "Wasn't my grandfather's magic stronger than mine? I tried to use the andaba charm against them before you got here, but nothing happened."

"Your heart was so full with love that you were actually able to use that emotion to strengthen your andaba charm," my mother says with a smile. "You used zandara and andaba together to harness your greatest power, Eveny."

I shake my head in confusion. "I don't know how I did that."

"And that's the key, sweetheart. You didn't think about it. It was instinct. At long last, you trusted yourself." My mother puts a hand on my cheek. "You should be safe for a while. You've destroyed half of Main de Lumière's leadership, and from the sound of it, one of the other leaders is dead too. It will take them years to regroup, and perhaps when they do, the remaining leader will be willing to work with you the way Gerdeaux was suggesting. You have a chance to change everything."

I nod. "What about Aunt Bea?" I choke back a sob as I look down at my aunt's crumpled, lifeless body. From across the clearing, I can see my father approaching. Beside him, Caleb carries a limp, unconscious Peregrine.

"Your aunt knew what she was doing, sweetheart," my mother says gently. "She loved you so much that she willingly gave her life to save you. And now she'll be with me, on the other side. Believe me, Eveny, it's beautiful there, and you'll see us again someday. But right now, you have a life to lead here. It's your destiny."

The words fill me with both sadness and peace. I know that Aunt Bea spent every day missing her sister, and now, they'll be reunited. But that doesn't mean I won't mourn my aunt or regret the troubles that passed between us these last few weeks. I know I'll be moving through the guilt and grief of her death for a long time to come.

"Sandrine," my father whispers, coming forward to embrace my mother. "My Sandrine."

"Oh, Matthias," she says, and they hold each other for a very long time. I can see the love between them, and it's enough to make me start crying again. This is the family I was supposed to have, but it was never meant to be.

After a moment, my parents reach for me and fold me into their embrace. But already, my mother is fading, her warm touch cooling.

"I love you both so much," she says, pulling away and looking at my father and me. "More than anything in the world, I wish I could stay here with you. But the Rose of Life only works to bring a person back once. I designed it that way so that it could never be abused and so that spirits could ultimately rest in peace. Someday, you'll understand that it's better that way."

The floodwaters are ebbing, but they're also seeping into the ground beneath us, diluting the blood Aunt Bea spilled. Some of the Rose of Life petals are drifting away in a small stream, and as the things that brought my mother here are washed away, she's vanishing too.

"Take care of each other," my mother says, looking first at me and then at my father. "Promise me that."

"I promise, Sandrine," my father says as I nod, too choked up to speak.

"I'll love you both forever," she says as her body fades back into a shadow of itself. "Remember, Eveny," she adds, her voice already very far away, "love will always save you."

"Wait!" I call out, suddenly panicked. "Mom? Who killed you? Can you tell us?"

But it's too late. She's already gone in a swirling cloud that vanishes into the pale light of the rising dawn.

A few hours later, I sit huddled in the living room of my mansion, one of the only places in Carrefour that hasn't been destroyed. I'm holding hands with Chloe and Peregrine, both of whom are conscious now. We cast a charm an hour ago, invoking cowslip, St. John's wort, and bay leaf to help heal our wounds, and already, the knife gashes in my arms have closed up, and the smoke lingering in my lungs has cleared.

"How are we going to come back from this?" Chloe says.

"We'll rebuild," I say. "We'll start over, and we'll use zandara to heal the town."

"But that won't bring back the people we love," Peregrine says in a small voice. Audowido slithers up her leg and curls himself in her lap, and she begins to absentmindedly pet him.

"No, but it will honor their memory," I reply. "We'll make Carrefour great again."

Arelia, Margaux, and Aunt Bea weren't the only ones we lost. Oscar, Patrick, and their fathers were found slaughtered in the graveyard just behind Peregrine's home. And almost everyone from the mothers' sosyete—including Sharona, who died at the hospital an hour after the showdown in the clearing—is dead too, with the exception of Cristof, who was apparently only spared because he was in the Périphérie when the carnage began.

The survivors are gathered here. Pascal, self-absorbed as usual, stayed alive by laying low in the house of the girl he was sleeping with at the time the fire broke out. Liv has returned after going home to make sure her father, brother, Justin, and Max were safe. Boniface—who can't seem to believe that my mother succeeded in imbuing the Rose of Life with power after all—is talking in hushed tones with my father in the kitchen. And Caleb is here beside me, his arms wrapped around me like he never wants to let go. I'm numb with the loss of Aunt Bea, and I know that the hole she's left in my life will be open for a long time. But right now, I'm worrying about Bram. No

one has accounted for him or my grandfather yet, and I have
a bad feeling about it.

"You're going to have to explain all of this to me tomorrow," Liv says.

"I'll tell you everything, I promise," I say.

"I can't believe the three of you are *queens*," she says,
shaking her head and glancing at Chloe and Peregrine, who
are tear-soaked and soot-stained.

"We need you now, Liv. As soon as we're recovered from
today, we'll add you to the sosyete." I pause. "That is, if you
want to join us."

She looks at me for a long time. "How could I say no to a
friend?"

"Eveny?" My father speaks up from the corner.

I turn to him, and for a long time, we hold each other's
gaze. Seeing for myself how much my mother still loved him
and realizing how ready he was to lay down his life for me
have made me view him in a new light. "Yes, Dad?"

"I'm proud of you," he says, his voice cracking with emotion. "So proud. I know your mom is too."

We're interrupted by a knock on the front door. My father
looks worried, and Caleb stands in front of me protectively.

"Let me see who it is," my dad says as he strides toward the
front hall. "Everyone stay here."

A moment later, he returns with Bram following him. I
gasp and leap up to embrace him.

"Hey," Bram says, hugging back. He's battered and

bloodied, but he's alive. "It's your grandfather, Eveny. He's the one working with Main de Lumière. I got him to admit everything. He wanted to destroy zandara, to leave you with no choice but to return to Caouanne Island."

"I know," I say.

He looks surprised. "I held him off for as long as I could, but his magic is stronger than mine, and he got away. I can only assume he's headed here."

I exchange worried glances with my dad and Caleb before turning back to Bram. "You bought us some time to regroup, Bram. A lot of people died today: Margaux, Arelia, all the protectors except for Caleb. And my aunt Bea."

"Oh no," Bram says, looking horrified. "I'm so sorry. I should have been here to help."

"You *did* help. If my grandfather had actually been there, maybe we'd all be dead."

Bram reaches out and brushes a lock of hair out of my face. "I'd do it again in a heartbeat if it meant saving your life." His eyes are so full of love and concern for me that it makes my heart swell and ache at the same time. It feels amazing to be loved like that, but I know it's for all the wrong reasons.

"I'll never ask you to do anything like that again," I say. "This is my battle to fight, not yours, Bram."

"It's *our* battle, Eveny," he tells me.

"Bram?" My father comes up behind me and puts a hand on my shoulder. I turn and am startled to see how worried he looks. He glances out the front window. "Where exactly did you last see my father?"

As if on cue, something thuds against the front door, and as we all turn to look, it splinters and explodes—not like it's been kicked in, but like a bomb has gone off. We duck as shards of wood, metal, and stone fly everywhere, and a second later, my grandfather appears in the dust that still hangs in the air. "I believe you were asking about me, son?" He looks weak, bruised, sallow. A blue vein bulges from the middle of his forehead.

"How could you do this?" my father cries, stepping forward, his fists clenched. "How could you destroy Carrefour and put Eveny in danger like this? She could have died, Father! What have you become?"

My grandfather chuckles as he steps into the house over the splintered door. Caleb springs to my right side, and Bram stays protectively on my left as we watch him walk casually toward us. I resist the urge to back up; I won't run from this man.

"My son," my grandfather says, his tone even and cold. "You have made so many wrong decisions in your life, but leaving Caouanne Island in order to ally yourself with this town was the worst one. I'm sorry that you got so attached to this place, but this was how it always had to be, from the moment you chose. You must realize that."

"No," my father says, "I made the right decision, because I made it out of love. Andaba and zandara have no choice now but to coexist. You can't wipe one out to save the other."

"Oh, but I can," my grandfather says. "It's already begun, Matthias. Look around you. You and Eveny have nothing to stay here for. The town is in ruins. All that's left are these foolish girls who contributed to its destruction." He nods toward Peregrine and Chloe, and Audowido hisses angrily.

"You're wrong," I say, stepping forward. "We have everything to stay here for. We'll rebuild Carrefour. I have no doubt about that. But know that for the rest of my life, I will always blame you for what happened here. How could you have allied with Les Jumeaux Noir?" I think of Aunt Bea, and anger surges within me. "The blood of the people we love will forever be on your hands."

"Maybe a little of that blood is on your hands too, Eveny." He shrugs. "You were so trusting and stupid. Just like your mother."

"What's that supposed to mean?" my father asks.

My grandfather looks back and forth between us, and for a moment, he seems to be considering something. "I'm an old man, my son. And this cancer is destroying me. I thought Les Jumeaux Noir would be my salvation, the salvation of andaba, but by defeating them, you've destroyed me too. So before I go, you might as well know the truth. You think I have no power over you? No power over Carrefour? You're fools, both of you. I've held the power all along."

He pulls out his Mind's Eye and beckons us closer. I take a step in his direction, but Caleb grabs my hand. "It's not safe," he says. "You can't trust him."

"I know," I say. "But he can't hurt me now."

My father nods at me, and together, we flank my grandfather and peer down at the smooth crystal. He closes his eyes and chants something softly, and after a second, an image appears in the Mind's Eye. I realize immediately what I'm seeing. It's the inside of my parlor, on the night of my mother's death. My mother and her sister queens are chanting, but I'm not seeing them from my perspective. I'm seeing them from the viewpoint of someone lurking in the shadows. It can only mean that my grandfather was there. I look at him in horror.

"I had to do it," he says, and his voice sounds far away, hollow. "I had to take away your reason to stay in Carrefour, Matthias. I had to make you and Eveny return to Caouanne Island."

My father stares at him. "What are you saying?"

But I already know. As I watch the scene unfold in the Mind's Eye, I see him snuff the lights out, creep through the shadows, and slit my mother's throat in one swift, clean motion before slipping back into the hall and away into the dark veil of the night. My heart feels like it's been split open as the image flickers out. *My own grandfather murdered my mother.* It's almost too much to bear.

"*You* did this?" my father says. "*You* killed Sandrine? The love of my life? The mother of my daughter?"

"You left me no choice, Matthias. I warned you. But the day you told me you planned to move back to Carrefour, that you couldn't bear to be away from your wife and daughter anymore, I knew I had to do something. I had to take away your reason for being here. And of course I couldn't harm Eveny without ruining the future of andaba, so I had to make you believe that your return would put her in danger." He shrugs and adds, "Well, it worked for fourteen years, didn't it?"

"You monster!" my father cries, lunging at my grandfather and landing a solid punch to his jaw. My grandfather flies backward, and my father lands on top of him, hitting him, tearing at him, like he wants to rip him to shreds.

But my grandfather doesn't cry out. Instead, he just takes it with an eerie smile on his battered face. "That's right," he says. "Kill me. Become a murderer like I am. You're no better than me, son. No better than me at all."

I reach for my father, and with Caleb's and Bram's help, I try to pull him back, but his hands are around my grandfather's throat, and he won't let go. He's crying, and so am I. "No!" I shout. "No. Don't do this, Dad. Don't become like him. That's what he wants!"

"But he killed your mother, Eveny!" he says, still pressing down on his father's neck. My grandfather is making gurgling sounds now, and his eyes are bulging out, but he still manages to look smug and satisfied. "He killed her, and it's my fault!" my father continues. "If I hadn't come into her life, your mother would still be here!"

"But *I* wouldn't be here, Dad," I say, and I'm relieved when I see his grip on my grandfather's throat loosen a little.

"But Eveny . . . ," my father says, his voice raw with emotion as he trails off.

My grandfather gasps for air as I go on. "What's done is

done, and it's not your fault, Dad. You saw it in Mom's eyes today. She loves you. You can't blame yourself. Don't let him turn you into something you're not. You're not a murderer. You're not like he is."

My father continues to sob, but after a moment, he finally lets go. My grandfather coughs wildly and puts his hands up to his bruised throat as I pull my father into an embrace.

"You're cowards," my grandfather says. "There's nothing worthwhile in either of you."

"It's quite the opposite, Father," my dad says, his voice shaking with fury. Out of the corner of my eye, I see Audowido moving across the floor toward us, and fleetingly, I wonder what he's doing. He's rarely away from Peregrine. "You're the coward. And now you'll spend the rest of eternity burning in hell. I'll call in every spiritual favor I have to make sure that's where you're headed."

My grandfather opens his mouth to reply, but before he can get a word out, Audowido has slithered up to my grandfather's shoulders and has begun to wrap his thick, muscular body around the old man's neck. He constricts more and more tightly, and my grandfather's face turns red as he gasps for air.

"Audowido, no!" I say as my grandfather wheezes and flails, his face a mask of terror, his eyes bulging out.

"Stop, Audowido!" Peregrine says, struggling to get up from the couch.

But the snake doesn't listen. He just contorts more and more around my grandfather's neck, even as I try to pull him off. He squeezes until my grandfather collapses, his eyes wide and unseeing. Then, the snake slowly unwinds himself and slithers back to Peregrine, who looks horrified. "He's dead," she says in disbelief.

"Did you do that?" Liv says, staring at Peregrine. "Did you make your snake kill him?"

"No," Peregrine says. "He did that all on his own."

My father sinks down beside the lifeless body of my grandfather. He's still sobbing, and I don't know whether it's because of the revelation about my mother's death, the fact that he came close to killing his own father, or because the man who gave him life is now lying dead in our front hall. I kneel beside him.

"You were wrong, Grandfather," I say, although I know he can't hear me anymore. "You said there's nothing worthwhile in my father or me. But my father loved you enough that despite everything, he couldn't take your life. Neither could I. My mother told me that love will always save us, and I believe her. Love always wins in the end."

I stand and help my father to his feet, and after a moment, he puts an arm around me and pulls me close. "We're going to be okay, Eveny," he says. "We're going to be okay."

I look around the room at my friends, my family, the people I love. "I know," I say. The worst is over. We've survived. Now it's time to move into the future.

EPILOGUE

*P*ointe Laveau's prom takes place six weeks later.
School officials considered not holding it, because
of the suspicious fire that swept through the town and killed
several students and teachers.

But Peregrine, Chloe, Liv, and I had volunteered to chair
the prom committee and make the dance happen. It's the
first step to restoring life and hope to Carrefour, and in that
spirit, we've decided to invite the whole town. Carrefour Secondary's prom will be combined with ours, and adults and
younger kids are welcome too. With a little bit of magic and
a lot of hard work—which has helped take our minds off the
tragedy that hangs over us—it has all come together beauti-
fully. Meanwhile, the police investigation into the death of the
mothers has concluded, with the police chief declaring that
the strange identical twins suspected of starting the fire were

also the ones responsible for the murders. The townspeople seem to have accepted the explanation.

The theme of the dance this year is "The Pride of Carrefour," and under a ceiling of twinkling lights at the Lietz Theater on Main Street, the walls are lined with photographs of people who were lost last month in what has come to be known as the Great Fire of Carrefour. All in all, the death toll was twenty-seven.

For the first time since I returned to town, Peregrine and Chloe seem to have bigger things on their minds than boys. Peregrine has come to the dance stag, and Chloe is here platonically with Pascal, who isn't trying to sleep with everyone for once. Liv, who has agreed to take the zandara oath and become a member of our sosyete, has come with a friend from Carrefour Secondary. Max and Justin are here together. Seeing them slow dance, their heads resting on each other's shoulders, gives me hope for the future of this town. Seeing everything around you destroyed makes you reevaluate what's important, and in the best of cases, losing people you care about inspires you to hold closer the ones you love.

I think that's what's happening with Caleb and me. He's my date to the dance, and unlike the Mardi Gras Ball in March where he was just doing his job, he's with me this time because he wants to be. The day after my grandfather's death, we'd strolled out to the garden together and made a promise: we wouldn't let the rules of the town dictate how we lived anymore. Neither of us wants to regret a single thing.

As my mother reminded us, love will always save you. And so we've agreed to rely on that—and on training and preparing for every possible danger that could come our way in the future. We also decided to sever the protectorate link between us permanently. After all, Peregrine's and Chloe's protectors, Patrick and Oscar, died in the attack, so it's the perfect time for us to start over without putting others in the path of danger. The future is what we make it, not what our ancestors dictated long ago.

I've just finished dancing with Caleb to Eric Clapton's "Wonderful Tonight," which my dad has told me was my mother's favorite love song, when Bram taps me gently on the shoulder. "Can we talk outside?" he asks, glancing uncertainly at Caleb.

"Of course," I tell him. I kiss Caleb on the cheek and follow Bram out the front door of the Lietz Theater, onto Main Street, where the town still smells of burning dreams. "I'm going back," he tells me hesitantly without meeting my eye. "To Caouanne Island. It's where I belong, Eveny."

I take his hand and smile sadly. I can't deny that with each passing day, I feel a little bit more for him. Thanks to the andaba charm cast long ago, it's inescapable. Besides, he's a good, kind person, and he risked his life for me and my family. But love trumps magic when it's strong enough, as was the case with my father and mother, and I believe my feelings for Caleb will overpower my feelings for Bram as long as Caleb sticks around.

I know that our paths will cross again someday. I'm Bram's sister queen, and I have a responsibility to Caouanne Island the same way I have a responsibility to Carrefour.

"Eveny, just don't let him break your heart, okay?" Bram says haltingly as he gives my hand a squeeze. "Caleb Shaw, I mean. He's a good guy, but I don't think he knows what he wants, or what's worth risking everything for. Until he can figure it all out in his own mind, he's no good for you."

The words make me sad, because on some level, he's right. "I'll be careful. Thank you for worrying about me, Bram," I say. "Thank you for everything. If you hadn't held my grandfather off, I wouldn't have been able to help save Carrefour. All of this could have been lost. I—and this town—owe you a great debt."

He smiles. "No debt owed, Eveny. Just promise me you'll keep an open mind about the future. I know you believe now that your life is here. But as you get older, you may feel differently. Just remember, I'll be waiting, if and when you decide to come home to Caouanne Island."

"Thank you," I say, hugging him tightly. "But please live your life. Don't wait for me."

"You know I can't promise that," he says. He lets me go, smiles sadly at me once more, and turns to walk away. I watch him until he reaches his car two blocks down. He turns, raises his hand in a long, frozen wave good-bye, and then he's gone.

I stand there by myself for a moment, just breathing in and out. I'm not sure what the future will bring, but I know one thing for sure: I'm *already* home. This is where I belong. And regardless of the fact that andaba and zandara will be pulling me in different directions for years to come, I'm making the decision now to take control of my own life.

The door to the Lietz Theater opens behind me, and I turn to see Caleb approaching, a look of concern on his face. "You okay?" he asks as he places a hand on the small of my back.

I search his eyes before nodding and leaning into him. He puts his arm around me and pulls me close. As I breathe in the familiar scent of him, I know his guard is down, that he's letting himself feel, instead of censoring his emotions. Right now, in this moment, he loves me as much as I love him.

"Yeah, I'm okay," I finally say. I turn, stand on tiptoe, and kiss him gently. He kisses me back, and for a moment, cradled in his arms, I feel safe and hopeful and secure.

But then he lets go. "Should we go back inside?" he asks. "Before the others start to worry?"

I smile. My fate is mine. It's not what zandara or andaba dictates. I can chart my own path. After all, I'm a Queen of Carrefour. I'm a Queen of Caouanne Island. I have the right to choose—and I choose simply to be *me*, whatever that means.

"No," I say. "I think we're just fine out here." I kiss him again, and this time, he responds with an intensity that speaks volumes.

I can hear my mother's words in my mind, far away but clear. *Love will always save you.* That's what I'm feeling so strongly right here, right now: love in its purest form. Love that doesn't exist because of magic, but that exists despite it.

"I love you," I say. "Whether you like it or not, Caleb Shaw, I love you."

Pain flashes across his eyes quickly and then it's gone. "I love you too," he whispers. He kisses me gently on the forehead and says, "Now, do you want to dance, or what?"

He holds out his arms and I melt into them. "Forever," I say. And as we sway to the music wafting onto the street from inside the theater, I realize that whatever the future brings, everything's going to be all right. Love will save us. And if I have love in my heart, and if I always believe in its power, I might just be able to save the world.

Acknowledgments

As was the case with *The Dolls*, I couldn't have written this novel without the generosity and hard work of my literary agent, Holly Root; my partner in crime, Nick Harris; and my editors, Sara Sargent and Viana Siniscalchi. You guys rock!

Thanks also to Wendy Toliver, my longtime writing buddy. Not only did you give me great notes—again!—but you put on the world's best writing retreat, during which I wrote a huge chunk of this book. I honestly don't know if I could have finished if not for that lovely, inspiring time spent in the Toliver lodge. So thanks to my Swan Valley writing friends: Jay Asher, Allison van Diepen, Emily Wing Smith, Aprilynne Pike, Linda Gerber, and of course Wendy. Your books are all amazing, by the way! Can't wait to see you all again!

Jerry Gandolfo from the New Orleans Historic Voodoo Museum was very helpful to me in my initial research stages, but it's important to underscore here that zandara and andaba are *not* voodoo. I used a handful of similar elements to build Eveny's world, but voodoo itself is a complex, fascinating set of religious and spiritual beliefs and customs. Zandara and andaba don't incorporate religion in the same way that voodoo does, and they've evolved much differently over time.

Thanks also to the great folks at Waxman Leavell Literary Agency, The Story Foundation, and Balzer + Bray, especially Julianna Wojcik (with your awesome drawings that always cheer me up!), Alessandra Balzer, Donna Bray, Caroline Sun, Veronica Ambrose, Bethany Reis, and Nellie Kurtzman. And of course a warm thanks to Farley Chase, Kate McLennan, Heather Baror-Shapiro, Elisabetta Migliavada (and her wonderful team at Garzanti), and the great folks at Usborne, including Becky Walker, Amy Dobson, Hannah Reardon, Anne Finnis, and Stephanie King.

Finally, thanks as always to my wonderful family, especially my husband, Jas. Love you!